PENG
GREYHAWI
MAS

Rose Estes has lived in Chicago, Houston, Mexico and
Canada, in a driftwood house on an island, a log cabin in the
mountains, and a broken Volkswagen van under a viaduct. At
present she is sharing her life with an eccentric game designer/
cartoonist, three children, one slightly demented dog and a
pride of occasionally domestic cats.

Her other books include nine of TSR, Inc.'s ENDLESS
QUEST® series of books, as well as *Children of the Dragon, The
Turkish Tattoo* and *Blood of the Tiger. Master Wolf* is the first book
in the Mika trilogy. The other two volumes are *The Price of
Power* and *The Demon Hand.*

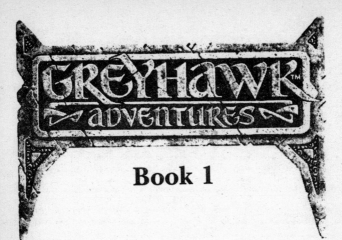

GREYHAWK ADVENTURES

Book 1

MASTER WOLF

by Rose Estes

Illustrations by Bart Sears
Cover illustration by Clyde Caldwell

PENGUIN BOOKS
in association with TSR, Inc.

PENGUIN BOOKS

Published by the Penguin Group
27 Wrights Lane, London W8 5TZ, England
Viking Penguin Inc., 40 West 23rd Street, New York, New York 10010, USA
Penguin Books Australia Ltd, Ringwood, Victoria, Australia
Penguin Books Canada Ltd, 2801 John Street, Markham, Ontario, Canada L3R 1B4
Penguin Books (NZ) Ltd, 182–190 Wairau Road, Auckland 10, New Zealand

Penguin Books Ltd, Registered Offices: Harmondsworth, Middlesex, England

First published by TSR, Inc. 1987
Published in Penguin Books 1988
Distributed to the book trade in the United States by
Random House, Inc., and in Canada by Random House of Canada, Ltd
Distributed in the United Kingdom by TSR UK Ltd
Distributed to the toy and hobby trade by regional distributors
ADVANCED DUNGEONS & DRAGONS and AD&D are registered
trademarks owned by TSR, Inc. PRODUCTS OF YOUR IMAGINATION,
GREYHAWK, and the TSR logo are trademarks owned by TSR, Inc.
1 3 5 7 9 10 8 6 4 2

Printed and bound in Great Britain by
Cox & Wyman Ltd, Reading

This book has been written in appreciation of
friendship—the highs, the lows—
for my sister, Jeniece Douglas,
and for Michael Douglas and Bert Weil—
friends and forever family

FOREST   LanD of GNolls anD HYeNas

Mika's camp

Pier RIVER   Eru-Covar

Wolf NomaDs

Quag

Chapter 1

THE BIG MALE WOLF lolled lazily in the deep recesses of the forest, enjoying the warmth of the late afternoon. Moss lay thick on the ground in this hidden spot, a tiny grotto etched out of the limestone that wove through the dense roanwood forest like the spine of a partially submerged dragon. With the exception of the male wolf TamTur and his constant companion, the man named Mika-oba, the residents of the forest—the Wolf Nomads—did not know of this grotto.

"Quit your teasing, woman, or I shall have Tam-Tur eat you and be done with you once and for all," growled Mika-oba as he scowled ferociously at the plump, blue-eyed female who had accompanied him to the grotto but refused to come close enough to grasp.

"Oh, Mika," Cilia giggled, "I am not afraid of Tam. He wouldn't hurt me. He likes me too much. And so do you. You wouldn't really let him eat me, would you?"

Celia's full red lips pouted prettily as she looked up at Mika from under the mass of tawny locks that framed her dimpled face.

"Don't be too sure of it," Mika said sternly, even as he felt himself beginning to waver, as always. "Tam obeys me in everything. He will do as I command. Do you wish to disobey me and find out who is right? Come here, now. The time for games is over."

"You don't play fair," Celia said with a tiny moue. "Even though I do not believe that Tam would hurt me, you'd probably set him on me just to scare me." But even as she flirted with the big, muscular man, whom she had known since childhood, she felt a familiar tingle of fear mixed with excitement and longing, and wondered what he would do if she ever really angered him.

He was really quite handsome, Celia thought as she walked slowly toward him, studying him through her thick fringed lashes. He was tall for a Wolf Nomad, at least six feet, and his well-developed body was a dark bronzed tan, even in winter when the sun seldom showed its face. His eyes were grey and his nose was long and slender. His mouth was well shaped and frequently curved up at one side as though he was enjoying a joke no one else shared. His lips, as Celia knew well, were soft and knew the secrets of her soul, not to mention her body.

"Oh, Mika," she sighed, abandoning herself to his embrace. Mika folded her soft figure in his arms and buried his face in her perfumed hair.

"One of these days, Celia, you will push me too far and I really will let Tam eat you," he murmured. "Or maybe I'll just do it myself."

Celia's reply, if any, was lost as Mika kissed her, and then there was no sound but the soft drone of insects and their own deep, languorous breathing.

Then, slowly, Mika became aware of another sound, a muffled shouting. Mika tried to ignore the voices, but they grew louder and carried with them the shrill edge of alarm. He sat up, dropping Celia abruptly onto the moss.

"Mika!" Celia complained crossly.

"Quiet," Mika commanded, listening intently. More voices could now be heard coming from all directions.

"Mika, where are you going?" cried Celia. But Mika was already gone, sprinting through the forest with TamTur at his heels.

The cries of alarm grew louder as he raced toward the camp, the detritus of leaves and moss thick beneath his feet. He darted nimbly between the huge roanwood trees, leaping fallen trunks with ease, flashing in and out of the few stray beams of sunlight that managed to creep through the dense leafy branches high above his head.

As he passed the outlying border of the camp, he saw that the women's cook fires were deserted and that no one, save one small babe, lying forgotten on a deerskin, was to be seen.

A babble of voices could be heard emanating from the Far Fringe, an outlying strip of land where the great forest halted at the edge of the open plains.

Mika hurried toward the Far Fringe, his heart thumping in his chest, wondering what disaster could have happened that would so affect the camp.

Indeed, it seemed that the entire camp, several

hundred men, women, and children, had gathered at the Far Fringe and were milling about, their voices raised in loud unintelligible cacophony. And everywhere, there were wolves of all sizes. Stirred by the commotion, they were racing around the mob of humans, adding their yips and howls to the uproar.

Mika forced his way through the crowd until he had reached the very center of the throng and was able to look down at the awful object of their attention that lay on the ground.

It was a man, or what remained of one. He was dressed in a soft, beige kidskin tunic, richly embroidered with cobalt-blue and gold threads and beaded with turquoise, a uniform that identified him as a member of the Trader's Guild, the powerful and exclusive organization that controlled the traffic of merchandise over the whole of Greyhawk. Such men were normally inviolate, safe from attack by all who would benefit from their commerce.

Mika-oba ran a shrewd hunter's eye over the man, leaving the ministration of water and healing herbs to others already bent to their tasks. But as Mika took in the multitude of wounds punched in the man's flesh and saw the quantity of skin hanging in strips from his body, he knew with certainty that no amount of medicine would keep the man alive.

The man writhed weakly, and garbled words poured from his torn lips, a meaningless stream of gibberish. A lesser man would already be dead, but the trader continued to struggle, still driven by whatever terrible compulsion had carried him this far.

Curiosity prompted Mika-oba to move closer, to hear what the man was trying to say, wondering what could have caused him to travel when his wounds dictated that he pray to the gods and ready himself for the death that was so obviously near.

Mika's face grew somber and a shudder ran through him as he realized the torment the man must have experienced as he escaped his attackers and sought help. Mika knew without a shadow of a doubt that he himself would never be able to endure such pain, and he made a strong mental note to actively avoid placing himself in any position that might allow such a thing to occur.

"Oh, Mika, isn't it terrible?" whispered Celia who appeared suddenly at his side, gazing up at him, her long curved lashes thick with sparkling tears.

"Don't look, Celia," he said, pressing her soft hair against his bare chest.

"But, Mika, what could have happened to him? Who could have done this? Maybe it was an army of orcs and they're coming this way. We'll all be killed! Oh, Mika, I'm frightened!" Celia wailed as a shiver of terror caused her to squeeze Mika even more tightly.

Mika cleared his throat, feeling Enor, Celia's father and the chief of the Wolf Nomads, staring at them with stern disapproval, and he regretfully separated himself from Celia and her fears.

"I'm sure it's nothing," Mika said calmly, knowing that the last great army of orcs had been driven from the plains long before his father's time. "Probably just bandits."

"Orcs!" cried Celia, determined to be frightened. "Or maybe goblins, thousands and thousands of them! We'll all be murdered!"

"It was probably no more than one or two robbers, scum from the dungeons of Yecha," Mika said firmly.

"Hill giants," squeaked Celia, closing her eyes and shivering with fear.

People were turning toward Celia, starting to listen. Mika-oba glared at her, knowing all too well how persistent she could be once she seized on an idea.

"Hush your yammering, Celia," he growled. "I'll find out what happened. I'm sure there's some simple explanation."

Steeling himself against the unpleasant task, although in honesty he had never minded blood so long as it was not his own, Mika-oba sank to one knee and picked up the man's hand. Stripped of nails and skin and pale with the loss of blood, it resembled nothing more than a lump of raw meat.

"Who did this?" Mika asked forcefully, yet hoping with all his heart that the man would be unable to speak. "Where were you? Tell us, so that we may avenge your death!"

Mika's father, Veltran, chief shaman, healer, and magic-user, knelt at the man's head, eyes shut, trying to commune with his spirit, urging it to live.

Veltran's small, withered body hunched over the injured man, his myriad of grey braids hidden beneath the snarling wolf skull he wore over his head. A thick luxuriant pelt hung from the skull, covering his thin body, and the two front paws crossed over his bony chest.

He held a staff of roanwood in one hand, the head of the staff embellished with a carved wolf's head, the teeth bared in a snarl. Wisps of fragrant smoke issued from the staff as Veltran waved it over the injured

14

man, allowing the row of wolf tails that were tied along its length to brush over his body.

Mika knew that his father was so completely absorbed in his efforts that he was unaware of anything else that occurred around him.

But others were. "Do not speak of death," hissed Whituk, a shaman of lesser standing who crouched at the man's side. "The dark spirits lurk above us and will come if they are called," he said angrily, glaring at Mika with a baleful eye.

Celia gasped softly and rested a tiny hand on Mika's shoulder. Her touch tingled through his shoulder and nudged Mika-oba over the edge of reason. Ignoring the shaman's angry warning, he gripped the wounded man's hand firmly.

The man's eyelids were gone, crudely cut from beneath his brows. His nose had also been removed, leaving a dark gaping hole that burbled darkly with blood, showing the stark whiteness of bone and cartilage beneath. The brown, blood-edged eyes stared upward, dulled with pain and exhaustion, seeing nothing.

"Speak, man! Tell us who did this!" Mika implored, closing his ears to the disapproving murmur of the shaman.

Slowly, the man's eyes focused, taking in the trees above him and the circle of anxious faces. He turned his mutilated face toward Mika and strained to speak, but only a dry croak emerged from his broken mouth.

Mika lifted the man's head, trying to ignore the thick, warm blood that smeared against his arm, and tipped a skin full of honeyed ale to the ravaged lips.

The man drank greedily, then sank back.

"Kobolds," he said in a wavering voice. "We were . . . coming from Yecha. They struck as we were fording the river Fler . . . Hundreds of them. You must send help."

The men crowded around him murmured loudly at the man's message, and the word *kobold* echoed excitedly through the gathered throng. Celia shivered and squeezed Mika's arm, as though chiding him for doubting her.

A disbelieving frown creased Mika's broad brow and he stared down into the man's blood-smeared eyes, probing out the truth.

"Kobolds?" he asked dubiously. "Why would kobolds dare to attack a caravan while it was under the protection of the Tiger Nomads? Kobolds are stupid, but they do not go to their death so senselessly."

"No Tigers," said the man, his voice sinking to a whisper. "A rider came . . . when we were in sight of the river. Said they were needed back in Yecha—a crisis. Said you Wolf Nomads would pick us up . . . as soon as we crossed the river. . . . Left a guard, then most left us. Kobolds attacked when we were midstream . . . heavy losses. You . . . must help or all will die. The princess . . . so beautiful . . . The kingdom, great wealth, all depends on her safety. I promised the king I would protect her. . . . I rode. I . . . promised to bring help."

"Princess? What princess? What kingdom? What wealth?" asked Mika-oba, suddenly interested in the man's welfare.

"Great wealth . . . so beautiful . . . the princess . . ." muttered the man. For a moment, his eyes glim-

16

mered, and he seemed to see Mika-oba clearly for one brief second. His eyes burned feverishly and he said loudly and clearly for all to hear: "You! You must go. You must save her. I pass her safekeeping on to you!" and then his eyes glazed and he fell back against Mika's arm.

The crowd gasped at the man's words, and Mika felt their eyes focused on his back. "He's sick, doesn't know what he's saying. Raving. Delirious. Anyone can see that," Mika said quickly, cursing his dumb bad luck.

"I don't think so," said Whituk with a nasty smirk. "He was very clear. Said what he had to. Certainly placed his mission in the right hands. Found the best man, all right."

"I don't think he meant me *specifically*," Mika said hurriedly, sweat breaking out on his upper lip. "I think he was referring to the clan in general. After all, what could one man do—if the story is even true?"

Veltran emerged from his state of trance, sorrowfully crossed the man's hands on his chest and spoke softly. "Rest easy, friend. We will ride to the aid of your party. Some of our men must be there already. They will turn the tide of the battle. Kobolds are no match for men of the Wolf Clan."

"All dead," whispered the man, his eyes no longer seeing. "They came . . . and they are dead. You must send . . . more . . . help." His arm slid from his chest and fell slackly to the ground.

Whituk moved to help, but Mika knew that the man was beyond them now and had joined the spirits of his ancestors. He rose slowly, his mind churning, and his eyes met the steady gaze of the chief. Enor was grim.

"It cannot be," said Enor, his bronze face a sickly shade of yellow. "I sent twenty of our best men. The Guildsman said a strong party was needed, and I sent the best. They could not be dead. The man has to be wrong. . . ."

But his voice was thick with dread and Mika-oba was touched by a cold chill, as he recalled those who had left without him. Hansa, bold and cunning and friend of his childhood, as well as Gunnar and Hondred and Belo and Haj. The best of the young men of the clan. Had he not chosen to frolic with Celia, he himself would have been among them. He shut his mind to the small voice of his conscience that recalled how unlikely that would be, since he always chose to frolic.

Relief flooded through him, vying with anger and grief, as he realized that even if they were dead, he was still alive.

"We must all go," said Enor-oba, son of the chief and Celia's brother. "The death of this man is a blot on the honor of the Wolf Clan. We must ride to the river and hope that we are in time to avenge the caravan." Enor-oba gave Mika-oba a sneer, confident he had upstaged him in the bravado department.

That was just like his dull-witted boyhood rival, his mouth racing ahead of his brain. And yet . . . Mika toyed with the idea of riding along, prompted no doubt by the mention of a beautiful princess and great wealth, as well as the conviction that any kobolds, should they really exist, would be long gone by the time he got there. Before he could decide if the risk was worth the reward, his father spoke.

18

"You cannot go, Mika-oba. Your place is here with the clan," Veltran said, climbing to his feet wearily, his face pinched with fatigue.

"We must pray for guidance and say the words that will keep the clan from danger. Others will go. Others will fight. I need you here to help me. You have much to learn before you are able to take my place."

Left to his own devices, Mika would undoubtedly have recalled the ferocity of kobolds and found some way to wriggle out of the confrontation, but forbidden by his father, the mission took on new appeal; the danger receded.

The image of the unknown princess took shape in Mika's mind. He pictured long, black flowing tresses, a delicate figure, a wealthy and grateful father, and a few cowardly kobolds hiding in the rocks. Surely the messenger had exaggerated. And even if he had not, surely the Wolf Nomads had defeated them before they themselves were killed.

Mika turned to his father and said loudly for the benefit of the others, "Veltran, honored father, I hear your words and the wisdom they hold, but I would serve the clan best if you would let me go."

Celia sighed in an admiring fashion and stroked his arm lightly. His father started to speak, but Mika-oba, now fully committed to folly by Celia's touch and his own greedy instincts, held up his hand to forestall his words.

"Father, we sent the best of our men to meet that caravan. They are the future of the Wolf Nomads. If they are in danger, so is the entire clan. They must be rescued. I am the best bowman of those who remain, and the best fighter in hand-to-hand combat. I know that I must take my place at your side in the future and I will do so, but let me go now and Whituk will help you say the prayers and pray for guidance."

His words echoed bravely in his own ears, and as he spoke Celia murmured her approval. That was enough to bring him to his senses and almost as soon as he spoke the words of folly, Mika was silently praying that his father would forbid him to go.

Veltran paused for a long moment, during which time Mika-oba's hopes crawled upward only to be dashed an instant later.

Whituk was glaring at Mika still, his anger never far from the surface, always furious that he would be passed over as the chief shaman of the tribe in favor of Mika-oba whom he viewed as a lazy, insolent upstart.

Whituk spoke out in a shrill voice. "The man passed his mission on to Mika-oba. I heard him with my own ears. Mika-oba must go! It has become a matter of honor!"

"Honor is as important as duty," Mika-oba's father said solemnly, looking up to Enor as though for confirmation. His sad, tired eyes looked at Mika through heavy lids. His face was a somber map of wrinkles under the grinning wolf skull. He considered his son soberly.

"I will give you my leave if Enor wishes it," Veltran finally said, and gesturing with his right hand, he invoked the protection of the gods. Mika's heart sank, and he smiled weakly at Celia.

"His strong arm would be useful," agreed Enor, placing his large tanned hand on the shoulder of the chief shaman as though in thanks for his sacrifice, and turning, began barking out the names of those who would accompany them.

All told, there were two score and four who left the camp before the sun reached the top of the trees. They rode the small, shaggy horses of the steppes that could continue the pace, carrying both rider and baggage, long after a long-legged horse of the lowlands had dropped in its tracks.

Each man was accompanied by the wolf that had bonded to him shortly after its birth, a wolf completely loyal to him alone and wild and ferocious to his enemies.

The Wolf Nomads wore heavy leather tunics that covered their hard muscular bodies from neck to knee, flexible yet tough enough to deflect all but the most direct of sword blows.

Their arms were bare to enable them to use their weapons more easily. They carried a wide variety of weapons from the smallest, sharpest knives to huge battle-axes, massive maces, longswords strapped on their backs, and tall, powerful roanwood bows with quivers full of sharp-tipped sablewood arrows.

Their hair, worn free in times of peace, was scraped back up and away from their faces and braided from the hairline down to the nape of the neck in a tight queue, then covered with a form-fitting leather skullcap that flowed into the top of their tunics. Many such helmets were topped with the snarling skulls of wolves that had died in honorable combat, and wolf tails dangled like fringe.

What little flesh remained to be seen was painted with a dull blue-grey clay that gave them an eerie,

otherworldly look that often served to rout their enemies before a single blow was struck.

Their feet were clad in knee-high boots made of the
same thick leather that protected their bodies. They
provided little warmth and no comfort, but comfort
and warmth were supposedly the last things of interest to a Wolf Nomad riding out to war. Not so to
Mika, however, who regarded the extreme discomfort as one of his primary objections to war—next to
death, of course.

They rode on and on westward across the endless
rolling plains, settling down to a steady, ground-
eating pace that would bring them to their destination before the sun rose.

Fathers, Mika-oba thought glumly as he rode
through the long night, his tail-bone grinding pain-
fully on the hard spine of his horse. The horse, a
haughty grey with a decidedly nasty temperament,
struggled against Mika's every command, bucking
and nipping as it ran, making the miles even more
miserable. Mike would have preferred another
horse, but this one had been a gift from his brother at
his manhood rites, and he was stuck with it for life.
Fathers. The problem with fathers was that they were
always so serious and had absolutely no sense of humor.

Enor, father to Celia and chief of their tribe of Wolf
Nomads, was always asking Mika what his intentions
were. Mika did not think it was wise to tell him. Fortunately, there were many other suitors for Celia's
hand, so the issue had not been pressed. But Mika
knew that it was only a matter of time before he was
forced to make a serious decision.

His own father, Veltran, was even worse than Enor, insisting that Mika sit with him for hours on end and learn vast quantities of nonsensical chants and boring lists of stinky weeds and their various uses.

But no matter how hard Mika tried—though when he was being completely honest, he had to admit that he had never tried terribly hard—he could never remember the chants. The rhymes were tricky and strange, and Mika always felt slightly ridiculous repeating them.

The words had a habit of turning themselves round in his head, sometimes producing quite startling results, like the time in the spring when he had accidentally turned a woman into a cat. She had strayed in front of him just as he was chanting. It was not his fault that she had been pursued into the forest by Tam and a horde of very hungry wolves.

Fortunately for the woman, his father had placed a hold spell on the wolves and reversed the chant, turning the cat back into a woman. That was a rather ticklish spell, but Veltran was a high-level magic-user, as well as a shaman. The spell was child's play for one with his skills, so in the end, there was no harm done.

Mika thought it was very unfair of Celia's brother, Enor-oba, to suggest that he had done it on purpose. The fact that the woman was Celia and Enor-oba's mother, a hateful, prune-faced crone who came between him and Celia every chance she got, had absolutely nothing to do with it. Mika was quite certain that it was an accident—well, almost certain, and had no problem looking Celia in the eye and telling her so. Celia, in turn, had no problem believing her beloved. And the chief, Enor, in his wisdom, chose to overlook Mika's indiscretion.

But the chants weren't the real problem. Mika-oba knew in his very heart of hearts that he wasn't cut out to be a shaman, a healer, or a magic user. Lofty and noble ideals were needed for the job, and Mika knew himself well enough to know that he simply didn't possess those qualities. Or perhaps he did, but if so, they were well buried under the desire for good times and available women.

He knew that he'd never be the shaman his father was. That was obvious to Mika, and he wondered why his father persisted in the training that was so painful for them both. Mika scowled into the dark night and heaved a deep sigh.

"Soon, my brother, soon," called a man who rode an arm's-length away, mistaking his sigh for impatience, "our swords will drip with kobold blood!"

"None too soon for me," Mika replied heartily, inwardly damning the fool who would choose killing over a warm bed and a warm woman. TamTur, racing alongside his horse, howled into the night. At least his wolf was hungry for action.

It was all his brother's fault, mused Mika. If he hadn't died, none of this would be happening. Veltran-oba had been his father's apprentice since childhood and was content to spend many long hours puttering around in the forest collecting bits of bark and weeds, fungus and flowers, and scarcely even looking at any of the many beautiful girls who hung around him, oohing and ahhing over his stupid plants, while yearning for the stature that was attached to the wife of a shaman. Veltran-oba had been a serious fellow, but he had taken his brother's disinterest in stride and had even been amused upon occasion by Mika's antics.

But while Mika had not shown any great aptitude for magic and healing, he had become proficient at weaponry and lovemaking, both of which he had learned to handle well and with great precision.

Everyone had expected Veltran-oba to don his father's mantle when the time came, but he had died two winters ago in the sickness that also robbed Mika-oba of his mother and younger sister. Twenty-seven others went to their ancestors at that time, as well, their lungs filled with thick white fluid that choked the breath off in their throats while they burned and trembled with a great fever. It had been a hard winter.

Until the sickness, there had been few clouds on Mika's horizon, other than keeping Celia satisfied and her father in the dark. He and the other nomads spent their time sleeping, hunting for roanbuck in the forest, eating great quantities around the burning campfires while telling stories of wolf heroes, singing songs, drinking mulled mandrake, and spending long hours in mock battle. Life was nearly perfect.

Through luck and good breeding, Mika-oba had been gifted with a magnificent body and handsome, almost noble features. Men thought him a boon companion, and women vied for his favors. He was adept at sword play and most other forms of combat. Fortunately, due to a strong and lasting peace brought about by the Merchant Guild in spite of the grumbling of Wolf and Tiger Nomads alike, there had been few opportunities for serious warfare in many decades. And Mika always had a good excuse when it came to avoiding the occasional kobold battle or bandit-hunt.

Mika had imagined, when indeed he bothered to stretch his thoughts that far, that things would always go on as they were. Enor-oba, the chief's eldest son, and Mika's rival in everything from weapons to women, was destined to be chief one day. His brother would follow his father, and he himself would go on gaming, wenching, hunting, and escorting the seasonal caravan to Yecha or Eru-Tovar across Wolf Nomad lands.

Mika enjoyed these trips as they allowed him to explore the novelties of the cities. He found the immensity of the ocean at the outer edges of the city of Yecha boggling beyond belief. Its vast stretches of endlessly moving waters called to him, cajoling him to leave his land-locked home. The salt-laden breezes caressed his mind like a woman's hand and dared him to discover its hidden secrets.

The intricacies of the city itself were no less fascinating. Used as he was to the lofty trees of the roanwood forest and the empty rolling plains, it was difficult to grasp the suffocating complexity of the city. It seemed that there was too much to see, more than was possible to fit in one's eye. Each and every scene needed to be studied closely to take in all the details, but that was impossible, for nothing ever stood still.

Yecha was the capital city of the Wolf Nomads, founded many centuries earlier by those of the clan who saw the need for a permanent site from which they might sell their loads of roanwood, trade for sablewood and other necessities, and hold their councils with the other nations of Oerth.

These early men of vision had been regarded by the nomads as martyrs who had reluctantly given up the freedom of the forest so that their brothers might live better lives.

The city had grown over the years, having been added onto and built upon until now there was a vast populous of men and women who, though they called themselves Wolf Nomads and wore wolf insignia on their clothes and banners, had never stepped foot in the forest and actually seemed to prefer living in the city! It was all but incomprehensible to Mika.

But even Mika had to admit that the city was an exciting place. Framed by huge, thick stone ramparts that flew the wolf banner, it was crammed with exciting and foreign sights and sounds that flooded the senses like a rare wine.

The streets themselves were narrow and twisting, filled with a wide variety of people—peddlers with packs, hawking their wares; burly countrymen pushing their carts heaped with produce still warm from the earth; painted harridans wearing filmy silks, flanked by massive ebony eunuchs baring naked, curved swords; not to mention ordinary merchants and traders from cities across the whole of Greyhawk, all of whom mingled freely with the everyday citizens of Yecha, exhibiting a multitude of strange manners of dress and customs.

Mika could not imagine how one could possibly live in such a place permanently without losing one's mind. It was barely possible to see the sky, for the buildings were frequently two layers tall and sometimes as many as six, towering higher than the oldest roanwood tree and often leaning out over the narrow streets below.

And the noise! There were no bird songs to be heard and few birds, other than the filthy gulls that flew overhead, laughing shrilly as they dropped evil white deposits on the angry citizenry below. Thin, mangy dogs roamed underfoot searching hopefully for chance morsels and hoping to avoid the prowling wolves that roamed the city freely. At night, the shadows were thick with the massive shapes of rats, their flashing white teeth sharper and more deadly than a cutpurse's knife.

And while he found city men strangely hostile and suspicious of a simple country boy like himself, their women had proved more than willing to make up for the rudeness of their mates.

But all of that would soon be over. Once he became his father's apprentice, there would be no more trips to the city and no more burgher's wives, only dusty old scrolls and stinking weeds.

Following the directions of the dead messenger, the Wolf Nomads approached the banks of the River Fler while mist still curled above the dark waters.

During the long, cold, uncomfortable ride, unremarkable except for the incessant howling of the wolves that flanked them on all sides, Mika-oba had cursed the foolhardy words that had placed him in such danger. Much as he regretted the death of his friends, if indeed they were dead, riding into the arms of a kobold army and getting himself killed would do nothing for his friends, not to mention his own valuable and irreplaceable self.

Although he was very curious about the mysterious princess and her wealth, Mika was determined to stay well to the rear of any battle, maintain a low profile, and return home to the adoring Celia with his skin intact.

Unfortunately, Enor-oba, Celia's hateful brother, had plans of his own, which he implemented as soon as they were within a mile of the river.

The band of nomads had dismounted and staked their horses out after walking and wiping them down to prevent crippling founder. The wolves paced excitedly, dark eyes shining, fangs glinting, knowing by some strange means that blood was about to be shed. TamTur, more disciplined than most of the wolves, heeled to Mika's command, his eyes bright with blood fever.

Enor called the men together as they checked and adjusted their weapons. They grouped in a circle on a small rise, waiting for Enor's strategy.

"We must make our approach before the sun brightens the sky," whispered Enor at last. "But to do so, we must know the disposition and placement of the enemy. Who among you wishes the honor of gathering this information?"

"I would gladly volunteer, Father," Enor-oba said rapidly, before anyone else could speak. "But Mika-oba is the very best among us, by his own admission. I will pass up the honor in deference to Mika-oba's greater skills. I swallow my pride and ask you to allow the better man to go. Send Mika-oba." His tone was serious, yet his dark eyes betrayed his inner malice.

Mika glared at Enor-oba, who crouched less than a

hand span away fingering the long white scar that ran down one side of his face.

"I could not take such an honor upon myself," Mika-oba said between clenched teeth. "You go, my brother."

"No," Enor-oba, said firmly, looking at Mika with mocking eyes, stroking the scar softly. "I cannot count the times you have told me that you are the better man. Now, when the stakes are so high, I bow to your greater abilities."

Mika thought he heard a murmur of suppressed laughter among his companions, though all presented somber faces as they waited for his response. But before he could reply, Enor clapped him on the back and said, "Good lad, I know that this is a simple task, but one that you will relish. Spy out the way of things and return in safety." And there was nothing more to be said.

Muttering blackly to himself, trying to think of a spell or an herb that would cause Enor-oba great discomfort while stopping short of actually killing him, Mika set about making his preparations for the dangerous reconnaissance.

Mika removed the light-grey wolf tails from his helmet and checked to make certain that there was nothing on his person that would reflect light. Satisfied, he smeared all exposed skin with a layer of hastily prepared mud, wrapped his dark cloak around himself, and then quietly slipped away from the others with Tam beside him, skipping with excitement.

He moved silently across the dark prairie until the sound of the river could be easily heard. Then, with TamTur following close at his heels, he made his way downstream, hoping to find a spot that would allow him to view the enemy while remaining unseen.

Creeping among the large rocks that lined the river, Mika and the large wolf gradually worked their way toward the shallow ford in the bend of the river where the caravans traditionally crossed.

After some time, they reached a pile of large rocks perched on the edge of the bank which would provide both the height and the cover he desired. Mika sank into the shadow of the rocks, motioned TamTur to stay, and began to climb, cautious not to disturb the balance of the rocks. He was eventually rewarded with a clear view of the battleground. It was not an encouraging sight.

The caravan was stretched across the river. One wagon rested on Wolf Nomad lands. Three wagons stood axle-deep in the river itself, and six wagons remained on the far side of the river in Tiger Nomad territory.

The dead were strewn around the wagons like leaves after the first frost. The thin cold light of the descending moon outlined their still forms, and Mika-oba was able to pick out at least twelve dead humans and a scattering of wolves. More than a hundred kobold corpses littered the ground, but the messenger had placed their numbers much higher. Mika allowed himself a moment's hope. Maybe the kobolds had been driven back and had abandoned their intended prey!

But even as he allowed such wishful fancies to cross his mind, thin cries erupted from the beleaguered wagons. Answering calls to the left drew his attention, and despair washed over him as more than two

hundred kobolds emerged from the flank of the foothills, almost exactly opposite his position on the far
side of the river, and began advancing on the wagons.

A meager flight of arrows streaked from behind the
wagons and fell short of the kobolds, striking none.
The kobolds, armed with javelins, short spears, axes,
and clubs, continued on in relentless waves.

Mika stared at the kobolds, fascinated in spite of
himself, for while he had never actually seen one, he
had heard them described in great detail by those
who had.

He knew that they were small, barely three feet
tall, every inch packed with diabolical cunning.
Their skin was a tough, horny substance that covered
their body like scaled armor and could deflect all but
the most direct hits from blades and arrows. The dig-
its of their feet and hands ended in sharp claws that
could inflict infection and disease by the merest contact.

Their heads were ugly, bare skulls ridged with a
hard, horny crest, and bestial snouts whose mouths
were filled with jagged teeth.

Their presence here at the river was odd, for they
were subterranean creatures most often found in
dank, dark places like caves or overgrown swamps.

They had obviously chosen their moment of attack
carefully, preferring darkness to the painful brilliance
of daylight. Mika knew that the pupil of the kobold
eye was similar to that of a cat and opened in darkness to utilize whatever light was available. Kobold
night vision was exceptional, as it must be for the
dark underground environs they normally inhabited.
Their human enemies, on the other hand, were both

hampered by the dark and exhausted.

Mika-oba groaned at the kobolds' steady progress, knowing that those sheltered behind the wagons would soon be overcome unless the Wolf Clan could cross the river quickly and come to their aid.

The odds did not look good, but Wolf Nomads were not known for their cowardice, and given the stubborn, pig-headed code of valor that Enor lived by, Mika knew that the chief would not stop to consider the odds, but would order his men into the fray.

Mika did not relish the thought of dying under a swarm of kobolds. Nor did he wish to be taken alive; he had heard rumors of what kobold women did to male human prisoners—placing them in cages and using and abusing them sexually until they begged for death. But what other alternative was there?

Mika thought for a minute, then, spying a smooth rock the size of his hand, he picked it up and considered it. Perhaps he could knock himself out and then wake up conveniently after the battle was over. No one would even miss him. He tapped himself on the head experimentally. Damn! Pain, hurt! Just then, there was a soft slither, and Enor-oba crept to his side.

Silently heaping malediction on the fellow, Mika dropped the rock, signaled Enor-oba to follow and quietly rejoined the waiting band.

"It's not good," Mika reported somberly, hoping that he could persuade the chief to abandon his plan. "It appears that most of the men are dead. I counted many human bodies, both traders and nomads. There cannot be many left alive. I also observed a large army of kobolds. They are advancing on the caravan even now. We are hopelessly outnumbered and I fear that it is already too late to rescue the few survivors. Our losses would be great."

Enor's face was cold and hard. "A Wolf Nomad does not know the meaning of defeat as long as he is still alive! We are born for a life of fighting. If death comes, so be it, as long as it is with honor. I know you would not have it otherwise, Mika-oba."

The chief placed his arm around the shoulders of the younger man and gazed deep into his eyes. "I know how your sword lusts to avenge the death of your friends. I know how your heart longs for battle. Well, you shall soon have your wish.

"Come, men, we must act immediately if we are to save them," said Enor, and Mika knew that there was nothing that he could do or say to convince the chief to change his mind.

Mika stamped his feet and shook his sword with the rest of them, while inwardly raging at the foolhardiness that could so easily cause him to forfeit his life. All Mika truly wished for at that moment was to be safely at home, tucked away in a dark nook, enjoying Celia's favors. It was not his intention to die on the blade of some stupid dwarf of a kobold just to save a wagon load of trade goods. All thoughts of rescuing the mysterious wealthy princess had long since vanished from his mind. Somehow, he must see to it that he was positioned in the rear when they attacked.

"We must cross the river and outflank the kobolds," droned Enor, his arm still wrapped around Mika's shoulders as the men conferred in a tight huddle, wolves crowding in at their feet. "Our only hope will be to trap them between ourselves and those in the wagons. We must not allow them to slip past us and reach the foothills where others of their kind are sure to be hiding."

"Mika-oba must lead us," Enor-oba said with quiet persistence while Mika cursed him silently. "He is, after all, the best bowman among us."

"That is true," Enor said, turning to Mika with a smile. "It is a position of great danger and I would not ask it of you, but I know that one of your prowess would demand it.

"Then, too, you have never had the opportunity of war to exhibit your abilities, since we have been cursed with this lasting peace. Friendly competitions are all right, but there is nothing like a good battle to get a man's blood running and show what he is really made of. I know that you must welcome this opportunity. All eyes will be on you, Mika."

Mika's heart shriveled within his breast. All thoughts of hiding in the rear were now banished by Enor's words. What misfortune! With a surge of panic, he looked from face to face around the circle of warriors, and saw nothing in their eyes but readiness.

"Light!" croaked Mika-oba, his voice shakier than he wished. "Light can be a weapon, honored chief. You are right, I do welcome the challenge, but there are so many kobolds, I dare not risk one of us, not even myself, over such a foolish thing as pride, until all of our comrades are safe. As you know, kobolds hate bright light. If we could fashion flares or large bonfires, it would hurt their eyes and deflect their aim."

"And make ourselves better targets, too," muttered one of the younger men whose older brother had been among those sent to accompany the caravan. Others nodded in agreement.

"Besides, there are no trees this far south of the forest and nothing but rock on the other side of the river," said Enor. "I am afraid we will have to rely on arms and if some of us fall, so be it."

"Grease bushes!" said Mika-oba with a sudden burst of inspiration. "We'll use grease bushes. Spread out and collect as many as possible. Fill your cloaks and wrap them well, for we will have to cross the river, and they must remain dry if they are to serve the purpose."

There was some indecision among the nomads, for not all of them were convinced that Mika knew what he was talking about, but in the end, unable to suggest an alternative plan, Enor nodded his approval and they did as directed.

Mika-oba smiled to himself as he hacked through the tough stem of a squat, round grease bush, piling it on his cloak with the others he had wrested from the hard ground. He pictured the devastation they would cause while allowing him to remain away from the kobolds.

Grease bushes were so named because they stored pockets of a pitch-like substance in their dry branches. Wise travelers avoided their easy abundance and sought other material for building campfires, for while grease bushes burned easily and well, heat caused the pockets of pitch to explode and coat the unwary with spills of clinging fire. With any luck, the kobolds would discover just how painful that could be.

36

Their cloaks were soon filled and the Wolf Nomads followed Mika as he picked his way downstream.

Enor dogged Mika's heels, pushing him on more quickly than he liked. The wolves were in the lead, running silently, tongues lolling, canines gleaming white in the occasional flash of moonlight. The cries of battle were swept toward the party by the winds, faint yet filled with the despair of death and, even more horrible, blood curdling kobold yelps of victory. Even Mika felt his blood stir as his feet carried him ever closer to the battle.

Once past the bend in the stream, the river swung south and then straightened for its descent into Lake Quag. Here, the banks rose steeply and the river rushed at a rapidly increasing speed. In its lower reaches, the water foamed and hurled itself around jagged rocks fallen from the sheer cliffs that framed it on either side. Fortunately, Enor and his men were able to cross before the river entered the narrow divide.

The water was cold and pulled at their boots, attempting to trip them and suck them beneath the dark current. Holding their cloaks on top of their heads, they carefully waded across the watery boundary, climbed out onto the rocky shore, and entered the land of the Tiger Nomads.

The wind was frigid, carrying the cold winds of the Land of the Black Ice from far to the north as it swept down across the desolate tundra. Water clung to their legs like icicles, and their heavy leather boots and tunics were stiff and hard. But this was scarcely noticed, for all their attention was focused on moving as rapidly and quietly as possible. All knew that the kobolds' hearing, framed and funneled by their large pointed ears, was as acute and well-developed as their fabled night vision.

The nomads could hear the cries of battle clearly now, and it seemed that the kobold voices were harsh with the sound of victory.

Driven by the fear that they would be too late, Enor urged his men forward, and they swarmed over the rocks heedless of the noise, hoping that the moving water would swallow the sound of their passage. Mika ran at their side, begrudging every step and hoping that his plan would work.

To their right rose the black bulk of the base of the foothills which marked the short range of mountains that marched along the edge of the river. Their flanks were eroded by deep arroyos that carried the spring runoff into the river. Because of the depth of the arroyos, the battle could only be heard and seen when one stood on their crests. The men scrambled up and down their steep sides, frustrated at the amount of time lost to their passage.

The wolves flowed up and over with ease, the hard scrabble of their claws and panting of their breath the only sounds, and they appeared to be no more than swiftly moving shadows. Tam was breathing heavily and nipping at Mika's heels, stirred by the Wolf Nomads' shouts, which resounded from the wagons.

To Mika's sorrow, they finally crossed the last of the arroyos and peered over its edge, taking advantage of its shelter and position above and behind the kobold lines.

The closest wagon lay a scant hundred paces away on a sand beach at the edge of the water. Seven Tiger

Nomads were crumpled in various poses of death, the striped bodies of their tiger companions close beside them, constant even in death.

The sight of the Tiger Nomads and their fallen beasts wrenched something deep inside Mika-oba. Wolf and Tiger Nomads had few ties, sharing little but the same ancient warrior heritage, favoring distance rather than close contact.

Tiger Nomads were brave men, accustomed to living simply and harshly according to the laws that guided them, and in company with their fierce, bonded tigers. These deaths, more than the greater number of fallen traders, brought home the meaning of the deadly game they were about to enter.

The Wolf Nomads crouched at the lip of the arroyo, looking down on the rocky slope of land that stretched between themselves and the bend of the river. The ground was covered by a frenzied army of kobolds that screamed and yelled and waved their weapons in the air as they closed the gap between themselves and the remaining survivors.

"Pray the Great She Wolf your plan works," whispered Enor. And Mika did so fervently as he pounded the point of a war arrow into the base of the grease bush. The moon was nearly set and the sun had not yet cleared the tops of the mountains to the east. It was the time which men fear most, the time of grey darkness when spirits most often join their ancestors.

All around him, men followed his lead and forced their arrows into the dry bushes, while wolves crouched at their sides, tense and anxious, whining high-pitched cries that were feverish with excitement.

"The bushes are heavy," grunted Mika-oba, "and will pull the points of the arrows down, but they must fly only a short distance, and we are above the target. Pull hard, aim high, and it will work." And he fervently hoped that he was right.

Hasteen, brother of the missing Haj, struck a firestone with a hissing intensity and, barely waiting for Enor's cry of "FIRE!" each man shot his arrow high into the air above the kobold ranks, then bent with scarcely a pause and pounded home another.

The air was filled with a fiery rain as the brightly burning bushes pelted down on the unsuspecting kobolds, showering them with explosive bursts of hot burning pitch.

The night was rent with screams of pain as the burning pitch burned the kobolds' scanty raiment and continued searing their horny skin. Writhing in anguish and rage, the kobold leader, an ugly brute half again the size of his followers, turned and scanned the rocks behind his ragged army, seeking the origin of the unexpected attack.

Mika-oba knew that the element of surprise was over. The kobold would soon spot them and direct his followers to attack the attackers. Rising to his feet at Enor's signal, Mika shrieked a hair-raising wolf cry, and waved nomads and wolves onward down the slope toward the kobold army.

Suddenly, just as the last of the men had passed him, a hard shove from behind pushed Mika off balance and he was forced to run downhill as fast as he could go in a desperate attempt to remain on his feet. With utter horror, he found himself overrunning his companions and plunging well ahead of the front line on a course that would soon place him squarely in the middle of the kobold lines.

A shriek of terror lifted from his throat and his comrades, taking it as a cry of courage, increased their strides and closed behind him in a solid wedge, propelling him on, their own wolf calls drowning out his piteous bleats of fear.

Axes, swords, pikes, and javelins raised above their heads, screaming madly, the Wolf Nomads, terrifying in their blue war paint with their ravening beasts beside them, caromed down the hill and slammed into the rear of the kobold army.

Chapter 2

ULULATING WOLF WAILS rose from the throats of
the Wolf Clan as they slashed their way through the
astonished kobolds. A chorus of elated wolf cries answered them from the wagons. Hasteen and several
of the younger nomads perched on the lip of the arroyo and continued firing flaming grease bushes into
the churning ranks of the kobolds.

Mika, finding himself suddenly alone but surrounded by kobolds on the rocky slopes, seized his
battle axe and began whirling round and round,
while screaming like a madman. Blood flew—kobold
blood—and hope grew that if he could just keep
swinging, the wretched creatures would not be able
to get close enough to hurt him.

Tam crouched at his feet, just below the arc of the
blade, snarling, ready for any kobold foolish enough
to venture within reach of his open jaws. Some did,
and Tam feasted on their blundering bodies.

A short distance away, the kobold leader roared in
anger and beat out the fiery sparks on his orange tu-

nic with his horny palms while urging his followers to stand fast and attack the newcomers. A few did as he directed, but the majority were too confused and frightened by the flames, which continued to rain down on them. Those few kobolds that did manage to reach the attacking Wolf Clan did not live long enough to regret their mistake.

Emboldened by the presence of their rescuers, twenty-odd survivors emerged from behind the wagons and joined their comrades.

The battle was long and fierce, but the advantage had been tipped in favor of the nomads, and as the first light of dawn crept over the eastern edge of the hills, its cold bright light so painful to the kobold's sensitive eyes, the nomads seized the initiative and pressed the creatures into a total rout.

Screaming their wolf cries, the nomads moved about them with axe and sword, hacking and slashing, killing kobolds in large numbers.

The wolves and the few tigers that remained alive were charged with a maniacal blood lust. Their eyes glittered crazily and their open jaws revealed sharp teeth that drooled with dark kobold blood.

The crazed animals seemed to favor prey that moved, and they brought down one fleeing kobold after another. A few kobolds, more clever than their unfortunate companions, took advantage of this tactic and dropped to the ground and played dead, crawling off after the bloodthirsty animals had passed them by.

Toward the end of the bloody battle, Mika-oba, who had grown both weary and dizzy, found himself face to face with the kobold leader. Its rusty brown hide was burned and bleeding in a dozen places, but fury still glowed in its orange eyes.

"You have won the day," the kobold growled in a guttural voice as it circled Mika-oba wielding a broken shortsword, searching for an opening, "but you will lose in the end. . . ."

Mika-oba responded in a cool, doubting tone, "It is you who will die, and we who will dance in your blood. . . ."

But the kobold was smarter than Mika-oba thought, having survived more than a few battles and learned from them as well. He opened his muzzle as though to speak further. When Mika-oba hesitated, the kobold lashed out with his sword and slashed Mika-oba diagonally across the chest. Only his fast reflexes saved him from a fatal blow.

Mika struck out with his axe and the kobold ducked low, letting the heavy blade swish harmlessly overhead. He used the opportunity to cut at Mika's knees with his bit of broken sword. Mika felt the blade nick him and leaped back, wishing that Tam had not abandoned him to join in the frenzied killing of the kobolds in retreat.

Mika and the kobold drove back and forth on the rocky slopes, neither able to gain the advantage. Mika was tiring, his muscles stiffening and trembling with fatigue. He knew he had to kill the kobold before he grew too tired to lift the heavy axe.

Giving a loud shriek, he raised the axe above his head and swung it in short, tight circles, driving the kobold back. The kobold could only retreat and soon found itself plastered against a stony outcrop.

As Mika raised his axe for the final blow, the kobold's brutal face snarled up at him with unremitting hatred. Then suddenly, before he could bring the axe down on the kobold's horny head, something sped past him with a harsh exhalation of air and thunked into the kobold.

The kobold shrieked and clutched its chest. Black blood erupted through its scaly fingers as did the shaft of a spear. As it sank to its knees, the kobold's face contorted, and Mika realized with a shock that it was smiling!

". . . Iuz . . . will . . ." gasped the kobold, struggling to form the words, but they did not come, and with a final shudder, it toppled onto its face and died.

"Iuz will do what? What about Iuz!" screamed Mika-oba as he grabbed the dead kobold and shook it violently. Enor materialized beside him and with some effort extracted his spear from the kobold's dead body. Then the chieftain noticed Mika's wild expression and grasped him firmly on the shoulders, intending to calm him.

"What are you doing?" Enor asked. "The creature is obviously dead. It has gone to its ancestors, if there is a place for such as these after death."

"Enor, it said something about Iuz right before it died," said Mika.

No Wolf Nomad could help but be disconcerted over the mention of the evil demon, lord of the Middle Lands in whose name untold acts of horror had been committed, and whom even the Wolf Nomads, whose lands bordered his, had cause to fear. Iuz had been ominously quiescent for generations. There were rumors about his presence from time to time, and there were unfounded reports of his foul deeds, but nothing certain or reliable. Why would Iuz be aligned with lowly kobolds?

"Iuz," Enor muttered uneasily, prodding the dead kobold with his toe. "I hope you are mistaken, Mika, or that the creature was lying. Let us pray that it is so. The demon lord has not been heard from in years, and I would have it remain that way."

Enor stood up beside the dead kobold and stared around him. The field was littered with dead and dying kobolds and a few injured wolves and nomads. Enor gazed off in the distance, where the main body of kobolds, perhaps forty or more, had gathered together for a last stand at the edge of the river. But it was a doomed affair, for the sun was rising, growing in strength and brilliance. Its bright rays shone down, blinding them to the flight of arrows and the final slash and cut of sword and axe. Soon, the last of them were dead, their black blood flowing into the rushing waters of the River Fler.

But Mika was seized with doubt and indecision. Had he heard the kobold leader correctly? So frightening was the thought of Iuz, drummed into his imagination from childhood and the lessons of his father, that he was more than willing to believe that his ears had tricked him, or that the kobold had lied. Enor was equally willing to forget the implications.

"Come, Mika, pay this one no more mind," directed Enor, pulling him away from the dead kobold. "We must tend to the living and eliminate those few of the enemy that may have survived."

Mika rejoined his companions, and they combed the battlefield carefully, aided by the wolves and tigers, searching out those humans and kobolds that still lived. They found only one suffering human, a wagon driver, who soon perished of his wounds, although grateful to die in the presence of men and with the sound of prayers in his ears to guide his spirit to the afterworld.

Many kobolds had survived, although bearing horrendous wounds that would have killed a man. They taunted the Wolf Nomads with curses and animal cries and died with smiles on their muzzles as the Wolf Men plunged swords through their hearts.

Mika was troubled by a lingering doubt, and whenever possible, out of the hearing of other nomads, he tried to question all kobolds who came before his sword. He also searched their foul-smelling clothing for documents, but they were either without knowledge or without fear and gave up nothing except their worthless lives.

"Leave them here as a warning to their foul brethren," Enor directed his clansmen as the sun rose slowly in the cold sky. "Perhaps it will give them reason to think before they attack another caravan. We have given the Guild our word of protection. Wolf Nomads do not make promises that they cannot keep."

"They will remember the lesson we have taught them today," Enor-oba said pompously, and Mika was saddened to see that the chief's son had come through the battle without even a scratch.

"To attack a caravan under the protection of the Wolf Nomads is to attack the Wolf Nomads themselves . . ." Enor-oba continued as the men began to drift away, disinterested in his somber pronouncements. Even Enor turned from his son and began directing the removal of the last few wagons across the river and into the safety of the Wolf Nomad territory.

"You men," called Enor, pointing at the widely scattered groups of nomads. "Check the area. I want to be certain that every last kobold is dead before we leave."

Mika was tired. His arms ached and his back was stiff and caked with sweat. All he wanted was to sit down and rest. He didn't want to look for kobolds. He had seen more than enough kobolds to last him for a long time.

But he knew from long experience that it was no use arguing with Enor. "I'll check the arroyos," he cried, and received a brief wave of acknowledgement from Enor, whose attention was focused on the work with the wagons.

The rest of the men were searching the area between the arroyos and the river. No one was near him. Satisfied that he had the area to himself, Mika slipped over the edge of an arroyo and wandered along its length, searching wearily for a concealed spot in which to sit and rest.

Such a spot soon presented itself, a small cut in the bank near the head of an arroyo where he was hidden from casual observation. He sank down on a large boulder, rested his back against the steep slope and closed his eyes with a hearty sigh.

TamTur circled in place several times, then sank to the ground, curled himself into a tight ball, his silvery brush covering his nose, and fell into a deep sleep.

Mika relaxed in the warm sunlight, allowing the tension to flow out of his stiff muscles, and congratulated himself on surviving the battle, despite the shove from . . . Enor-oba, no doubt.

His thoughts drifted, considering the wagon train. It had appeared quite ordinary, no different from any other caravan, and certainly not the repository of a beautiful princess and great wealth. Ah, the princess! He had almost forgotten about her. Had the messenger lied? Was it all an elaborate hoax to ensure the rescue of his comrades? Mika thought not, but he would have to get a closer look at the surviving wagons . . . after a brief, well-deserved snooze.

Mika had been seated for only a short time, enjoying the warmth of the sun on his face and chest, when he felt a strange tingling cover his body. He opened his eyes abruptly.

A small kobold stood directly in front of him, blocking the rays of the sun. Mika cursed his own stupidity for placing himself in such a tightly wedged position where he could not easily wield either axe or sword.

They stared at each other for a long moment, each studying the other. The kobold wore a badly singed orange tunic and its bony crest sagged crookedly above its eyes as though it had been broken by a direct blow. Then, even as Mika considered rushing the creature, overwhelming it by sheer bulk, a second figure appeared in the narrow opening.

Mika-oba could not tell whether the creature standing against the sun was human or not, draped as it was in a heavy dark cloak from head to toe, its features completely concealed by deep, unnatural shadows. The kobold lifted its wrinkled muzzle and spoke to the figure that stood a mere hand span taller.

The kobold seemed to speak with great deference, and its cringing posture suggested fear.

The small dark figure leaned on a thick staff and stared at Mika without movement.

After a few moments of the silent staring, Mika grew increasingly uneasy. There was something quite frightening about the small figure that filled Mika with a sense of dread. He backed up, but there was nowhere to go. The silence stretched on like an unending scream.

Mika shook himself mentally, attempting to shake off his unreasoning anxiety. What was he afraid of? The Wolf Nomads had won, hadn't they? He raised his arm and started to draw his sword out of the sheath that hung between his shoulder blades, taking a step toward the odd pair.

He flexed his massive shoulders—intimidatingly, he hoped—and rattled his sword. He took another step, hoping they would back off, but the twosome stood their ground firmly as Mika-oba approached. His blade snicked through the air, making a most satisfying sound, rather like the sound of a neck separating from a head, Mika thought with a rush of humor. Yet still the pair did not flee. It was definitely unkobold-like behavior. But when he noticed the kobold shrinking back in a most satisfying manner, he drew in a great mouthful of air for his attacking wolf cry, and rushed forward, sword raised high.

Slowly, almost leisurely, the small, dark figure raised a shrouded hand and pointed at Mika, the tip of its cloak and the bountiful folds describing lazy movements in the air.

Mika felt as though he had slammed face first into

51

a pile of sand. The faint tingling he had felt earlier had been but a hint of what he experienced now.

His entire body was wrapped in a numbing cold. Yet he felt as though he were being stung by bees from the top of his scalp down to the soles of his feet.

His heart slammed against his ribcage like a hawk caught in a cage, hurling itself against the bars, determined to escape or die in the trying.

His blood roared in his ears and pressure built behind his eyes till his vision blurred and he could sense only vaguely the kobold and the dark creature approaching him as he stood frozen in place, sword still raised above his head.

"Should I kill 'im, Master?" the kobold asked nervously.

Mika felt sweat pouring down his face, and he strained every muscle in his body, attempting to lower his arms and crash the sword into his enemy. But he could not move his arms. In fact, he could not move anything at all. All he could do was stand there, frozen, and wait for the dark creature to decide his fate.

The cloaked figure did not answer immediately, but walked around Mika-oba as he stood there, with eyes bulging and sweat running down his body, looking like some strange statue dedicated to a rightfully forgotten god.

Mika-oba was in pain. He was cold and his body itched unbearably. He was even a little frightened. But most of all, he felt stupid. Incredibly, overwhelmingly stupid. He marveled at the degree of his stupidity and knew that he deserved to die.

"Can I do it now? Do you wants 'im dead?" the

kobold repeated helpfully.

In spite of the fact that he had just decided he deserved to die, it was quite another thing having the kobold agree with him. Mika-oba silently heaped foul curses on the wretched beast and wished with all his might that its tongue would wither in its head.

"I could stab 'im, real easy like," the kobold offered, completely unaffected by Mika-oba's ardent wishing.

The cloaked figure completed its circuit around Mika's stiffened body and waved the kobold into silence with a twitch of its hand. The kobold fell quiet instantly.

Mika's vision had cleared a little and he was able to focus on the darkness in the center of the hood, yet he could not make out any features, human or otherwise. It was as though the cloak were held up by nothing but blackness.

Then he ceased to wonder about anything, even his fate, for once more he was seized by the incredible cold that seemed to enter his skull and grow more and more intense until there was nothing left of the world but pain.

After several lifetimes, the pain receded and left him still standing, sword above his head, only vaguely aware of his tormentor.

"So he doesn't knows nothing?" queried the kobold, its voice seeming to come from a great distance. "Can't I kills 'im anyways?" it whined in a disappointed tone. Evidently the answer was negative, for Mika-oba continued to live, although it took him a while to ascertain that fact and even longer to regret it.

As the pain left his body, he stood, still locked in place, sword held high above his head, still cursing himself for being such an ignoramus.

The kobold and the robed creature had vanished. Mika felt ill, not only from the all-too-unpleasant physical effects left over from the encounter, but from the knowledge that he had just had a brush with a dark magic-user. One did not need to see a sign hanging around someone's neck to recognize such a spell-caster. Mika-oba had deserved to die for his negligence and realized that he was alive only because the magic-user had spared him.

After a while, the pain and the cold and the stinging left him and it appeared fairly certain that he would live. But still he could not move. Not even one little finger.

He prayed that none of his companions would come searching for him and find him in such a state. He would be the butt of humorous songs and jokes for centuries to come.

He heard a wide yawn behind him as TamTur stirred, stretched, then got to his feet, having slept through the entire incident. Perhaps the magic-user had arranged it thusly.

Tam walked around Mika, sat down on his haunches, yawned shrilly, then placed his head to one side and stared at Mika-oba curiously. He circled Mika several times, then with a movement that must have been the animal equivalent of a human shrug, TamTur curled himself into a ball at Mika's feet and went back to sleep. Thanks a lot, pal.

Mika grunted and strained and willed his muscles to move. Finally, aided perhaps by some stray gust of wind, he did move. Forward. And down. He could not even close his eyes as he smacked, face first, onto the hard earth and lay there without moving for several additional lifetimes.

"Mika! Mika-oba!" called a voice.

"Mika! Where are you!" cried another.

"Oh no," Mika groaned inwardly.

"Here he is!" cried a voice filled with relief. Hands seized his shoulders and turned him over roughly.

"Mika! What a place to take a nap!" Hasteen said with admiration shining in his eyes. "Have you no fear? There might easily be more kobolds sneaking around. Come on, the Guildsman has broken out a wineskin in gratitude for our help.

"Enor sent us to find you. Everyone wants to grip the arm of the man who saved our lives." And he extended his hand to Mika.

To Mika's amazement and joy, he found that he could move, albeit stiffly, and felt no worse for his experience than he had after a night of drinking honeyed ale. Taking Hasteen's hand, he rose to his feet and walked shakily down the slope with a sleepy Tam trailing behind.

"I can't take all the credit," he said with a nervous laugh to cover his confusion. "After all, I did have help," he said, yawning widely. "Tell me, how many men did we lose?"

During the trek back to the caravan, which now rested on the Wolf Nomads' side of the river, Mika-oba learned that the majority of the Wolf members who died in the raid had come from a clan that lived closest to the river and were, for the most part, unknown to him. Only two of their own clan had died before killing more than a score of kobolds apiece. Their widows would be well regarded.

The wagons were drawn in a circle, and drivers, tradesmen, and Wolf Nomads mingled freely, passing jugs of root liquor and Celadian wine and chewing on dried sticks of venison. Celebratory voices were raised in boasting and song. The survivors were heroes, and happy to be alive.

"Why do you suppose they did it?" asked one of the wagon drivers, a big burly Yechan who wore a bloody rag tied around his head. "I ain't never known kobolds to be that brave and I never heard tell of any around here before."

"And they ain't known for cooperatin' with each other, neither," added another man who seemed to be in charge of the mules that pulled the wagons. "I never seen any two of 'em who could get along fer longer than a heartbeat."

Enor-oba was equally puzzled by the attack but passed it off with a casual comment. "Kobolds are stupid. They don't need a reason for anything, they just do it."

Mika-oba had never spent much time pondering the intelligence of kobolds, but reason told him that it took a certain amount of mental ability to gather several hundred kobolds and mount a concerted attack on a heavily guarded caravan.

Mika was scarcely able to enjoy the fine Celadian wine or pay much attention to the comments and congratulations of his comrades, so deep was his feeling that there was something very wrong about the raid. The kobold who mentioned Iuz, the encounter with the magic-user . . . Everything pointed to something exceedingly strange afoot. But Enor had shrugged it off. And Mika knew nothing really—just misgivings and an incident without proof, clues . . . Who would listen to him?

Even after the wagons set off across the plains, Mika-oba considered confronting Enor with everything that had happened, but the thought of relating the humiliating experience with the magic-user turned his ears red, and he knew that he could never speak of it to the chief. He put it aside in his mind. It was an isolated incident, he told himself, of no great importance. There would be no further mischief.

He was bolstered by the reaction of the Guildsman, a small, thin, bald man with bright blue eyes, who clasped his hand and regarded him with a thoughtful eye.

Mika had ridden up alongside the Guildsman in an effort to peer into one of the wagons. Now that danger was past, his thoughts returned to the wealthy princess . . . if she existed. All the wagons looked more or less alike, but Mika couldn't help but notice that the caravan leader never strayed far from the side of one that looked to be pulling an especially heavy load. When Mika leaned over to get a better view of the wagon, the Guildsman's smiling face blocked his view. He engaged Mika in conversation about the kobold battle, but in Mika's opinion there was something shifty, evasive, about the man. And he never did get a clear look at the wagon.

"Forget them," the Guildsman said of the kobolds with a dismissive gesture. "Kobolds are as unpredictable as they are stupid. We will see no more of them now that we are out of the foothills."

"What is your cargo?" Mika asked with interest. "Are you carrying anything unusual, something special that would draw their attention?"

"Nothing more than the usual imported wines, lengths of sablewood, and spear points required by our brothers to the east for their continued daily existence," the Guildsman said with a shrug. "Certainly nothing that would attract an army of kobolds."

"Nothing like a beautiful princess or coffers of fabulous wealth?" Mika said in an offhand manner, watching for the man's response.

"Don't I wish," said the Guildsman with a rueful chuckle. "It would make this job a lot more interesting."

"That is what your messenger told me," said Mika. "The kobolds had ripped him up pretty bad. I can't imagine anyone suffering like he did to reach us to get help unless you carried something of great importance."

"We were friends," said the Guildsman. "And he was a brave man. Would you not do such a thing to save the lives of your friends under such circumstances?"

Mika was silent, wondering what he would do in such a situation and hoping that he would never have to find out.

But in spite of the man's words, Mika was convinced that the Guildsman was not telling the truth. There was more here than met the eye, and it had nothing to do with kobolds.

"Well, it's good to be underway again," sighed the

Guildsman, attempting to change the subject. "All thanks to you good fellows! There'll be more than a few coppers in it for you once we get to Eru-Tovar! I'll show you a good time and give you my thanks in full once we arrive in safety. No more kobolds! I've had my fill!"

Mika edged his horse—the stubborn grey stallion that fought his every command—closer to the wagons and slowed him to a walk. The Guildsman rode up next to Mika, and kept up a stream of meaningless chatter that Mika ignored. Seemingly more heavily loaded than the others, the wagon creaked along. Its driver was even less informative than the Guildsman.

The driver stared at Mika with a sullen expression on his large moon-shaped face. His arms and upper body swelled with huge muscles, and the reins were all but lost in his ham-like fists. Mika noticed that, while all the other wagons were pulled by a team of two mules, this wagon was drawn by four. Like the other wagons, it was laced tightly shut fore and aft, revealing no clue of its contents.

"What's in the wagon?" Mika asked the Guildsman one more time, the question unmistakeably sharp and brazen.

"Nothing that's your concern," replied the Guildsman, all banter gone from his tone. "Mind your own business, nomad, and let me mind mine."

Mika touched his hand to his forehead in a derisive gesture and rode away, more certain than ever that his suspicions were correct.

The Guildsman was no ordinary merchant and there must be something special secreted in the wagon. Somehow, he intended to find out what it was.

Chapter 3

THE CARAVAN MOVED slowly across the rocky plains, jolting from one uneven slope to the next. The mules bent to their thankless task, heads down, eyes to the ground, and plodded along stolidly.

The wagons themselves were solidly made of roanwood, purchased from Wolf Nomads who did a thriving business in the hardwood which was difficult to cut but impervious to rot and weather. They were covered with hoods of tanned cowhide stretched taut over rounded ribs, which kept the rain off the valuable cargo.

The wheels were huge, reaching halfway up the sides of the cowhide covering. They were made of roanwood saplings, bent and shaped while wet. Once dry, the formed saplings were married to hot hammered metal. A good wheel made by a master wheelwright could last a careful man a lifetime.

The mules were huge, brown shaggy things with foul tempers, but they were better suited to the terrain than oxen or horses. In the early days, the wagons had been larger, with four huge wheels, and the teams had consisted of four, six, and even eight mules capable of carrying larger loads and earning the Guild even greater profits. But the challenge of the terrain had quickly put an end to that.

As one left Yecha, the land was smooth and gently rolling. Sweet grass and cultivated fields stretched for many miles to the east. Then the smooth terrain ceased abruptly, giving way to rock and alkaline earth where only greasewood bushes could find sustenance.

The earth grew increasingly barren and rocky as it plunged through the rugged foothills of the Yatil Mountains, with only small pockets of greenery at the edge of the River Fler. And always the wind blew down from the glaciers in the frozen north.

Once across the river, the land opened onto the true stretches of the steppes, seemingly endless expanses of open plain. But the ground was stony and forbidding, and only greasewood and stringweed, a tough fibrous grass, were able to survive and in turn nourish the mules that could eat almost anything.

The large, heavily laden wagons struck rocks often, sometimes tipping over and spewing their cargo across the ground, killing or maiming the draft animals and drivers and often damaging the wheels themselves. The stony ground made passage difficult, causing many horses to stumble, go lame, and become victims of the roving packs of wild wolves that found horses a tastier than usual meal.

Oxen were tougher but required more forage and more water than the steppes provided. They also traveled more slowly, and their ponderous pace pronounced their doom, for traders used up their provisions and died or were slaughtered long before they found more friendly land. And so the merchants and traders had reluctantly traded the larger wagons for the smaller carts that could travel more swiftly and easily over the difficult ground.

The land was the least of the problems actually; there were far greater dangers from other quarters. While the plains were the domain of the Wolf Nomads, they were also home to a large number of wild creatures, from the tiniest of poisonous spiders to fierce packs of wild wolves.

Thieves, murderers, brigands, and all manner of desperate rogues also wandered the steppes—outcasts of Yecha and Eru-Tovar who had been banished from the cities for their crimes, an easier and far more cruel punishment than imprisonment.

Here the hapless criminal was permitted to live. But there was no shelter, no food, and more than a thousand treacherous miles between Yecha and Eru-Tovar. These men were fair prey to the more bloodthirsty of the Wolf and Tiger Nomads who hunted them from horseback like pigs, if the wild animals did not get them first.

Some, of course, did survive by some manner of miracle, and they in turn preyed on the caravans, seeing them as the only means of sustenance in the desolate territory.

The danger from wild animals and desperate men provided both Tiger and Wolf Nomads with steady and profitable work accompanying the caravans across their lands. The nomads found the work much to their liking, for they enjoyed nothing more than hunting wild animals and dangerous criminals for sport and would have done so even without getting paid. As a system, it worked well. There had been few incidents in Mika's lifetime. Until now.

The caravan lurched slowly across the plains, heading for the Wolf Nomad camp where it was agreed that the worst of the wounded would remain until they were well. They would be replaced by Wolf Nomads who, including some of those who had gone on the raid, would accompany the caravan to Eru-Tovar.

The wagons progressed at a snail's pace, the mules' bells tinkling melodically. But one wagon, the secret wagon as Mika had dubbed it, moved more slowly and much more heavily than the others, its wheels chunking from one rock to the next. The four mules that pulled it were the most immense mules Mika-oba had ever seen. But despite their great size, the weight of the wagon's load lathered their backs and lips with thick white foam.

The Guildsman was tending to duties at another part of the caravan. Mika saw his opportunity once again and angled his horse closer to the secret wagon, hoping that the ends of the wagon might now be unlaced. They were not. The driver threw him a scowl, and Mika noticed that he wore two knives at his belt and looked as though he knew how to use them. The man watched him closely as he brought the grey alongside the laboring wagon.

"Ho, brother. It is well that we are away," Mika said genially, smiling across at the man in a friendly manner. "An evil business. How did your cargo fare?"

The man did not answer, merely leaned forward and slashed the reins down cruelly on the mules' backs.

"Hold, brother," Mika said pleasantly, although a hint of something hard had crept into his voice. "No need to harm the beasts; it looks as though they are giving you their all."

The man turned his head toward Mika and spoke quietly but with force. "I am not your brother, and my cargo and animals are none of your concern. Go away."

TamTur growled deep in his throat, and Mika did not have to look at the beast to answer the question. He waved his hand in a command gesture, forbidding the wolf the right to attack.

"I was merely passing the time of day, brother," Mika said, using the term purposefully now. "I am not well versed in the ways of the city, but out here on the plains, it does not pay to be rude intentionally. One never knows when one might need a friend."

The man's dark eyes held Mika's gaze without flinching and Mika knew that this one would never call for help no matter what the circumstances.

Mika slowed his horse and fell back, allowing the wagon to pass him. He studied it carefully. Front and back were still tightly sealed. The wheels groaned in protest against the heavy load, and the axle complained in a shrill unending shriek that grated on the nerves. TamTur whined and shook his head, the high-pitched noise hurting the tender membranes of his inner ear.

Mika brought the grey to a halt, allowing the

wagon to pull away, studying it as it rode low to the ground, and decided that he would have a closer look at it and its mysterious cargo once they reached camp, whether or not the driver or Guildsman approved. If there was a beautiful princess inside, she was yet to be glimpsed, and not a whimper of complaint or request issued from the wagon as it groaned along the route.

They reached camp at nightfall, greeted while they were still far out on the open prairie by a host of young, semi-naked boys daubed blue, riding bareback, and accompanied by their wolves, most of which were still leggy and ungainly with puppyhood.

The boys rode wide circles around the caravan, yipping and caroling wolf cries, parodies of the calls that would be used later in more serious encounters. They carried lances, some of which bore banners bearing the wolf emblem, and others that streamed long wolf tails.

They were answered by the returning warriors who wailed their own wolf calls into the cold night air. Their cries set off the wolves, which reared their heads and joined their voices in an eerie chorus that hung on the ear and sent shivers up and down the spines of those in the wagon train.

The sound of their voices brought people hurrying to the edge of the forest and crowding out onto the Far Fringe. Mika rode to the fore, placing himself next to Enor and Enor-oba, looking casual and unconcerned, his eyes searching for Celia.

Enor-oba looked at Mika with hatred, his hand going to the white scar on his face, almost without thought. "You shall not have her," he said through gritted teeth.

"What?" asked Mika, startled.

"You shall not have my sister," repeated Enor-oba. "You may have my father fooled, but not me. You are a coward and care only for yourself. I will do whatever is necessary to expose you as the scoundrel you are. Believe me, for I mean what I say."

Mika looked into Enor-oba's eyes and saw the hatred that burned there.

"What has set your ears on end, brother?" he asked with an easy smile. "We have competed since our earliest days. We crawled into the same den together and took our cubs from the same litter . . ."

"Yes, and you took the one I wanted," Enor-oba said bitterly, "and left me the female runt."

". . . so why declare me enemy now, after so many years?" Mika continued, the smile still on his lips.

"I know that you are a coward who wants nothing more than to laze among the women," Enor-oba spat. "Had I not seen to it, you would have stayed at the rear throughout the entire conflict. I prayed that you would die, but you survived and now others will think you a hero. I know the truth and have had my fill of your posturing. I will see to it that others know as well. Including Celia. Especially Celia."

Mika saw that Enor-oba meant what he said, and that no words of his could change the man's mind. Besides, every word that he said was true.

He looked into the hate-filled eyes and grinned complacently, remembering the day shortly after their fifteenth year, when they had completed the last and the most important of the requirements for their initiation into adulthood, the acquiring of a wolf cub that would bond with them and remain loyal to them unto death.

The taking of a cub was no easy matter, for while a pack only had one dominant male and female that bred and produced cubs, there might easily be up to six other members of the pack that guarded, fed, and helped raise the pups.

A cub had to be taken young, before it had bonded to its wolf parents. And it was difficult to approach them at such an early age, as the wolves stayed close to the den.

Mika-oba and Enor-oba had both spied out the same den, yearned after the same large, black male pup, whose only other sibling was a small, runty female.

On the day of the taking, Mika had tricked Enor-oba into believing that the cubs had been moved to an alternate den. Enor-oba had believed Mika and had crawled into the den in search of the cub.

Later, Mika protested innocence and denied any knowledge of the fierce lone wolf that had taken up residence in the den. He had even offered to help his father mix up the ointment that would prevent the long deep wound on Enor-oba's face from scarring and festering.

The next day, while Enor-oba lay abed with his face mysteriously bloated to a grotesque size and his eyes swollen shut, Mika had brought him his new black wolf pup to admire. Enor-oba would not stop howling and had to be forcibly restrained from trying to strangle Mika.

By the time he recuperated, the only cub left was the tiny female that never attained full size and would

obey all commands except those of Enor-oba. Mika
grinned at Enor-oba, the memory still bright in his
mind's eye.

Still smiling, Mika touched his heels to the ribs of
the grey and caused it to leap away in a spray of
gravel and dirt that showered down on Enor-oba as
Mika rode for camp whooping and hollering exuber-
antly.

There was much commotion in camp as the
women dropped what they were doing and hurried to
the sides of their men.

"You are well?" asked Veltran as his eyes sought
evidence of injury on his son's body.

"Yes, Father, I am well," sighed Mika-oba as he
clasped the older man's fragile shoulder, taking in the
sight of his tiny shrunken body, draped as always in
the heavy wolf headdress and pelt.

Veltran's eyes, though blue, were faded and dull,
and wrinkles criss-crossed his face in a cruel map of
his years. Mika saw the weariness and pain that he
carried with him like a visible burden. His father had
become an old man without his even noticing.

Suddenly, he felt shamed and he realized for the
first time how hard the death of his mother, sister, and
brother had affected his father, how precious he himself had become.

"I'm fine, Father," he said gently, as they walked
along the line of wagons that had entered the camp
and creaked to a halt.

"There are many wounded to be tended to. I will
help you as best as I am able."

"You are not hurt?" asked his father, placing a thin
hand lined with prominent veins on Mika's tanned

arm.

"Just tired and stiff," replied Mika. "It was a long ride and I will welcome my bed tonight." Or Celia's, he thought to himself.

"What casualties?" asked his father, walking quickly toward the lead wagon and fumbling for the large pouch of healing herbs that he always carried at his waist.

"Ten dead, all told. Only two from our camp. But many are wounded; they are all in the first three wagons."

"I am glad you are unharmed," Veltran said, pausing beside one of the wagons. "You are all that the gods have left to me, and my heart falters at the thought of losing you. I will not rest easy until you wear the robes of the high shaman as I do and put the danger of war aside. Promise me that you will not do this again. Promise me!"

Veltran gripped Mika-oba's wrist with surprising strength and his rheumy eyes stared intently into those of his son.

Mika squirmed under the intensity of his father's gaze, wanting to please the old man, but unwilling to commit his life to the gathering of smelly weeds and the memorization of reams of confusing spells.

"Promise me," urged his father while Mika hesitated, trying to think of some reply that would satisfy his father without binding him to some awful vow. On the other hand, there were definite advantages to curing beautiful maidens. And there was the gratitude of young wives and the comforting of grieving widows to consider.

"Promise me!" insisted his father, leaning closer.

Mika opened his mouth, still not knowing what he would say, when suddenly the cowhide covering of the wagon they were standing alongside ripped open and a spear thrust through the opening and rammed deep into his father's side, emerging between the ribs on the opposite side of Veltran's body, the black obsidian blade dripping with dark arterial blood.

Veltran opened his mouth, but no sound came out and he collapsed in a crumpled heap on the trampled grass.

Mika reacted instantly, ripping his sword from its sheath. He slashed the cowhide coverings from the wagon frame, revealing the kobold, a pale dingy beige from the loss of blood from a dozen wounds, laughing up at Mika-oba. Ocher blood ran from the corner of its mouth, and its filed teeth were bared in a grimace of hatred.

Mika plunged his sword through the chest of the kobold, skewering it on the razor-sharp blade, then pulled the blade down through the body, slicing it in two.

Black blood poured from the body, staining the sides of the wagon as Mika wrenched the horrible creature out onto the grass and hacked off its head which still bore the hateful leer, knowing that it had paid its death dues with the life of a human shaman.

Mika continued to slash at the kobold long after it was dead, hacking and slicing it into tiny bits of bloody flesh and bone.

Then, tossing his sword aside, he dropped to his knees beside his father and tenderly lifted the man in his arms.

"Father, Father, I promise! I give you my word!"

he cried. "I will be the man you wish me to be! Please don't die!"

There was a terrible roaring in his ears and his vision clouded, shutting out everything else in the world.

"Mika! Mika-oba!" said the voices, falling on his ears like incessant rain. "Mika! Mika!" and he felt the hands pulling on his arms, taking his father away from him.

His eyes filled with tears and he lashed out at the hands, feeling satisfaction as he struck them aside and heard the gasp of their breath. Suddenly he was filled with rage and the need to cause pain. He threw back his head and howled. Falling to his knees, he screamed out his anger and his pain till his voice was ragged and his throat was raw. TamTur crouched beside him as he knelt on the grass, and head thrown back, the wolf joined his voice to Mika's. Together their howls careened up and down, mournful cries of grief that keened and shivered on the wind.

At last there was no more left inside of him. He was drained. Empty. Hands led him away, took him to his own hearth and covered him with blankets. But soon he rose and with unseeing eyes, withdrew into the forest with TamTur at his heels to do his grieving and sing his death songs alone.

Chapter 4

FILLED WITH GRIEF that was deeper than he would have imagined himself capable of, Mika-oba plunged into the forest and tried to lose himself in its vastness. Like a wounded animal he sought out its darkest corner and lay there hoarding his pain, all that was left of the man who had been his father.

Voices were heard dimly on the first day, and torches flitted through the forest like giant fireflies during the night. The voices grew louder on the second day, calling his name like a relentless echo. But Mika did not answer, unwilling to share his grief with others who did not matter. Somehow he felt that to accept their kind words and soft glances, to allow them to ease the pain, would somehow diminish the reality of his grief, and would put his father firmly into the land of the spirits.

Mika knew that by now the body would be placed atop a pyre of roanwood and that his presence was both required and expected. It was one of the most sacred rituals of the Wolf Nomads, the burying of a shaman. But he was not ready to appear, to watch the flames consume the small body. The man that had been his father still lived as long as he remained silent, remembering.

On the fourth day, his body rebelled and his mind was sluggish and would not focus. TamTur had renewed his efforts to cause him to rise, pawing at him, raking his sides with long claws. The memories of his father faded and refused to be recaptured. His stomach growled and his throat ached with lack of moisture. TamTur watched anxiously as Mika stumbled slowly to his feet, knowing that it was time to go. His grieving was done. He would return to camp and become the man his father had wanted him to be. He would don the cloak of shaman which had been in his family for generations. He would study his father's works until he knew them by heart. He would collect every green stuff known to man and learn its uses. He would become a tribute to the memory of his father.

The new resolve lasted all of a mile before he remembered how much he disliked gathering weeds and how they made him sneeze.

He pulled himself up short, lecturing himself sternly as he walked. "I will do it. I will! I know I can do it!"

"But you don't want to," whispered a tiny voice, filling his mind with visions of stinking weeds and dusty scrolls that unfolded to his knees covered with tiny printing, all to be memorized.

He pressed his hands over his ears to shut out the tiny voice inside him and tried to think noble thoughts.

He pictured how pleased Enor would be, as well as

Celia. Perhaps . . . yes! Now was the time. He and Celia would be married and would have children, all boys, of course, whom he could train to follow in his footsteps. None of that nonsense about women and playing around, he would see that his boys grew up straight and somber as befitted future generations of shamans and magic-users.

Enor-oba and Whituk and the others would be dubious, of course, thinking it all a joke, but Mika would convince them eventually. Soon, he would be a respected and valuable member of the clan, the chief's right-hand man. Maybe . . . in time, he might even become chief himself. And he would name his firstborn Veltran. Everything would work out fine.

It was curiously silent as Mika entered camp. Women were moving about their chores silently, eyes to the ground. There were few children about, and those few who were visible were playing quietly, no running around or loud games. No one seemed to notice him. It was as though he was invisible. People seemed to fade away as he approached, turning in the opposite direction as if they did not see him, or entering their huts, almost as though they were avoiding him for some reason.

He made his way to the center of the camp and there, just as he expected, were the remains of the still smoldering pyre. The heavy scent of burned flesh still hung over the camp and Mika bowed his head and whispered, "Be at peace, spirit of my father. I will honor your memory always."

TamTur whined low in his throat, mincing sideways nervously with the smoky scent of death in his nostrils.

75

"Everything is all right, old friend," said Mika, dropping a hand to the head of the great beast. "Come, I must find Enor and tell him of my plans, relieve him of his concern. I am sure that he will be anxious to have me don my father's cloak and responsibilities as soon as possible."

As he drew near to the largest dwelling, the building that housed the chief and his family, the camp grew quieter still and a woman appeared briefly in the doorway of a hut, snatched the arm of a child who was seated outside, and dragged it hurriedly inside.

A hush seemed to fall, almost as if the camp were holding its breath. Mika looked around him, puzzled at the silence. There was no one to be seen. Not one child played in front of one campfire, not one woman bustled about doing her daily chores. Not one wolf cub scratched at the midden heap for a bone. All windows were drawn and door flaps sealed as though the inhabitants were readying themselves for a storm or for war.

Mika was confused. Had something happened while he was gone?

Mika approached Enor's lodge, a large wooden affair with tall painted posts beside the door, cleverly carved to depict generations of wolves, piled one atop the other's shoulders.

As he drew near, the door creaked open and Whituk stepped out, an unpleasant smile on his narrow lips. His stringy grey locks were draped with a mantle of brightly colored feathers and shells and crowned with the whitened skull of a great wolf whose empty eye sockets gleamed with the yellow of topaz.

A heavy robe of black wolf pelts hung from his

shoulders, the neck and armholes edged with white wolf tails. The familiar pouch of herbs hung from a belt at his waist. In his scrawny fist he clutched the shaman's staff of office.

Mika stopped in mid-step, stunned as though he had been dealt a blow to the head. His mind whirled as he tried to think of some reason why Whituk would wear his father's robes and carry the staff of office which should, by right, be his.

Rage began to build within him the longer he looked upon the vision of the lesser shaman, whom he had never liked, wearing the familiar robes.

Whituk, never a stupid man, undoubtedly realized his danger and, clutching the staff tightly, stepped back and thrust open the door calling out: "Mika-oba has returned, honorable chief. Perhaps you might step outside and speak to him."

Mika breathed deeply, sucking his anger down, and resolved to speak calmly and gently. This was surely a misunderstanding that could easily be set right. Enor was a just and intelligent man and a wise chief. He would settle everything.

Enor emerged from the hut, followed by Enor-oba and several of the lesser chiefs, all of whom stared at him with cold disapproval, although Mika also discerned a smirk of pleasure curling at the edges of Enor-oba's thin lips. Celia peeked from the corner of the door, her small face shadowed with worry, before Enor-oba stepped in front of her, blocking her from Mika's sight.

"So, Mika, you are back," said Enor, a deep frown creasing his forehead. "Whituk here thought you had gone for good."

"No, I am here as you can see. I was in the forest, saying my farewells to my father."

Whituk snorted. "In the forest. A dutiful son would have been at the funeral pyre where he belonged, saying the prayers that would speed his father's spirit to the land of our ancestors. A good son would have . . ."

"Would have what, Whituk?" demanded Mika, a steely note entering his voice as he moved within a pace of the shaman and stared into his beady eyes.

"We each must grieve in our own fashion and say our good-byes as we see fit. No other man may say what is right at such a time," said Mika.

"What matters is that I have returned and am here now to take the place that is mine by birthright. To wear the mantle that now seems to be on your head. To don the robe that sits on your shoulders. To carry the pouch that hangs at your waist. To hold the staff that is in your hands. I have returned and now ask you with all due respect to give me that which is mine."

Whituk shifted nervously. His eyes flitted sideways, unable to hold Mika's gaze, and his knuckles whitened as he clutched the staff more tightly. He began to edge away, attempting to slip behind the body of the chief. Mika's hand shot out with the speed of a ferret going for the kill, grabbed the shaman, and dragged him forward, lifting him up to the level of his eyes so that the man's toes barely touched the ground.

"Do not play with me, Whituk. I have asked you nicely to give me that which is mine by birthright. I do not wish to be unpleasant. Do you understand me?" He surprised himself with his vehemence. He gave the shaman a gentle shake that tipped the wolf skull down over Whituk's eyes and rattled him as though he were a sack of bones.

"They're mine!" hissed the shaman. "I'm head shaman now. Tell him, Enor!"

Enor stared at the shaman with open distaste, then sighed deeply and signaled for Mika to let the man down.

"Come inside, Mika. We must talk," he said heavily. Turning, he entered the building without even looking to see if Mika would comply.

Mika's heart sank at the somber tone in the chief's words, and he lowered Whituk to the ground with only token roughness, which was still enough to send the man reeling dizzily into the embers of a nearby fire.

Mika found the chief seated before the fire in the lodge.

"As you know, it is the duty of the firstborn son to sing the death songs, lead the prayers, light the pyre, and send the spirit on its way to the hunting grounds of our ancestors. With your brother's death, that responsibility became yours."

Mika opened his mouth to speak, to explain the deep grief that had come over him, making it impossible for him to share his feelings with anyone or take part in the ritual. Enor held up a hand, silencing him.

"With your father's passing, once the pyre is lit and his spirit safely sung on its way, according to our custom, as you know, the mantle, the robe, the staff, and the pouch became yours, as well as the title of head shaman, healer, and magic-user."

Mika's shoulder's straightened and a weight lifted from his heart. Enor had spoken the words he himself would have said. The words detailing the custom that would ensure his rightful place in the clan.

"But you were not here and we could not find you, even though we delayed the building of the pyre and allowed your father's body to remain in his dwelling place from one sunrise to the next, risking the danger of his spirit slipping away and becoming earthbound forever. We could not find you, even though we searched the farthest corners of the forest and called your name until our voices rasped in our throats. You did not answer, though you must have heard us."

Enor stared at Mika with a keen piercing look from his dark eyes, as though begging him to deny the fact, his great beaked nose giving him the look of a questing eagle. But Mika hung his head and tried to swallow the lump in his throat, for he had indeed seen the torches and heard their voices and had not responded.

Enor sat quietly, waiting for Mika to reply, stroking the long wolf tails that cascaded over his shoulder among his thick black braids. Mika had always thought of Enor as an old man, but in truth, he was no more than in the middle of his years. His body was firm and well-muscled and there was nothing wrong with his eyesight, which saw far more than Mika gave him credit for. Enor had great hopes for the young man to realize his potential, but the clan as a whole was his responsibility and no one member, no matter the circumstances, could be allowed to disrupt it.

The silence stretched out to an uncomfortable length. At last, just as Celia gave a tiny hiccuping sob somewhere in the shadows, and a pine knot cracked on the fire, spreading a bright shower of incandescent sparks that sprayed through the air and fell on Mika's legs, Enor spoke.

"Failing to find you, we continued the ceremony without you. You, as you well know, are the last of your line. But your father could not go unsung into the spirit world, nor could his staff lie unclaimed.

"There must always be a shaman and magic-user; no clan would be safe or complete without one. And so, even though some few begged me to defy tradition and wait until you returned, others, many others, spoke out, saying that it was not possible. In the end I bowed to their voices and Whituk inherited the staff."

Mika lifted his head, which had become heavy and unwieldy, and stared dully into Enor's eyes. He saw pity and compassion as well as intelligence in the large brown eyes, and he hoped he might yet explain himself and beg for a reversal of the decision.

But Enor had not become chief by birth alone, and quickly he spoke again, cutting off the younger man before he could begin his plea.

"There were other things that entered into our decision beside the fact of your absence," he said. And one by one, Mika heard a listing of his misadventures over the years since the time of his youth. Taken individually, they had seemed no more than the pranks of an impish mind, but laid end to end, they made a formidable list that depressed even Mika.

"And finally," continued Enor, "it was felt that you had no real interest in the study of herbs and healing. Some were concerned with the fact that their lives might well rest in your hands one day. They were worried that you might make some terrible mistake, by accident or intent, rather than heal them. To be honest, I could not deny that it was a real risk.

"Eventually, you would have recognized that the time for jokes was over and tried to do your best. But Mika, you should have been studying these many years past, and none, not even you, can deny that you have spent your time in other ways.

"As chief, I had to agree that the well-being of the clan would be best served by other hands. I am sorry, Mika. I would that it had been otherwise."

"What . . . do I do now?" Mika asked quietly. "Am I still part of the clan?"

"That is a difficult question to answer," said Enor, looking into the fire.

"There are only two answers," said Mika. "Yes or no."

"Yes, there will always be a place for you at the fire," Enor answered heavily. "But I do not think you would find much comfort there now . . .

"Every single member of the clan pays for his space at the fire with his services. Even the women and the children contribute. And it must be so. If it were otherwise—the whole supported by the actions of the few—the clan would perish. This has happened to many clans. There is no room around the fire for those who do not bear their share of the burden.

"Up until now, your presence was paid for by your father's diligence. But that is no longer true.

"We must ask what you would do if you remained. Are you a hunter? A warrior? Would you be a shaman's apprentice under Whituk? Mika, you are none of those things. You play at all and master none."

Mika's face burned with shame and he looked down at his tightly clenched hands. TamTur lay by his side and whined.

"Then I am banished," Mika said in a low tone.

"There is a way . . ." Enor said. "But let us drink a cup of mulled mandrake and smoke a pipe of wolfsbane to take the sharp edge off the words that have been spoken here."

Mika did not object and sat motionless, his thoughts whirling in his head while Celia crept out of the corner and knelt at her father's side. Uncorking the narrow mouth of a bulge-bottomed gourd, she poured two shares of the thick gold brew into copper mugs and placed them on the stones that ringed the central fire.

While they were waiting for the wine to heat, Enor took down a long slender bone pipe from its hook on the carved rafter. It was a soft, pale shade of yellow, worn to a creamy patina by generations of reverent hands. The shaft was delicately incised with a frieze of running wolves, and the bowl itself was carved to depict a snarling wolf's head.

Enor filled the open mouth loosely with the powerful narcotic weed which was normally used only during political or religious ceremonies. He passed the pipe to Mika and lit a splinter from the fire.

Mika took the pipe without comment and, as Enor touched the flame to the tobacco, inhaled deeply. The hypnotic smoke filled his lungs, and almost immediately, he felt the tight bands of pain ease from his heart and mind.

Enor took the pipe as it was passed to him, but he did not inhale. Instead, he permitted the sweet smoke to dribble out of his mouth untasted. Mika did not even notice.

When Enor judged that Mika was ready, he handed him the mug with a brimming share.

Mika gulped the hot liquor in a single draught and held out his mug for more, unmindful of the hidden power of the potion.

Celia studied him carefully as she poured out the second portion and placed it beside the fire, her big blue eyes reflecting her concern. But Mika only stared at his cup, refusing to meet her eyes and see the pity that he knew would be there.

Enor held his counsel and allowed Mika freedom of drink, smoke, and his own thoughts, knowing that the powerful narcotic tobacco and hypnotic drink would soon ease the worst of the young man's pain and make him more malleable.

After six mugs, Mika was able to focus on the flames and consider their beauty, rather than comparing them to the color of Whituk's blood, if he had any. After eight cups, he felt at peace. Almost.

"What is this solution you have in mind?" he asked between numbed lips, slowly setting the still-full cup down on the ground in front of TamTur.

"It's the caravan," said Enor, watching curiously as the wolf inched forward on his front paws and quietly lapped up the contents of the mug.

"The caravan?" Mika asked stupidly, wriggling his fingers to encourage the return of feeling.

"Yes, the caravan," Enor repeated patiently. "You remember the caravan you helped rescue."

"Oh, THAT caravan," said Mika, and his face grew dark. "Damn kobolds."

"We have serious problems with the caravan that only you can solve, Mika-oba."

"Not 'oba' any more," Mika said solemnly, wagging his finger under Enor's nose. "Just Mika. Plain 'ol Mika. Only Mika-oba while father is still alive. Father's dead. Gone. Mika's all alone now." Mika stared into the fire, pondering the sad turn of events.

"Yes, I know," Enor said with a sigh, already regretting that he had allowed the young man the freedom of the gourd and the pipe. Two drinks of mandrake were more than enough for a normal man. Three would render even the strongest unconscious. The pipe had been pure overkill. Yet he had wanted to avert the violence that he knew lurked just under the surface of Mika's control and spare him the consequences of precipitous actions.

Mika had all the qualifications needed to become a truly great Wolf Nomad one day if he were able to channel his superior strength and intelligence instead of wasting his talents on wenching and pranks. As chief, it was Enor's duty to see that that happened. As a father whose daughter was infatuated with Mika, it was even more crucial.

"The caravan, Mika," he repeated. "Those kobolds didn't just happen to be there. There haven't been any kobolds in our territory in decades; we cleared them out long ago. No army of kobolds could have crossed our lands without our knowledge. They had to have been transported there magically. Such a deed would have required a very powerful magic-user. As only you and I know, that magic-user may well be—" Enor paused "—Iuz . . .

"The question is, why would someone be after the

caravan, and is that someone Iuz?"

"Yes, why?" echoed Mika.

"I have asked the Guildsman, but he denies any knowledge."

"Sneaky bastard," muttered Mika. "Don't like 'im."

"Mika, listen to me carefully," Enor said, taking Mika's chin in his fingers and turning it so that Mika was forced to look him in the eye.

"The contract with the Guild is all important to the clan. It pays for our spear points and our axe heads, our saddles and our blankets, our salt and our grain, and many other things that you have come to take for granted. Without them, we would soon be little more than savages in the forest."

"Savages," said Mika, struggling to keep his eyes open.

"Mika, I want you to accompany the caravan. Be in charge, keep it from danger. Make certain that it arrives in Eru-Tovar safely."

"Safely," said Mika.

"Something in that caravan is of great value. Find out what it is and protect it, no matter what. If you can do that, those who spoke against you would be proved wrong and you would gain a place at the fire."

"The princess?" asked Mika dimly. "The messenger said there was a princess . . ."

"They have been here four days," said Enor meaningfully, "and we have seen no princess. That was a dying man's clever lie intended to incite our bravery. But Wolf Nomads need no special incentive to keep their vows."

"Mika's brave," slurred Mika, slumping forward

as Enor released him. TamTur gave a great snore beside him.

"Yes, I know you're brave. You have never had a chance to prove it, Mika, but I know that the courage of the Wolf Clan runs deep in your veins," agreed Enor. "That's why I want you to go. You must leave immediately. Time is important, and we have already lost four days that the men could travel because of the ceremony. But I knew that sooner or later, you would come back."

"You can count on me," said Mika, thumping himself hard on the chest. He tumbled over backward. He started to rise, then, with a grunt, collapsed on top of TamTur, and within seconds his snores were mingling with those of the wolf.

"Come," said Enor, holding his hand out to his daughter. "We will leave him now. Let the idea take hold in his mind as he sleeps. The worst is over. He will take the caravan to Eru-Tovar, and when he returns, he will be able to get on with his life."

"Will it be dangerous, Father?" Celia asked, her lip trembling as she looked down on the man she thought she loved.

"Yes," Enor said truthfully, "very dangerous. And it will surely be a test of his determination. He will need his wits about him if he is to complete the mission, and he will not be able to blame anyone other than himself if he fails. It will be the making or the breaking of him."

"Do you think he will succeed, Father?" asked Celia.

"By the Great She Wolf, I don't know," sighed Enor. "I just don't know."

Chapter 5

MIKA FELT SO TERRIBLE the next morning, he could conceive of no danger greater than moving. Opening his eyes was sheer agony. He was afraid to turn his head for fear that it might fall off his neck. His mouth tasted like the bottom of a midden heap, and someone, probably Whituk, was beating a drum somewhere nearby. It pounded incessantly. Mika groaned. He thought he might die. He hoped that it would be soon. Suddenly, bright light flooded the room, cruelly lancing his brain like fire.

"Hush, Mika," said a soft voice that rumbled like boulders clashing together. "Here, drink this. You'll feel better soon."

Groaning, trying to uncross his eyes, Mika crawled shakily into a seated position in front of the long dead fire. He took the carved wooden mug Celia handed him and allowed her to help him guide it to his rubbery lips. The first scalding sip flowed down his throat and Mika recognized the acrid taste of roanwood tea, a well-known remedy for the after-effects of too much mandrake wine, one cure he was personally familiar with, although never could he remember feeling quite this dreadful. It seemed that he had slept where he had fallen, on the hard-packed earth floor of Enor's home.

TamTur groaned. His legs stiffened and twitched. He moaned again, a pitiful sound, one that Mika could sympathize with completely. "Celia, give Tam some, too," he whispered.

"Don't be silly, Mika. Wolves won't drink roan-wood tea. It tastes terrible," Celia said, cocking a well-rounded hip to one side and shaking out her mass of flowing hair. She had dressed quite carefully that morning, putting on her newest tunic of pale ivory doeskin, edged with velvety moleskin and hung with hundreds of tiny silver bells and turquoise beads, hoping to create an image that Mika would remember on the long journey.

"Please, Celia, don't argue, give him some," Mika groaned, burying his head in his hands and covering his ears to shut out the horrible jangling of the bells and beads.

Celia pouted but did as he directed, pouring a bowl full of the strong tea and placing it in front of the wolf. To her amazement, TamTur turned his head and began lapping the contents of the bowl from a recumbent position. Only when the bowl was empty did he rise, although somewhat shakily, and lean against Mika, his head hanging low and his tongue lolling from his mouth. The whites of his eyes were yellow, and even his whiskers seemed to hang limply from his muzzle.

"Oh, you're too awful. And that stupid wolf is just

like you, doing everything you do! I don't know why I bother to care!" Celia cried, and turning, she stomped out of the room, leaving the miserable pair wincing at the noise of her steps.

One at a time they staggered from the building and made their way to the stream where they soaked their aching heads in the icy water and made extremely brief ablutions.

Squinting against the clear bright light of morning, Mika walked back into the center of camp and was handed a hot plate of food by an older woman who had seen many mornings after mandrake and knew that, although it often seemed like punishment, hot food eased the ravages of the drink.

Mika seated himself on a log worn smooth by many generations of Wolf Nomads, and gingerly swallowed the scrambled hawk eggs, fried loin of hart, and hunks of toasted mealybread.

The elder woman appeared at his side, took the empty plate from his hands and handed him a large mug filled with fragrant coffee ground from kara beans and heavily laced with honey and a hair of the wolf, a dollop of mandrake.

"You'll feel better soon, lad," she said kindly, and took herself away, sparing Mika the effort of speech.

And surprisingly enough, he did. Whistling for TamTur, who had slunk out of the forest and obviously did not share Mika's renewed interest in life, Mika made his way through the camp to the Far Fringe where the caravan was still quartered, guarded by a full complement of twenty men. The men were fully armed and alert, an unusual circumstance, for who would be fool enough to attack a Wolf

Nomad camp?

Mika located the captain of the command and made his way to the man's side, delighted to find that it was Hornsbuck, a grizzled nomad with whom he had lifted many a cup.

Then, his step slowed as the strangeness of the situation struck him. If the caravan were truly in danger and truly important, why place Mika above Hornsbuck? Hornsbuck had long passed his fortieth winter and had seen much combat. He was far senior to Mika in warfare, weaponry, and the command of men.

Mika began to suspect that he had been given command in title only. Hornsbuck was really in charge and Mika had been fed the lie simply to ease him out of camp and avoid an unpleasant confrontation with Whituk.

Mika seriously considered turning around, taking a horse, and riding away, leaving everything and everyone behind. Starting new somewhere else.

But he did not own a horse, nor a saddle, nor did he have food or equipment for such a journey. *The whole supporting the few.* Enor's words rose up to confront him and he knew them to be true; he had not earned his place at the fire.

His detractors, those who had spoken against him, were undoubtedly waiting for him to fail, to allow some harm to befall the caravan. Well, he would surprise them! He would conduct himself in absolute propriety and deliver the caravan safely to Eru-Tovar. He would honor the memory of his father in the only way left open to him.

"We are ready to leave as soon as you give the

92

word," Hornsbuck said in a neutral tone. "Unless you wish to check the supplies and the men personally."

"No, Hornsbuck. I'm certain that nothing is lacking if you are in charge," Mika said with a smile, determined not to offend the venerable warrior.

Hornsbuck's huge grey-blond mustache and beard twitched in surprise at the compliment, and his green eyes gave Mika an appraising glance. Then, bowing slightly from his thickened waist, he strode off on muscular legs, bowed from many years of life in the saddle.

Mika returned to camp to dress himself in the soft leather tunic, waist-high leggings and gloves that comprised the normal traveling gear. He left off the wolf-skull headpiece all of the others wore, in deference to his still-pounding head, which he now recognized was pounding of its own accord and not from any drumming of Wintuk's.

When he returned to the caravan, the men were mounted and ready to leave. Wolf banners hung from tall staffs and fluttered in the cool morning air. Wolves of all sizes and colors circled the horses of their human companions, yipping sharply and howling with excitement, anxious to be on their way.

The sharp-spined, grey stallion was as ornery as ever. As he mounted, the stallion whipped its blocky head around and attempted to nip his leg. Mika kicked it in the muzzle and pulled back sharply on the reins, causing the beast to rear up on its hind legs in an attempt to shake him from its back.

Mika clung expertly, hugging the massive ribcage with his knees, determined to rid himself of the obstinate creature one of these days. Moving to the front of the caravan in a bone-jarring trot that amplified the pounding in his temples, he gave the signal to move out.

Reining in on a slight rise, with the grey high-stepping in place and champing at its bit, Mika watched with a critical eye as wagons, wolves, guards, and the heavily loaded supply wagon paraded before him.

As the last of them passed, he turned to look back toward camp, thoughts of his father rising unbidden before him.

Enor and Celia broke free of the crowd of well-wishers and relatives who had gathered on the edge of the Far Fringe to see the caravan off and walked out to where he stood.

Mika was not pleased to see that Celia was accompanied by Matin the Pleasant, a tall, well-built, good-looking young Wolf Nomad who had his arm wrapped around her narrow waist in a conciliatory—and most proprietary—manner. Lurking over Celia's shoulder was Enor-oba, smirking with satisfaction. The smile on Celia's fair face was more ambiguous—hurtful and coy.

"Here," said Enor as he handed a leather pouch up to Mika. "This holds your father's spell book, magic scrolls, his healing herbs, and ungents. They were his personal property and as such belong to you now.

"You possess the basic knowledge necessary for healing which could come in useful if you run into trouble on the plains. And if you don't, you can always study.

"There's nothing to stop you from becoming a

magic-user if that is what you wish. It's up to you, Mika. You can become as much . . . or as little, as you choose.

"Some of us will be interested to see what you decide. Take care of yourself and the caravan. May the Great She Wolf guide your steps and bring you back safely."

Celia seemed more interested in tracing Matin's jaw line than in saying good-bye, but her father turned to her and called her name sharply with a frown on his face.

"Oh, yes! Well, good-bye, Mika," Celia said prettily, her dimples creasing her rosy cheeks. "Try not to get yourself killed. And don't worry about me, I'm sure I'll be fine."

Matin said nothing, merely grinned at Mika and pulled Celia closer, causing her to giggle and protest laughingly.

Anger merged with suspicion as Mika glared down at Celia, noting the handsome tunic that showed her figure in all its soft curves. Had he only imagined the tears and concern?

It would serve her right if he got killed! Muttering to himself, he kicked the stallion hard and rode swiftly after the departing caravan, TamTur at his heels.

Chapter 6

THE COLD, BRISK AIR of the plains was a welcome relief to Mika's throbbing head, and despite the ragged lope of the grey stallion, he soon shook off the last remaining effects of the mandrake. TamTur also seemed invigorated by the rush of cold air and took off to run at the side of a small, dun-colored female.

Mika smiled, urging the horse into a canter as he rode alongside the wagons, eyeing them in a speculative manner, inspecting each for potential problems. All seemed in good condition except the secret wagon. It still rode low to the ground, and its axle squeaked so loudly that Mika felt it must be heard in Yecha.

Holding his hand to his head, Mika swung his horse away from the wagon and made a note to implore the Guildsman to have some of its mysterious load transferred to another wagon and to grease the noisy axle. The same driver rode atop the high seat and glared at Mika in the same hostile manner, causing him to reflect that the man just might learn a few manners on the trip.

After a short mounted conference with Horns-buck, they agreed to follow the usual trail, skirting the edge of the Burneal Forest to take advantage of the ample water, game, and firewood there.

The forest route would add several days and many miles to their journey. It would be far shorter to head directly across the plains, angling sharply toward Eru-Tovar. But there were disadvantages to such a route. Firstly, there was no water on the open plains, and while the mules might handle the shortage with few complaints, the horses would not, and heavy water bags would only slow them down.

Then, too, there were the brigands to consider. These men, desperate as they were to survive, generally avoided the forest, for they had few if any weapons and found it difficult to defend themselves against the many dangerous creatures that lived in the forest, not to mention the nomads themselves, who killed them on sight.

These dangerous men were often to be found on the plains, and so great were their thirst, hunger, and desire to live that they would attack caravans against even overwhelming odds.

All things considered, Hornsbuck suggested, and Mika was quick to agree, that there was little advantage to the direct route.

The first day went smoothly and they traveled more than twenty-five miles by nightfall. Drawing the wagons into a circle, mules and horses staked outside to give early warning in case of attack, they made camp.

A hunting party entered the forest and was lucky

enough to encounter a large doe which they quickly brought down with a well-aimed sablewood arrow. As the meat roasted over the fire, Mika and Hornsbuck discussed the journey.

"If we are able to hold to this pace," Mika said thoughtfully, "we ought to make Eru-Tovar inside of twenty days."

"Something will go wrong," growled Hornsbuck, taking a deep swallow of the honeyed mead that he allowed himself at the end of each evening. "An axle will break or a mule will die or the provisions will spoil and we'll have to hunt. Something always goes wrong; you can count on it. Better figure twenty-five days at least."

"Nothing will go wrong," said a deep, firm voice from the shadows. "And it is most important that we arrive in Eru-Tovar no later than ten days hence. We've already wasted enough time while you practiced your barbaric rites, burying that witch doctor."

Mika started to rise, anger clouding his mind, but Hornsbuck's massive hand closed over his shoulder and forced him to remain seated.

"That witch doctor," said Hornsbuck with controlled fury, "was a great healer, sir, and he died long before his time, thanks to a kobold who, may I remind you, was hidden in one of your wagons. He was also this lad's father."

"My apologies, sir," said the man as he moved into the circle of light cast by the firelight. It was the Guildsman.

"My words were ill-chosen out of concern for my schedule, which has been badly affected by the events since we left Yecha. It is most important that we arrive no later than the twelfth of Harvest Moon."

"But that is only ten days hence," Hornsbuck replied in a genial tone, still gripping Mika's shoulder firmly. "That is not possible."

"It is possible if you take a more direct route," insisted the Guildsman.

"Sir, that is a most dangerous path," said Mika, once more in control of his temper. "We deem it wiser to take the forest route, which will ensure the safe arrival of your cargo."

"I did not think that danger was an important issue with you Wolf Nomads," said the Guildsman. "I thought you cut your teeth on daggers and fought wild boars for sport."

"We are not afraid," Mika said stiffly, "but only a fool risks his skin when it is not necessary. We will travel as fast as possible and perhaps shave some time off our reckoning if there are no problems with the wagons."

"You will find nothing wrong with my wagons, my drivers, or my animals. And you forget, wolfman, that you are but the guard. I represent the Guild and have the final word on all matters. It is my decision that we take the direct route."

"You may represent the Guild, sir, but I am responsible for our lives, including yours, and I will choose my own path," Mika said hotly.

"I should have known that Wolf Nomads lack the courage of their cousins, the Tiger Nomads," sneered the Guildsman. "When I reach Eru-Tovar I will speak to the Guild and tell them of your cowardice. They will not take kindly to the late arrival of this valuable cargo. I will convince them that we have made a mistake in entrusting our caravans to your craven care. The time for treaty-making is almost upon us. I will see to it that we sign an exclusive arrangement with the Tiger Nomads. They are men and do not run weeping like women at the mere thought of danger."

Mika stared at the Guildsman, his thoughts in turmoil. No more than one night out and already he was faced with a terrible decision. Mika looked at Hornsbuck for guidance, hoping that the man would step in and take charge. But Hornsbuck merely twirled his beard between his fingers and stared at the ground.

Mika thought fast. Loss of the valuable Guild treaty was a powerful threat. Enor would not be pleased if Mika brought the caravan in safely but lost the treaty. It would hardly be a fitting tribute to the memory of his father. And it would scarcely win him a place at the fire.

Finally, he struck on what he considered to be his only option. "All right, Guildsman, we will take the overland route, but let it be known to all that it was by your directive. If we fare poorly, the blame will rest on your shoulders alone."

Hornsbuck sighed at Mika's words, but the Guildsman smiled coldly and, bowing in mock respect, retreated from the fire.

"Mika, lad, why did you fall for that old trick? Could you not see that he was prodding you, hoping to bruise your pride until he shagged you into doing his bidding? Go after him. Tell him that we will stick to our original plan."

TamTur looked from one face to the other, sensing something was wrong. His large, intelligent hazel

101

eyes reflected concern, and he stared after the Guildsman and growled.

"No," said Mika, regretting his decision. "I must do as I said. We cannot afford trouble with the Guild. We will take the overland route. We will leave at dawn. We must make certain that all waterskins are filled and that the men ride armored and fully armed."

Hornsbuck nodded unenthusiastically and rose to give the new orders, a glance of contempt over his massive shoulders indicating that the earlier camaraderie had cooled. Probably the man considered Mika a fool, but the Guildsman's threat to the caravan treaty could not be ignored.

"Great Mother Wolf, what have I gotten myself into?" Mika muttered, kneading his forehead with his fist. Then, unwilling to sit in the firelight, a clear target for the certain hostility of his men, he rose and stalked into the darkness that lurked on the far side of the wagons.

He roamed for an hour or longer in the forest, the fragrance of ferns, pines, and roanwood a soothing balm to his troubled mind. He paced the unfamiliar forest floor with little or no thought to the carnivores whose home it was, or to the savage, aboriginal humans, thought to be the remnants of the original Flannae Folk, who lived in the forest and attacked with deadly stealth.

TamTur was well trained and could be depended on to scent out all danger and prevent it before it occurred. It was a pity, though, Mika reflected, that the wolf could not monitor his wayward tongue as easily as he warded off physical risk.

One day, Mika's hasty words might place them into a situation that neither he nor Tam could handle. Once again, Mika resolved, albeit once again too late, to think before he spoke.

Chapter 7

THEY BROKE CAMP well before dawn, hurriedly downing chunks of dry mealybread and mugs of steaming coffee.

The mood was sullen and tense as the men turned the caravan away from the shelter of the forest and headed out onto the open plains.

All day the party watched their back trail, and scouts rode before them and to either side, searching for threats that did not materialize. They were lucky, and as evening drew near, they found a large pool of clear water in a depression at the foot of a small hill covered with thick sweet grass. The loosely hobbled horses and mules drank deeply and ate their fill and, their bells tinkling pleasantly, settled down to graze through the night.

"The Great She Wolf, mother of us all, is guiding our steps," Mika ventured as he sat down next to Hornsbuck who was eating a peppery dish of beans and hart meat.

"One day. It's only one day. Don't be getting your

hopes up. They're out there and they'll be on us in the flash of a wolf's tail as soon as they spot us. We're too rich a prize to pass up. Horses. Weapons. Armor. Goods. If you were stuck out here, wouldn't you risk all for a try at us? After all, what have they got to lose?" muttered Hornsbuck as he shoveled the hot mixture into his beard-shrouded mouth.

Wiping the bowl clean with a hunk of mealybread, Hornsbuck tossed the dripping piece into the air where it was caught adeptly by his wolf, a great grizzled male named RedTail, which bore an uncanny resemblance to the nomad.

RedTail's fur was heavy and thick, a strange shade of reddish blond that Mika had never seen in other wolves. His body was thick and muscular, almost stocky, with none of the long, lean grace normally found in wolves. His muzzle and ears were short and stubby and covered with a network of old scars. His bright green eyes followed Hornsbuck's every move, and Mika knew that the bond between them was great. Heaven help the man who tried to hurt Hornsbuck!

"Too much open space out here to suit me," Hornsbuck said. "Gives me the shivers."

Mika looked out past the fire and nodded his agreement. Hornsbuck was right; the plains were a desolate place, nothing but rock, scree, greasewood, and an occasional salt bush all the way to the horizon and beyond. By comparison, the spring seemed a magical place and one he would be loath to leave.

"Have you been here before?" Mika asked the older man. "This seems like such a good spot. Why has no one set up a base camp here, used it as a way station or even a trading post? The water is exceptional, sweet and satisfying to tongue and thirst. I've told the men to empty the waterbags and fill them with water from the pool."

"Water. Pah! I never touch the stuff myself," said Hornsbuck and setting his bowl down on the ground he poured himself an ample portion of honeyed mead from the large skin that hung from his saddle. He settled himself comfortably in front of the fire.

"As for this place, I dunno, something funny about it if you ask me, which you did. I've never seen it before. It's not on the map, and I've never heard anyone talk about it. And there's no rogues hanging about. Water on the prairie would draw them like trolls to flesh.

"Only thing I can figure is that there was a rain, just a little one, see, and it filled the pool and brought on the grass. I've known it to happen that way in the desert sometimes. Probably this place will be dust again in a day or two. Just luck, that's all. Doesn't mean anything. We'll still have to be on our toes if we want to reach the city with all our body parts attached."

The older man's sour words depressed Mika, and he felt a strong chill of misgiving pass through him.

"What do you figure is so important about this cargo that it has to reach the city in such a short time?" Mika asked, suddenly losing his appetite and giving the remainder of his meal to Tam.

"Who knows?" answered Hornsbuck, easing the heavy beaten metal buckle that cinched the leather tunic around his ample girth. "Guildsmen. Merchants. Pah! What kind of life is that for a man, mewling and haggling over cloth and foodstuffs and fancies that no one really needs. And for what, piles of coins! Fie! May the Great She Wolf take them all and lose them in the forest!"

"You think that's all it is?" Mika persisted. "I wouldn't think that even a Guildsman would ask us to take this risk for profit alone. It has to be something more."

"Don't go looking for trouble, lad. It will find you soon enough all on its own," advised Hornsbuck, growing more mellow as he quaffed his brew. "If there were something valuable on board, we'd know about it. Yon narrow-nose Guildsman would have told us to keep a special eye out, but he has not. This caravan is no different from a hundred others. Go to sleep, lad. Save your strength for the morrow."

But Mika could not stop thinking, and long after Hornsbuck had lapsed into a nest of deep, rumbling, mead-scented snores, Mika lay awake, his arms laced behind his head, staring up at the night sky, pondering the problem.

Hornsbuck's analysis of the situation appeared sound, with one exception—the heavily laden, squeaking wagon. It *was* different from the others. True, Mika had not been told to guard it specifically, but the driver was well-armed and looked as though he could protect himself and his cargo if the need arose.

Mika had continued to observe the wagon all day long and noted that even though it was heavily weighted, it kept pace without difficulty, thanks no doubt to the extra pair of mules.

Although he could find no complaint with its speed, the shrill screeching of the axle signaled their presence to every brigand and rogue within hearing distance. What could the wagon hold that would weigh it down so?

Perhaps it was gold. Gold bars were very heavy and would certainly weigh a wagon down and cause the Guildsman to take great risks. No doubt it was being sent to ransom the supposed mysterious princess who had been kidnapped and was being held somewhere by who knows what variety of fiends. Mika would rescue her, slay the brutes, and have the gold—and the royal beauty—as his reward. . . .

Or maybe it was precious stones being sent to Eru-Tovar to pay homage to a god some nobleman had offended. Yes, that was it. Enor was right. There was no princess. The dead messenger was just trying to sidetrack the Wolf Nomad and appease his gods. But Mika could think of no god who could not be honored in Yecha as well as Eru-Tovar, the gods being much the same, with the exception, Mika shuddered at the thought, of Iuz, demi-god of oppression, deceit, and pain.

Many of those who worshipped the dark god made their home in Eru-Tovar. But why would anyone make an offering to Iuz? Many answers, all unpleasant, immediately filled Mika's mind before he could turn his thoughts in another direction.

"Hornsbuck, you know that wagon, the one that squeaks . . ." Mika began, but only snores replied, erupting from the nomad's slack lips.

"Come on, Tam," Mika said, determined to have a talk with the driver of the wagon. Maybe he could learn something about the cargo and either confirm or deny his suspicions.

Most of the drivers had abandoned their wagons and were lounging about the central fire finishing their meal. Some few were casting knucklebones with the nomads, thinking them dull country fellows, but Mika knew from long practice, that his fellow nomads could hold their own gambling with any race and likely emerge winners.

The men crouched on their knees in a circle that had been swept smooth of grass and stone and were throwing a pair of highly polished knucklebones, the ridges of which had been incised with various numbers. The idea was to bet correctly on which combination of numbers would land face up. Nomad pouches would be many grushnicks heavier by morning.

The wolves were curled up near their chosen humans, licking their rough footpads and grooming their thick pelts. Some were already asleep, noses tucked beneath their thick brushy tails.

The driver of the squeaking wagon had not joined his associates in their various endeavors but instead sat upon the hard seat of his wagon, alert and watchful.

"Ho, driver," Mika hailed the man in a friendly manner. "How went your journey today?"

"Well enough," the driver said grudgingly, seemingly reluctant to pass even those few words.

"Good," said Mika. "But I think that you would do even better tomorrow if you did not have such a heavy load to pull. Share your load out among the other wagons tonight so that the weight is more evenly distributed."

"No," said the driver in a steady voice.

"What?" said Mika, startled. Drivers were generally no more than drunkards off the streets or out of the jails who agreed to take the job rather than rot in prison. They had little or no character and usually vanished into the nearest tavern as soon as they reached their destination. There, they drank themselves into oblivion until their funds ran out and they were tossed in jail once more, their only escape another driving job. None had the spine to stand up to a Wolf Nomad, much less defy one!

Mika gaped at the man, then repeated his request a little less pleasantly, thinking that perhaps the man had misunderstood.

"No," the man said quite clearly, not at all intimidated by Mika's manner. "My beasts are able to bear the load. They will keep up with the rest."

"But you are very heavily weighted," persisted Mika, wondering at the man. "The axle squeals as though it is in pain. Aside from the fact that the strain might break the wheel and cause us to waste valuable time, the noise alone could easily attract just the sort of villains we seek to avoid.

"Do not be a stubborn man. I am commander of the caravan, and I am giving you a direct order to divide your load among the other wagons. Just what is it you carry that is so damned heavy?"

"No," repeated the man for the third time as though he had not heard any of what Mika had said. "I will not shift the load, and what I carry is none of your concern." And his hand tightened on the handle of his knife.

Mika's eyes bulged and he took an angry step toward the man, his hand shifting to the handle of his own knife. Tam snarled and paced restlessly, awaiting Mika's command.

Mika reached out, intending to pull the man from his seat and thump him on his ears to improve his hearing, which was obviously faulty. But before he could do so, the Guildsman appeared out of the shadows at the rear of the wagon.

"What's the problem, now, Master Wolf?" he asked coldly, giving a sarcastic twist to the title, deliberately removing any hint of respect from his voice.

"I gave this man a direct order and he defied me!" Mika said in a strangled voice. TamTur started a growl that rumbled deep in his throat, adding his quiet menace to Mika's words.

"What's the problem, Cob?" the Guildsman asked, directing his question to the driver in a normal tone of voice.

"He told me to divide my load. I said no," replied the driver, his hand still on the handle of his knife.

"Quite right," agreed the Guildsman. "This load is not to be touched until we reach Eru-Tovar.

"But it is too heavy," said Mika, his face growing flushed. And he repeated his earlier arguments.

"No," said the Guildsman. A sneer spread across the driver's face.

Mika started to speak, then stopped, a smile crossing his own lean features. No need to get into a fight that he could not win. Their voices had already attracted the attention of several nomads and drivers. After all, he thought smugly, there was more than one way to skin a rabbit.

"All right," he said calmly. "But be warned, if there *is* trouble and you lag behind, none will turn back for you. You will be on your own." And as he strolled away, Tam lingering threateningly, he was pleased to see a look of consternation on the driver's face as he began to speak to the Guildsman with much waving of arms and hands.

Late that night, after the last of the grumbling gamblers was sound asleep and the fire had burned down to embers, Mika rose from his bedroll as though he were going to relieve himself, and slipped into the darkness that lay beyond the wagons. He paused to make certain that no one had noticed or followed him, then quietly made his way round the perimeter until he was within two wagon lengths of his goal.

Stealth was a skill that Mika excelled at, somewhat surprising in a man of his great size. But he could rival even TamTur when he set his mind to it, and he did so now.

Together, man and beast crept closer and closer to the secret wagon. Mika looked at Tam and smiled, no words necessary. Tam's tongue lolled out of the corner of his mouth, and he seemed to grin in return. Many was the time that they had crept up on some unsuspecting prey together in a similar fashion.

It was Mika's intent to slip inside the wagon and find out for himself what the mysterious cargo was. The value of the secret cargo soared higher and higher with each thinking. It wasn't that Mika wanted the treasure for himself, it was just that, well, the commander of a caravan needed to know what he carried. Yes, that was it. After all, how could he protect them adequately if he didn't know what he was protecting? It was his solemn duty to investigate.

Mika was within one wagon of his objective when he stopped for one last check. The moon was conveniently tucked away behind a dark cloud. Everything was silent other than the occasional cry of a night bird and the dull tink, tink, tink of the mules' bells as they snorted and muttered through their dull mule dreams.

Satisfied that none was about, save he, Mika began to slither forward. Suddenly, out of absolutely nowhere, there appeared near the rear of the wagon the figure of a tiny, wizened little old man dressed in a tattered robe! With a start, Mika crouched behind a bush, almost unable to believe what he was seeing.

How could it be? Where had the man come from? There were no trees or bushes for him to have hidden behind; the land was entirely open except for the small hill that lay in the opposite direction. It was as though the man had materialized out of the night itself!

The more Mika stared at the old man, the more familiar he looked. Was it? Could this be the same cloaked figure who placed the stun spell on him at the River Fler? The dark cloak was gone, but the posture was the same and with gnawing fear Mika knew the figure at the river and the man before him were one and the same. But why was he here?

As Mika watched, the old man looked in all directions and then gestured at the wagon with both hands. It seemed to Mika that the wagon and the air around it became hazy . . . fuzzy. Mika blinked, mistrusting his eyes and wondering if they were clogged with sleep.

The view remained the same—blurry. It was as though the old man had placed a spell on the wagon.

The old man began to unlace the tightly stretched hide that sealed the back of the wagon. Magic-user or no, Mika was not going to stand, well, lie idly by and watch someone else steal his priceless cargo.

Mika grasped the single crystal bead that hung from a fine gold chain around his neck and quickly uttered the words to a simple globe of invulnerability spell.

This spell, which he had taken special care to master, created a magical buffer around his body for five feet in all directions and protected him from all spells up to the fourth level of ability.

It seemed unlikely that the old man's abilities would exceed third-level spells.

The magic buffer was also capable of repelling the stun spell that had frozen him like a statue back at the arroyo. He had a score or two to settle with the old man. Next time he'd be more careful whom he enchanted. Once the spell was in place, Mika stood up slowly and began inching toward the little man.

Mika glanced down and saw that Tam was at his side, creeping forward on silent paws. A low, ominous rumbling sound that Mika felt more than heard uttered from Tam's throat, but evidently the little man had exceptional hearing for he whirled around instantly.

Seeing Mika and Tam, the old man permitted a smile to cross his wrinkled face. He took his hand from the back of the wagon and fumbled in a pouch hung from his waist. Then he began to mutter in a low voice and gesture in the air, pointing his skinny hand in their direction.

Confident that his spell of invulnerability would protect him from anything the little man might do, Mika advanced swiftly, a nasty smile on his face.

Suddenly, Tam leaped forward.

The old man gestured sharply and snapped out one last guttural word. No sooner had he spoken than a huge wind rose up out of nowhere and slammed into them.

Mika was shielded from the wind by his spell, but Tam had left the area of protection and the wind struck him full force, tumbling him head over tail through the air and smashing him to the ground some distance away.

Mika only had time for a brief glance, ascertaining that Tam was not seriously hurt, before a number of brilliant balls of fire began streaming from the old man's finger tips and arcing directly toward him.

He cringed, throwing his arms up over his face and head, even as he told himself that the magic missiles were but a lowly first-level spell and could not harm him. But the missiles were impressive and even frightening. Had he not been shielded by his spell of invulnerability, they would have killed him easily.

Mika had gone no farther since the old man had begun his attack; now, growing more confident, he took several steps forward. Out of the corner of his eye, he saw that Tam had gotten to his feet and was advancing again.

The old man looked at Mika and smiled gently, then wiggled his fingers. A great bluish white light obliterated him from sight and headed straight for Mika.

Mika barely had time to blink before the light exploded around him, striking the shield and bouncing off with a loud booming noise. Mika opened his eyes, temporarily blinded, and heard a shrill yipping, trailing away to whimpers. Tam! All of a sudden, Mika felt a strange tingling running up and down his back from the top of his head to the soles of his feet.

He stopped running and looked down, trying to remember where he was going and why. Nothing occurred to him. He looked around, puzzled, and saw Tam.

Tam looked very strange. He was lying on his stomach with his head between his paws and his hind legs and tail stretched out behind him. His fur was standing up straight all over his body. He looked like a giant hedgehog. And he was stiff, unmoving. Mika stared at Tam, unable to think of what had happened to him. He looked very strange.

His mind a whirl of foggy, confused images, Mika turned around and saw the old man smiling at him. Mika put his head to one side and stared at the old man. He looked familiar, but Mika couldn't seem to remember who he was.

There seemed to be a lot of noise. Mika turned his head and looked between the wagons toward camp. He could see lots of people stirring around and beginning to run toward him. He wondered what they were excited about. Vaguely, he wondered if he should be excited, too.

The fuzzy feeling still gripped him, addling his brains and slowing his actions. He tried to loosen his knife from his belt, thinking he might need it for whatever it was that was happening.

The old man gave him a penetrating look from small dark eyes that seemed to have no pupils, and the smile dropped from his face. He glanced at the nomads and drivers and then took a step forward, raised his hand and pointed his finger at Mika.

Mika pulled back, knowing even in his confused state that something terrible was about to happen. He thought that maybe he should run, but couldn't decide in what direction.

As the old man began to chant, the first of the nomads appeared between the two wagons, swords raised and torches flooding the area with bright light. The instant the light touched him, the old man disappeared, simply faded out of existence as though he had never been!

Mika raised his hand to his eyes slowly and rubbed them, wondering if he had imagined the whole thing. He looked again, but the old man was gone, leaving nothing to show that he had been there, other than the loosened flap of hide on the wagon.

"Mika, what is it! Are you all right?" asked a nomad named Klaren.

"Old man," Mika said thickly, still wrapped in confusion. "There was an old man here. Uh, not here. There, trying, trying to get into . . . wagon."

"Where is he?" roared a large burly driver who wore a hostile scowl and waved a heavy cudgel above his head. "Must have been a bandit! Which way did he go?"

"Who?" asked Mika, forgetting what they were talking about.

"The bandit! The old man!" shouted the burly driver.

"Oh, was he a bandit?" Mika asked in surprise.

"I don't know. I never saw him! Where is he?" yelled the driver, beginning to get angry at Mika.

"Who?" asked Mika, totally bewildered and wondering why the man was yelling at him.

"Where's the old man?" said Klaren between gritted teeth.

"Oh. Him. Well, he was right there," said Mika pointing to the wagon. "He was a magic-user, I think."

The clamor of voices broke around him excitedly.

"What would a magic-user want with a wagon train?" asked Cob, the driver of the secret wagon, now wide awake, his brow furrowed with suspicion as he stared at Mika.

"I don't mind bandits, but I don't like magic," said the other driver, lowering his club and looking around him carefully as though the magic-user might be secreted among them.

"What's all this nonsense about bandits and magic-users?" said the Guildsman as he pushed his way through the throng. He looked at Mika and said, "Is this some of your doing? I will not allow you to stir up the men."

"No nonsense," mumbled Mika, fighting to shed the dazed feeling that shrouded his brain and tongue. "Old man came. Unlaced wagon. Tried to stop him. Threw a spell. Musta' been a magic-user."

"An old man, hmmm," said the Guildsman, sarcasm dripping from his tongue. "And can you explain just how you happened to be so conveniently nearby to foil his attempt?"

"Uh . . ." Mika said stupidly, flogging his stricken brain to come up with something, anything that would make sense, but nothing occurred to him.

"Uh . . ." he stammered futilely, trying to remember.

"I suggest that you had a little too much to drink and decided to have a look inside the wagon yourself," said the Guildsman. "Too bad you made so much noise and got caught."

After a shocked moment of surprise at the tone the Guildsman used, the drivers broke into hoots of laughter, drowning out any answer that Mika might have made, had he been able to think of one.

"By the Great Wolf Mother, you do not speak to a Wolf Nomad thusly unless you wish to guide your own wagons across the plains," roared Hornsbuck, pushing his way up to the Guildsman and spitting his words down into the man's face from his great height. "Apologize!" he roared.

"No offense," the Guildsman said coolly, carefully stepping back several paces. "I merely wondered if our young captain might not have had a little too much to drink and decided to investigate the contents of the wagon. He made some noise and, fearing detection, invented this ridiculous story of an old man who appears and disappears at will. I simply suggest that yon nomad's interest is far more likely than some mysterious magic-user who has most conveniently vanished."

"Mika?" growled Hornsbuck, looking at Mika for words of hot denial. But Mika could barely keep his eyes from crossing much less speak eloquently in his own defense.

Hornsbuck looked at Mika with disgust, Mika's very silence damning him in the older man's eyes. Hornsbuck spat on the ground at Mika's feet, then turned and shoved his way back through the crowd, flinging drivers from him like water off a dog's back.

Klaren gave Mika a shamed look, then followed Hornsbuck, trailing hoots of laughter from the drivers who were not unhappy to see the haughty nomads revealed to be no less human than themselves.

"Wait!" muttered Mika, but nobody paid him any attention.

"Tryin' to steal a little somethin' extry fer 'imself, 'e were," guffawed a rough-looking driver with only one eye. "I allus said them stuck-up sons of a she-wolf weren't nothin' special."

"Wonder if he found anything?" commented another, peering at Mika to see if there were any suspicious lumps concealed on his body.

Finally, Mika was left alone. Sinking to the ground, he cradled his aching head on his arms and tried to put his dazed thoughts in order, but it was impossible. As soon as he focused on one thought, it splintered into hundreds of others trailing confusion in their wake.

Mika sat there for a long time. At last, just as the moon was about to slip below the horizon, the fog lifted from his mind. He stood up shakily and saw the Guildsman leaning against the side of the wagon, arms folded across his chest, watching him.

"You know I did not take anything from the wagon," he said, his anger building rapidly.

"There was an old man, a magic-user, and he put a

spell on the wagon, I saw him do it. And I've seen him before. It was at the River Fler. He put a spell on me there that paralyzed me. He tried to kill me this time and would have succeeded had I not protected myself with a spell of my own.

"I can prove I'm telling the truth. Call the driver. The magic-user's spell seemed to affect him, too. Get Cob up here, if he can move. Let's see who's telling the truth!"

"That's not necessary," said the Guildsman, with a wave of his hand. "I've no doubt that you're telling the truth."

"Then why did you make me out a liar and a fool?" Mika hissed angrily.

"Because it would do me no good at all to have my men looking over their shoulders for the remainder of the trip, soiling their pants at every shadow," the Guildsman said harshly.

"Protecting us is your job, Master Wolf. Whether against bandits or magic-users. So do it! That is what we hired you for, to protect us. Or have you forgotten that? And how do I know that this magic-user is not after you instead of the wagon? After all, you are the only one who's seen him and the only one he's hurt.

"It seems entirely probable that you have irritated someone enough that they hired this magic-user and instructed him to turn you into a rock. I wish him better luck next time.

"I urge you to count your enemies and try not to cause any more trouble between here and Eru-Tovar or I shall keep my promise to speak to the Guild!" Fixing Mika with one last cold gaze, the Guildsman turned on his heel and stalked away.

Mika was shaking with fury, and he held his tongue with difficulty, wondering for the first time if it were possible that he himself was the target. Perhaps the wife of the baker back in Yecha had followed through with her tearful threats to tell her husband . . . No . . . he had kissed her and she had quite forgotten her complaints. Of that he was certain.

Mentally turning over a list of all who had grievances against him, Mika trudged slowly back to his own bedroll.

"Come, Tam," he called half-heartedly, noticing for the first time that the wolf was not at his side. But Tam did not appear.

Memory flooded back, and Mika remembered with a rush, the whirlwind sequence of events of his encounter with the magic-user.

The gust of wind had struck Tam in mid-air, while he was outside of Mika's aura of protection. It had tumbled him head over tail out of the direct area of confrontation. Yet Mika had heard him cry out, as the lightning bolt struck.

Mika was overcome with fear, and his heart began to pound as he looked around him, searching for the wolf. It was dark, yet Mika persisted and found the wolf at last.

Tam was still lying down, his muzzle on his paws and his hind legs and tail stretched out behind him. And he still looked like an enormous, very long, hedgehog.

"Tam!" Mika cried in alarm, rushing to the wolf's side. He placed a trembling hand on Tam's ribs and felt the great heart beating, albeit erratically, against his palm. Mika was weak with relief. Tam was alive, but stiff as a board.

Stroking Tam, trying to smooth the bristling fur down, Mika talked to the great wolf, knowing from his own experience that the wolf could probably hear him.

"You were far enough away from the lightning that it didn't kill you. Probably just gave you one hell of a good, stiff jolt. Stiff enough to stand your fur on end. Then he must have tossed in a stun spell for good measure. My spell of invulnerability protected me, but you, my poor TamTur, were too far away, so you caught that one, too. And you were probably as confused as I was.

"Don't worry, Tam. I'm here now."

Muttering soothing comments, Mika tipped the wolf gently over onto his side, slipped an arm under and around his body, and then lifted him off the ground.

Tam was nearly as tall as Mika from the tip of his nose to the end of his tail, and he was now as hard as a rock and equally as heavy. He was hard to hold on to, and he kept slipping out of Mika's arms. Once he fell to the ground and lay there on his back until Mika was able to heave him onto his shoulder and balance him there, teetering, with one hand on the stiffened tip of his tail, the animal's snout sticking out on the opposite side. He carried him like a furry log for the fire.

Mika had almost reached his own campfire when he startled a sleepy driver relieving himself in the shadow of his wagon. The trickle faltered and then stopped completely as the man stared at him with eyes and mouth agape.

Mika glared at him, daring the driver to speak as he strode past. "What's the matter?" he snarled. "Haven't you ever seen anyone walking a wolf before?"

Chapter 8

FALLING INTO A DEEP SLEEP after tucking his cloak around the stricken wolf, Mika had wakened to chaos and Hornsbuck's rough hand on his shoulder.

"Wake up! Mischief's afoot," he said gruffly.

Mika leaped to his feet, sword in his hand, ready for anything from bandits to kobolds. But all he saw was sand.

He blinked his eyes, hoping, wondering if it were some lingering affect of the spell. But when he opened his eyes the view was the same.

The pool of water was gone, as was the lush carpet of grass. In their place was a barren hill sprinkled with a thin covering of grease bushes and rocks. The men were staring about them with wide, frightened eyes, swords drawn uselessly against an unseen enemy.

"Magic. Illusion," Mika said. Thirst already clawed at his throat even though he had drunk his fill of the sweet water only a few short hours before.

"Oh, no," he groaned as a thought hit him and he

ran to the nearest pile of harnesses and packs and stared in dismay at the withered and empty waterskins.

"Gone. All gone," he muttered, more to himself than anyone else, remembering that it was by his order that the men had emptied the skins and filled them with water from the illusionary pool. It was some kind of magic delaying tactic, nothing more, he told himself. Or was it the prelude to something worse? Who was putting obstacles in their path?

The sun was rising fast over the edge of the horizon and already the mules were bawling for their morning drink. The horses, while quieter, were restless and shaking their heads from side to side.

The drivers huddled together, muttering in low tones and casting black glances at Mika.

The nomads were breaking camp and saddling their horses. Their years of training and self-discipline enabled them to exhibit a calm front, but Mika knew that they were surely filled with the same feelings of fear and uncertainty.

"We must turn back to the forest," Mika decided, drawing Hornsbuck to the far edge of the wagons. "No matter what the Guildsman says, we cannot continue without water. Even he will be forced to agree."

"I do agree," said the Guildsman, popping up at Mika's back. "But look yonder—storm clouds, coming this way fast. I warrant they will be here no later than midday. I say that we continue on. We should be able to fill our waterskins with ease, and the rain will bring on the grass. The horses and mules will feed well, and we will make good time."

"What do you think, Hornsbuck?" asked Mika, unwilling to do the man's bidding.

"He's right," growled Hornsbuck as he stroked his beard and squinted at the rapidly approaching front. "Black, heavy. Full of rain, no doubt. Be hell to pay if they catch us in the open. Never get back to the forest before they hit. Lose time. Might as well stay here."

Mika was forced to agree. Though he was anxious to have the trip over and done with, it made no sense to get caught up in a foul storm. So they saddled the horses, loaded the pack animals, and led the mules to harness, working quickly against the advance of the ominous curtain of billowing black clouds that stretched across the entire northern horizon.

The animals were nervous and allowed the humans to do as they wished. The mules showed the whites of their eyes and brayed long and loud, each outburst setting off others until the whole camp echoed with their cries. Even the wolves were affected and lifted their muzzles and howled forlornly till everyone, even the nomads, were half-crazed.

"I've never seen nuthin' like this 'afore," cursed the one-eyed driver. "Stupid animals."

But Mika had his doubts and eyed the storm with apprehension, wondering if it were truly an act of nature or another apparition.

Yet the storm was real and hit them before they had traveled more than a mile. It might have been better had they remained in camp, for they were barely able to turn the wagons into a circle before the curtain of wind and rain smashed into them.

The rain was cold and slashed down on their exposed skin with the force of hail, leaving men and animals feeling bruised and sore after only a few minutes' time.

The wind tore at them, whipping at their clothes and hair and screaming through the wagons, causing the hides to billow and pop, threatening to overturn those wagons that stood broadside to the force of the wind.

"Turn those wagons!" Mika screamed, and whipping the grey horse into the wind, rode up alongside three wagons that were in danger of tipping.

The wind seized his words almost before they were spoken, plucking them from his lips and hurling them away, unheard. Only by gestures was he able to tell the drivers what to do. So set in their ways were they that it was necessary to beat one of them with the flat of his sword before he would turn the wagon, so that the back end could take the brunt of the wind.

Using his sword, Mika then split the tough cowhide that sealed both front and back, allowing the wind to whistle through unimpeded, doing no damage.

Mika was quick to notice that the Guildsman himself was directing the placement of the creaking wagon and stayed close by its side even when it was in place, its wheels chocked firmly with stones. Many of the drivers had followed Mika's lead and opened their wagons to allow the wind through. But the secret wagon still remained tightly sealed.

Nor did the driver take shelter under or inside his wagon as many of the others had done. Instead he remained huddled on his seat as though standing guard.

The wolves, fearsome predators and fierce fighters, unafraid of anything that walked or flew, drew the line at rainstorms. They did not like the water, they hated the lightning, and they were nearly driven mad by the thunder.

Each dealt with the storm in the only way it knew, by crawling under the nearest wagon, digging a shallow hole, curling into a tight ball, and burying its head beneath its thick brushy tail.

The nomads knew from past experience that they would not emerge until the storm was over. May the Great She Wolf help them if it were ever necessary to go into battle during a rainstorm!

Mika himself, along with the other nomads, patrolled the perimeters of the wagons, water streaming off their already hopelessly wet heads and shoulders.

As soon as the main front had passed overhead and the wind abated somewhat, Mika and Hornsbuck directed the hanging of waterskins. They used the cowhide flaps to funnel water from the tops of the wagons into the waterskins, which soon bulged with the precious water that would carry the caravan safely across the prairie.

The storm seemed to ease the humiliation of the previous night, and Mika was pleased to note that the men obeyed his orders with no signs of rebellion. He was determined to see that it remained that way.

He was doubly determined to find out what was concealed in the secret wagon.

Thunder boomed and crashed around them, and lightning bolts split the dark skies and pierced the prairie. The rain continued to plummet from the clouds, turning the hard ground into a slippery quagmire on which the horses could find no firm footing.

The storm continued until mid-afternoon, but after the worst of it had passed, Mika, Hornsbuck, and the Guildsman decided that there was no advantage to staying put. They could scarcely get wetter, and everyone, humans and animals alike, would feel better doing something.

Everyone except the wolves. It was hard to stir them, and Mika felt sympathy for Tam. He had proved his mettle many times over, taking on fearsome adversaries, larger and more powerful than he, without a thought for his own safety. But once the wagons creaked forward, the wolves were exposed to the full force of the rain and could do little else but follow.

They did so unhappily, their fur matted and spiky with moisture, their tails curled low beneath their bellies, their feet glopped with clinging mud, and their yellow eyes sick with fear. They slunk alongside their humans, although a few chose to run along beneath the wagons.

TamTur ran beside Mika's horse, all but groaning when the grey kicked up water that splashed into his face. Mika met his eyes briefly and had to repress a smile at the look of disgust the wolf gave him. Mika shrugged, "I'm as wet as you are. Don't like it overly much myself. Just be glad we have water. We could be choking on our own dust."

Tam did not seem to appreciate Mika's logic and ran onward with his head down.

Mika forced the grey into a gallop, advancing until he found the scout who rode the forward point.

"How are we progressing?" he asked the man, a squinty-eyed dark-skinned nomad named Marek

132

from one of the Eastern clans along the River Fler, from whose ranks most of the casualties had come during the battle of the kobolds.

"All right. Better than I would have hoped," replied the man as he ran a well-callused hand over his dark braid. "The wind is behind us and is pushing us forward."

"The wagon wheels are sliding in the mud, easing the mule's loads," Mika added. "Almost like sledding."

"Whatever the reason, we're doing well and should make twenty, thirty miles today if we keep on as we are. That will bring us to Bubbling Springs, and we can make camp there tonight."

"Bubbling Springs?" asked Mika, totally unfamiliar with the geography of this stretch of the plains, having always followed the forest route.

"Sometimes there's as many as three springs there," replied Marek. "Sometimes none. But there must be water under the land; there's a large grove of trees that are always green, even in the dry years. We might have to fight for it though, because bandits are drawn to it like bees to honey."

"How many bandits? Would it be safer to avoid the area?" asked Mika.

Marek gave him a sideways glance from narrowed eyes, clearly surprised that a Wolf Nomad would avoid the chance for battle.

"I speak out of concern for the caravan, not out of my own preference," Mika said hastily. "Yon Guildsman places great importance on his wagons arriving safely and on time. Were it left to me, I would be the first to head for these springs and slaughter every bandit there. Rid the plains of the low-life!"

"Water the dirt with their blood!" added Marek, reassured by Mika's words. "No, we'd be safer in the woods and would have wood to burn as well, which we'll need after this wet day. Killing them as are hiding there will give the men a little bonus, cheer them up like. You can have first crack at them, being commander and all."

"No, I wouldn't think of depriving you of your pleasure," said Mika, who could not think of anything he'd less rather do than fight a bunch of desperate bandits.

"I shall kill one for you, sir," said Marek, his dark eyes bright with growing admiration.

"Do that," said Mika. "May the Great Wolf Mother, she who birthed the world, watch over you and keep you safe!" Smiling, he allowed the grey to drop back. The rain quickly blurred his vision.

"Fool," whispered Mika. "He'll never make old bones." Positioning himself among the wagons, he rode without incident throughout the remainder of the day.

As Mika rode, once again he pondered the secret wagon. But he could not decide on a plan that would provide him with enough time to enter the wagon and discover its contents. Sooner or later, he told himself, something would occur to him.

Marek had figured correctly, and shortly before dark, just as the rain was ending, the lean nomad rode back to pass along the news that Bubbling Springs could be seen on the edge of the eastern horizon.

Anxious to be done with hard wagon seats and saddles, wet chafing clothes, and the constant chill of moisture, drivers and nomads whipped their tired animals until they were within easy viewing distance of the woods. Smoke rose above the treetops in several different locations.

"Best take some men and see who's there," Mika advised Marek. "But be certain that they are bandits before there is any bloodshed. We wouldn't want to slaughter any innocents; it would cause too much trouble with the Guild if their bones were found."

Marek nodded his understanding, and taking half of the nomads, he rode swiftly toward the distant woods, wolves streaming behind him and the party.

For a time there was silence, then there was an eerie howl that climbed high and hung on the air, shivering the skin, followed by other wolf voices, the ululating cries of a wolf pack on the hunt, destined to bring fear to all who heard.

Those wolves that had remained behind circled wildly, then stopped abruptly, threw back their heads, and added their frenzied cries to those of their brothers. The howls almost covered the sound of human shrieks, but not completely.

Mika's stomach turned queasily, and for a moment he sympathized with the unknown humans who were going to their deaths violently, their throats ripped out by wolves or hacked to death by nomad swords.

After a while there were no more cries, and Marek and his companions rode back out of the woods and rejoined the wagon train.

"All clear, Captain," Marek said with satisfaction.

"You're sure?" asked Mika, not at all interested in

meeting up with some crazed survivor.

"I swear it on the Great Mother's tail," Marek said solemnly. "We hunted them out from under every bush and stone. We dragged them out of trees where they thought to hide, and we stuck a few with swords where they hid in holes in the ground.

"You may tell these townsmen that they have nothing to fear. There were but a dozen of the creatures, and they had no more than three knives among them, although they fought like wild men, and one of them even dared to throw a club at Klaren. Hit him, too!"

"Is he all right?" Mika asked anxiously, unwilling to lose even one of his men in case there was more fighting to come.

"He'll be fine after a good night's sleep," said Marek, noting Mika's concern with approval. It was always good to have a captain who cared about the welfare of his men. "The club did no more than crease his thick skull. Can you imagine the luck of such a one felling a nomad?" Shaking his head over the disrespect of the dead man, Marek took his leave.

Nomad though he was, Mika could very much imagine the situation. If he himself were attacked by someone bent on taking his life, he knew that he would fight with any means available to him, and he spared a moment of begruding respect for the brave, but dead, bandit.

Bells jingling cheerfully, the wagons rolled along smartly. A strange light, thrown into contrast by the dark clouds now far to the east, bathed the prairie with a glowing incandescence, transforming the bare rocky earth into shining gold and the puddles into pools of quicksilver. The freshly washed, electrically charged air was sharp and clear and held the rich scent of earth and wood smoke.

Although humans and animals alike were still wet, cold, and uncomfortable, their earlier misery was all but forgotten with the promise of food and rest as the wagon train entered the dripping forest.

Chapter 9

THE BODIES OF THE SLAIN BANDITS were dumped unceremoniously in a far corner of the woods where animals and birds of prey would dispose of them.

After double checking to make sure that no more of the would-be cutthroats were lurking in the small forest of dwarf roanwood, phost, and the occasional yarpick, the men set up camp.

It was undoubtedly the fruit of the thorn-studded yarpick that sustained the bandits who sheltered in the forest, supplementing whatever wildlife they might be lucky enough to catch.

Yarpick nuts were as large as a child's fist and were eaten whole or ground into meal. Mika was glad to see that the trees bore a heavy crop and decided that before they left, he would order drivers and nomads alike to knock the fruits from the trees with sticks and gather them into piles. Later, the tasteless fruit would be separated from the nuts which could be sold in Eru-Tovar as well as adding variety to their own foodstuffs.

The men would grumble, of course, but since the nuts were widely regarded as a delicacy, they would do as they were bid.

Right now, the first business at hand was to strip the horses and the mules of their waterlogged trappings and rub them down. It would not do to have sick animals. This done, they were hobbled and let out to browse on the sparse grass.

The men were no less anxious than the animals to be free of their sodden garments, and it was with a feeling of great relief that they rubbed themselves dry with rough cloths and stood in front of the bandits' fires warming their clammy bones.

Mika stood apart from the various groups of men and watched as they snapped each other's flanks with damp cloths and shrieked with mock rage, acting like children.

Mika knew that the play was harmless and even desirable in that it would relieve the tension of the last few days. Should it become necessary, the men would fight better, having had a brief respite of fun.

The wolves joined in the fray. A small, grey female seized the end of a waving cloth, ripped it out of the hands of the holder, and began racing around the camp with all the other wolves giving wild chase.

At any other time, Mika might easily have been among the naked throng, roaring out his bet as to which of the wolves would end up with the prize, but his thoughts were on other matters.

He sat down on a fallen phost tree, its phosphorescent glow lost in the still-bright evening. Later, its pearly aura caused by decomposition would be clearly visible in the darkness. For the moment, though, it provided a sturdy seat as Mika combed out his long dark hair, toweled it dry, and rebraided it into a thick central braid that ran from forehead to mid-back and was then doubled back on itself and tied at the nape of his neck with a length of leather.

Years of experience enabled him to do the intricate braiding both swiftly and neatly. As he tied off the braid, he chanced to look down, and there, lying on the carpet of wet forest leaves, was a single feather, pure white and the length of his hand.

Mika picked it up reverently, knowing from the size and color that it had come from the wing of a great snowy white owl, a huge silent messenger of the north that struck without warning, its prey dying with long, curved talons curling through their organs before their minds even grasped the fact that they were in danger.

Mika stared at the omen, ideas flitting through his mind, wondering if he dared, even as he laid his plans. Holding the feather gently, as though it were a precious gem, Mika located his saddlebags and, dumping his wet leathers on the ground, rummaged through his possessions until he found the pouch that Enor had handed him as he left the camp.

He untied the leather strings that held the pouch shut and pried it open gently, daring to hope that Enor had spoken truly, that it contained more than just herbs and vials of potions. He prayed that it held his father's book. The book that contained all the permanent spells, charms, and enchantments that he knew, and the scrolls that held those spells that could be used only once before they disappeared.

"It's here, Tam! It's here!" Mika said, looking

into the mouth of the bag and sighing happily. "Won't old Whituk be angry? I can see his face now—may he eat sour grapes forever!"

Tam wagged his huge tail from side to side, his eyes bright with the happiness in Mika's voice. He rested his huge muzzle against Mika's leg and whined shrilly.

"I think it's above my skill level, Tam," Mika confided. "I'll have to be very careful. I don't want to make any mistakes, not when I'm out of my body. But what could possibly go wrong if I read it carefully and memorize all the words?"

Tam groaned deep in his chest and pawed at his nose with his paw, hiding his eyes. Mika knew that it was probably just a flea, but it seemed as though Tam were laughing at him! Doubting him!

"Don't you think I can do it?" Mika asked, more hurt than he would like to admit. "Come on, you're supposed to be my best friend! Let's have a little bit of faith here! I bet I can do it! No! I *know* I can do it! And I'll find out what's in that wagon. You wait and see!"

But TamTur merely groaned louder and longer and lifted his muzzle to let out a short agonized howl.

"Fine friend you are," muttered Mika, and yanking the strings shut around the mouth of the pouch, he hung it from his shoulder and went to find dinner.

The wagons had been drawn into a wide circle inside a natural clearing in the forest. A small, dark spring that did indeed bubble rose from the ground at the far east end.

The horses and mules were wandering outside the perimeter of the wagons, browsing on grass and ten-

der leaves. The men had added armfuls of firewood
to the bandits' fire and now lounged before it, revel-
ing in its great heat as they ate their evening meal. A
feeling of contentment pervaded.

"A good day's work, Mika," growled Hornsbuck.
"Waterskins filled. Miles under our belt. Yarpicks to
eat. Did the men good to sink their swords into those
dungeon slime. Picked them right up. I always say a
little killing can do wonders for a man."

"Mmmm," said Mika, dipping his bowl into the
communal pot of beans, the remainder of the batch
from the previous evening now reinforced with even
more beans, bits of smoked dried rabbit, and too
much salt. Damp chunks of mealybread added to the
bulk.

Meals were terrible for the most part. The worst
part of every trip. Occasionally, the cooks were men
of inspiration, but more often they were whey-faced,
dour individuals, who were unhappy in life and were
determined to ruin as many other lives as humanly
possible. Their foul cooking generally accomplished
that mission with ease. Mika ate as few camp meals
as possible, making do with small game roasted on
spits.

"Gonna eat that?" asked Hornsbuck eagerly.

Mika passed him the bowl without comment and
Hornsbuck shoveled the gloppy contents into his
mouth along with parts of his beard which he spat out
regularly along with a fine spray of food.

"Can't waste good food," grunted Hornsbuck, between mouthfuls. "A man needs something to stick
to his ribs!"

Mika refrained from comment.

The evening passed almost too slowly for Mika. The men stayed awake for hours, talking and laughing around the campfire. Even the Guildsman was in a good mood and passed his wineskin freely, telling of his adventures across the whole of the known Oerth. Extraordinary stories about fabulous sea serpents encountered while sailing the turquoise depths of the Dramidj Ocean; of mystical meetings with the silver-hued, pointed-eared Olven Folk of the tiny kingdom of Celene; and of narrow escapes from painted savages in the jungles of Amedio. If the man were to be believed, he had led an interesting and charmed life. No wonder the Guild had chosen him to accompany the caravan.

Mika visited the sentries shortly after nightfall, speaking with each and every man. Tam followed, greeting the other wolves in the usual manner, sniffing noses and genitals.

"How goes it?" he asked the sentry who stood watch at the northernmost edge of the forest.

"Quiet," replied the man. "Nothing stirring. Just as well, there is no moon tonight. But BlackClaw will tell me if there's anything out there."

Mika studied the big black wolf appreciatively while keeping his hands to himself. No man touched another man's wolf unbidden. A wolf would react before it thought and could easily sever a man's hand or slice a vein with its great canines. They might regret it later, but by then it would be a little too late for apologies.

Mika urged the men seated around the campfires to end their songs and get themselves off to their bed-rolls. He wanted as many as possible to be asleep when he put his plan into effect.

Trying to look casual, Mika settled himself on a fallen phost log far enough from the fire that the eerie white glow was clearly visible. Then he opened the pouch and began leafing through the pages of the small leather-bound book, stifling the twinges of pain that came from seeing the tiny loops and curls of his father's neat handwriting.

"Pickles . . . pig warts . . . poltergeists . . . Here it is, polymorph," read Mika, his lips forming the words.

Looking up from time to time, he smiled at the men occasionally, but not in a manner that would invite company. Tam lay at his side watching with a mournful expression as Mika tried to commit the words of the spell to memory.

It was difficult. This was the part of magic that Mika always had the most trouble with. The words were confusing. Many of the words rhymed, yet most meant nothing when said individually. In and of themselves they were gibberish. It was only when you strung them together in the right order and said them with just the right intonation and emphasis that you got results. The speaker could only hope the Great She Wolf would guard his tongue and prevent him from forgetting a word or pronouncing it wrong.

If a word did come out wrong and the speaker was lucky, nothing terrible would happen. The spell would merely fail, canceled out by ineptitude. The only penalty would be being forced to learn it again, for all memory of the spell would vanish once it was used, even if used incorrectly.

It was when the speaker got the spell wrong and

145

was not lucky that the trouble began. For then, in spite of the fact that some element of the spell was incorrect, the spell worked—but incorrectly, frequently heaping devastating consequences on the inept magic-user who had conjured the spell improperly.

These effects usually wore off within the time span allotted to the spell. But sometimes, in the interim, the magic-user or an innocent victim would be killed, maimed, or altered irrevocably as had almost happened when Mika changed Celia's mother into a cat. Celia might never have forgiven him if Tam had actually eaten the cat.

In spite of his boastful words, Mika was very worried that he might get the spell wrong. One had to be at least at the seventh level to use the Polymorph spell, which allowed one to change from a human form into that of an animal.

Seventh level was still several years away in ability. Years of intense study. But nothing else would do! If Mika turned himself into a great white snowy owl, he could slit the top of the wagon with his sharp beak and slip inside. Once he had explored the dark interior of the wagon with his superior owl vision, he would let himself out and fly away undetected. The plan was foolproof. Who would suspect an owl?

Tam nudged Mika's leg with his nose. All right, all right. So Tam would know, but fortunately, he couldn't tell.

The words marched round and round in his brain, till he could repeat them perfectly, well almost perfectly. Each time he thought he had the spell memorized, he would go blank and forget a phrase or blither and mix two words up front to back. But he kept at it, goading himself with the thought of the wagon.

Mika stared into the forest dreamily. Pearls. That had been his latest guess. Pearls from the kelp beds. Lustrous beads that he could drape round his woman, all around and under the sweet soft naughty places, a great long rope of pearls.

Mika sighed deeply, looking off into the dark night, seeing Celia in his mind's eye reclining on the green moss wearing nothing but a string of pearls. Then, suddenly, out of nowhere, Matin appeared on the moss next to Celia, reached out for the rope of pearls and . . . Mika straightened up with a frown on his face.

"Problems, Captain?" asked Klaren sympathetically, appearing unseen and unheard at Mika's side.

"What! Oh! Um, well, just thinking about tomorrow. Plans. Strategy. That sort of thing," Mika said brusquely.

"Sorry to intrude, sir. Just wanted to report that all is quiet. The last of the men have turned in and we'll be ready for an early start. You should try and get some rest, too, Captain. It's been a long day."

"Thanks, lad. I'll be turning in soon," said Mika, not mentioning what he would be turning into. "Sleep you well."

"And deep," he muttered beneath his breath as the young nomad nodded and turned away.

Mika continued to study the elusive words until he was quite sick of them. Finally, he shut the book, stuck it in his pocket and, hanging the precious pouch from his shoulder, toured the camp once more.

147

It was as Klaren had said, everyone was asleep. Even the Guildsman snored as heartily as Hornsbuck, thanks no doubt to the largess of his wineskin.

Unfortunately, the wagon that was Mika's objective stood closest of all to the bonfire, which still blazed high against the damp of the evening.

Anyone or anything, even a great snowy white owl, that tried to enter the wagon would be easily seen.

Mika fretted, wishing that the circumstances were more to his liking. He considered waiting another night, possibly even longer, until conditions were more favorable, but his natural impatience, which always demanded immediate gratification, whispered, "Do it now. Do it now." And it was impossible to argue.

Mika and Tam walked deep into the forest, passing the second and then the third of the springs that had risen to the surface, then further still, forcing their way into the thickest, most tangled copse.

The light of a fallen phost tree drew him like a beacon, and he settled gratefully on its rough, shaggy surface, trying to still his hammering heart.

As the moment drew closer, he found himself filled with doubts. He might have turned back at that last moment, but Tam pawed at his knee and looked up into his eyes, whining plaintively, as though begging him not to try the spell. Mika's resolve hardened.

"It'll be all right," he reassured the wolf. Then he undressed, placing his leggings, cloak and boots alongside the glowing log. Why burden the owl with clothing?

He picked up the book and the feather, quickly

148

found his place and scanned the words one last time. For the millionth time he regretted that one could not read a spell aloud but must have it memorized. It was also necessary to close one's eyes and picture that which you hoped to accomplish, at the same time that you said the words.

Mika squared his shoulders. Then, he tucked the book back into the pouch and cleared his throat nervously. He sighed deeply and clutched the feather with determination. There was nothing left, he was as ready as he would ever be.

He closed his eyes and started chanting. One. Two. Three sentences done! Four. Five. Six. Uh oh, a slight bobble on his intonation as nervousness gripped his throat. Mika paused, waiting for the knowledge that he had failed. But there was nothing. Maybe it was still all right. He continued. Seven. Eight. Tam whined. Nine. Damn! Now his nose itched. Ten. Done! He kept his eyes closed, unable to look, knowing that he would soon be aware of whether the spell had worked . . . or failed.

Mika felt dizzy and a bit sick to his stomach. He put out an arm to steady himself and could not open his fingers. He opened his eyes and for a minute the world spun dizzily around him. Then it stilled and he found that he was looking Tam directly in the eyes.

Tam stared at him long and hard, then sniffed him softly, snuffling his scent through the big black nose that would be so easy to nip with a sharp beak, and then lay down on the carpet of dead leaves with a great sigh.

Nip Tam's nose with a beak? Whoa! Mika's eyes swiveled around, and he saw why he had been on a level with Tam. The spell had worked! He had really done it! He, Mika, a lowly, lazy, bumbling fourth-level magic-user had pulled off a seventh-level skill! He had always known he could do it. Why did everyone think this magic stuff was so hard?

Mika puffed out his huge fluffy white chest and took a step forward, feeling the need to strut, to get the hang of this owl stuff.

Then he stepped on a yarpick thorn that pierced the bottom of his foot and caused him to hop around the tiny clearing hooting with pain.

Wait a minute, this wasn't supposed to happen! Thorns weren't supposed to stick you if you were an owl! Owls had tough, scaly feet with long curved talons. You only got stuck if you had big, soft, floppy human feet with ugly toes.

Mika looked down with a sinking heart and letting out the owl equivalent of a human groan as he saw his own huge, big, soft, floppy human feet, complete with ugly toes, sticking out at the bottom of his beautiful owl body. He had goofed! Mika stomped around the thicket muttering curses. He circled around the log and walked right over Tam who followed his progress with mournful eyes.

Mika kicked a stump. It hurt. He tore a hunk of wood out of a branch with his beak. Blehh, it tasted terrible. Damn! What now? Would he be stuck like this forever?

Mika forced himself to calm down, glaring at Tam with fierce owl eyes, which he was not pleased to notice had retained their human vision instead of gaining the owl's ability to see in the dark. Curses! Why did nothing ever go right!

Mika continued glaring at Tam as though daring the wolf to give him his I-told-you-so look. But Tam turned his head, refusing to meet Mika's furious gaze.

Finally, unable to vent his anger on anyone other than himself, and unable to think of a solution, Mika shrugged his wings, which he had to admit were very handsome, and admired himself as he pondered the problem.

All right, so he'd botched things a little. But all things considered, they'd worked fairly well for a mere fourth-level magic-user. So he had human feet, the better to land with, except on little branches, of course.

He had to look on the bright side of things. It might have been worse. He might have gotten the feet part right and wound up with hands instead of wings. That would definitely have made flying difficult.

Well, there was no sense in standing around moping. Best to get on with it. Thinking calmly, he assumed that the strange combination would disappear with the dissolution of the spell. It was time to get on with the plan.

Mika flapped his wings once or twice, trying to get the feel of being an owl. But there were too many bushes and limbs in the way and he was unable to extend his wings to their full length. Ducking his head down, he pushed his way through the underbrush, a subdued Tam following along behind.

Actually, his feet worked pretty well. Probably better than those little stumpy feet that owls have. They probably should have been designed this way in the first place. Hmmm, maybe if the Great She Wolf were watching, she'd rethink the whole owl design.

Pondering the matter of owls, religion, and anatomy, Mika the owl stalked into a clearing, startling a mouse. It stared at him with immense eyes, then disappeared with a terrified squeak.

Mika stifled an immediate craving for mouse and looked up at the dark sky. No moon, just as the guard had said. Good. He patted Tam on the head awkwardly with one large white wing and then, concentrating hard, began to flap his wings.

It was easier than he thought it would be. The powerful wings forced the air beneath them, pushing it down against the ground, creating a resistance, and at the same time, his body just seemed to flow upward with the silly human feet trailing beneath him.

It was beautiful. It was glorious. It was magic. Mika flapped harder and harder, his large white body rising higher and higher in the dark night sky.

Mika could see the forest below him and the single bright eye that was the campfire. The wind sang in his feathers and rushed past his body, softly stroking it like a lover's caress.

He opened his great curved beak to taste the air. He reveled in the passage of air as it slipped through the tips of his wings, felt the sliding pressure against his body as he found a low riding thermal and rode it like a curling wave. And his feet . . . his feet were cold. Definitely cold. Like little nubs of ice.

Time to descend. It wouldn't do to be up here if the spell ended suddenly. Shivering at the thought, Mika turned his body into a soft curve and floated silently down, back toward the forest.

He judged his distance correctly but not his speed. Opening his wings to brake, he almost overshot the wagon and only stopped himself at the last minute by running along the top of the cowhide roof and stabilizing himself with his big human feet. See, they weren't such a mistake after all!

Mika looked around him cautiously, swiveling his head in all directions. He saw no one awake except Tam, who sat watching at the edge of the forest.

Mika lowered his great feathered head and studied the cowhide surface. Just plain cowhide, laced together here and there with thin leather strips; no problem at all for his sharp beak.

Feeling confident, Mika clacked his beak experimentally and then rapidly snipped a half a dozen turns of the leather, opening a hole the size of his hand . . . when he used to have one.

Excitement beat in his breast as he placed his eye to the hole and looked down into the dark interior of the wagon and saw . . . nothing. It was too dark.

Muttering owlish imprecations, he quickly snipped several dozen of the leather strips. No turning back now, it would be obvious that someone or something had entered the wagon, so he might as well do it right.

The hole gaped darkly, inviting Mika to solve the mystery of the wagon. Visions of gold and jewels and pearls filled his head as he leaned forward and looked inside. But still he saw nothing; it was as dark as a robber's heart, or, um, dark as a cave in there.

Mika leaned farther, trying to grip the edge of the cowhide with his toes, but there was really nothing to grip. Now, here was a case where talons would have served him better.

Mika stuck his head completely through the opening and hung upside down, determined to see, once and for all.

Suddenly, he felt himself losing balance. His human feet scrabbled helplessly on the smooth cowhide but found no grip, and he felt himself falling through the hole, falling straight down with no chance or room to flap his wings, and no hands to break his fall.

Awwkk! He landed with a thump on the top of his head. On something soft. Very soft.

He righted himself carefully, sliding first one foot then another along the curious softness. The softness which was also warm. And curved. Nicely curved. Hmm, it all seemed very familiar. Celia?

His toes found what felt like the edge of a bed and, flapping himself upright, he stabilized, then peered about, trying desperately to see what it was he had found.

But it was dark, too dark to see anything at all. There were sounds. The sound of soft breathing, little murmurs such as a woman makes while sleeping. And scents. A wonderful scent like cinnamon and cloves, maybe just a hint of celandon. Oh, if he could only see something!

All of a sudden, there was a harsh scratching noise. Then, as though in answer to his wish, a dim light flooded the interior of the wagon.

In the few seconds that it took his dazzled eyes to adjust to the light, Mika was stunned, unsure of what he was seeing, doubting his eyes, thinking it an illusion.

But as his vision cleared, he saw that he had not

been mistaken. He was standing on the edge of a bed, just as he had suspected. A bed of silk and the softest down.

Mika shivered. Sprawled delicately on the pink silk comforter was the most beautiful young woman in the entire world.

The Princess!

Her hair was a mass of curly black ringlets that covered the pillow cradling her head and shone with small blue highlights.

Her skin was alabaster white, lustrous as pearls, and faintly tinged with the most delicate blush of pink. Her lips, slightly parted, were tiny soft petals.

She was clad in the softest, most fragile gown of pink silk that clung to her voluptuous body like down on a ripe peach.

Her tiny hands were open, slightly curled, and Mika could all but imagine how they would feel on his . . .

At which point, out of nowhere, a sword appeared in front of his face, or more specifically, in front of his beak.

Belatedly, his brain began to function, assimilating facts, yelling messages: Light! Sword! DANGER! even as he flung himself sideways and rolled back on top of the sleeping beauty, reasoning, he hoped correctly, that whomever wielded the sword would not take the chance of endangering the girl.

Begging the indulgence of the strangely silent beauty, Mika pressed his fluffy form against the softness of her body, his head cradled between the twin mounds of her ample breasts. Any sword thrust capable of killing him would risk harming the girl. He prayed that the strategy would work until he could think of something else.

For a moment it seemed that his gamble had worked. A figure appeared in the center of the now almost blinding light, and slowly took shape.

Mika saw with a sinking heart the largest human being he had ever seen in his entire life. The man was a giant. A veritable giant. The small curving interior of the wagon bent him almost double. Standing erect, Mika had no doubt that the monster would top eight feet.

In addition, he weighed more than any two nomads put together, perhaps four hundred stones!

Mika was able to make his estimate without the confusion of clothes, for the giant wore only a square loincloth which was large enough to smother a two-year-old child.

His arms, chest, and thighs, devoid of clothing and hair, were immense and rigid with corded muscle. Mika doubted that the giant could lower his arms to his sides or knock his knees, so greatly distorted were the muscles that warped those extremities.

Mika formed all of his impressions in the blink of an eye, then became too frightened to blink his eyes and stared in fixed terror at the angry face so close before him.

The giant's head was bald and gleaming, his ears bracketing the white boulder of a head like two distended fungi.

His eyes gleamed in his doughy face like shiny chunks of anthracite and were made more harsh by the total absence of eyebrows.

His nose was a blobby affair, its various bends and

planes giving evidence of having been broken numerous times and set without the benefit of a healer.

His mouth was but a cruel slit through which his foul breath rasped loudly.

Clutched in one immense hand was an equally immense sword, the well-honed edge of which gleamed silver.

The giant snarled silently, and his face twitched into an awful grimace while his sword trembled barely a hand's span from Mika's quivering body. It was obvious that the giant was uncertain what he should do.

Desperately Mika looked at the giant, trying to formulate some plan of his own.

Then, the giant's hand shot out, grasped the back of Mika's neck and began to pull. But owls have no necks, and the man's hand found nothing to grab but feathers, which he pulled and tugged, causing Mika great pain.

Mika was determined not to be separated from the girl, so he opened his beak and gripped the scarlet ribbon that criss-crossed her dress, gently separating the girl's breasts, and hung on tight, clasping her generous figure with outspread wings. The sword hovered nearby, waiting for even the tiniest sliver of space so that it could slip between the girl and his body. He clutched harder. What a waste, he thought. Here I am pressed up against the most beautiful woman in the world, and I'm an owl.

Then the thought spun out of his mind as the giant gave up his painful tugging and began beating on Mika's head with the hilt of the sword.

Damn! This had to stop. Mika knew that he had to

get out of the wagon and soon, or he would be one dead owl. Letting go of the ribbon, he swiveled his head and sank his beak into the giant's arm. The sensation was very satisfying. Blood spurted in every direction and flowed down Mika's throat. Strange that he had never noticed how good blood tasted before.

The giant tried to shake Mika off his arm, but there wasn't enough room in the wagon to swing a cat, let alone an owl, and all he succeeded in doing was bashing his elbow against a wooden strut. He hissed angrily. The giant tried to pass the sword to his left hand, but Mika kicked out with his foot and the sword fell to the floor with a tinny clatter.

The wagon was shaking violently now, and out of the corner of his eye, Mika saw the cowhide covering behind the driver's seat start to open. Then the giant swung around, obscuring Mika's view. Mika bit down harder. The giant grunted soundlessly and fell against the cowhide. Mika heard a startled exclamation and guessed that the driver had been knocked off his perch.

Mika had only a second to hope that the fall had been fatal, for the giant was up to no good. Using his arm, the one Mika was biting, the giant pressed against the owl's throat, crushing him against the side of the wagon.

Against his will, Mika was forced to open his beak in an attempt to suck air into his lungs. As he did, the giant ripped his arm free and grabbed Mika by the chest, holding him out at arm's length while reaching for the knife that hung from his loincloth.

Time to leave! Mika kicked the giant full in the face with all his might and felt the man's nose squash beneath the hard, callused ball of his foot.

He rammed his big toe into the giant's eye, stepped on his shaved head with his other foot, and tore free of the giant's grasp, leaving the man nothing but a handful of snow-white feathers, as he scrambled through the hole in the roof of the wagon and flew away.

Men stood in the clearing looking upward, pointing at him as he flew above them. Well, he could fix that, and taking careful aim, Mika squeezed a sphincter muscle and was rewarded by the howls of the watchers below as they shielded their heads and ran for shelter.

Mika beat the air with powerful strokes and headed back for the safety of the forest. But shortly before he reached the coppice, he began feeling sick at his stomach and his vision blurred. Realizing what was happening, Mika circled lower and lower, attempting to land before he changed back into human form.

Everything grew vague. A huge tree loomed up in front of him, and putting his feet out, he touched down just as darkness washed over him and he saw no more.

Chapter 10

MIKA WOKE TO FIND HIMSELF sprawled naked on top of a large roanwood branch, more than forty feet above the ground. Off in the distance he could hear men shouting as they plunged through the dark forest. He could see the bright light of their torches. It would never do to be found like this. He had to get into his clothes and make an appearance. His absence would definitely be noted.

As he pushed himself up from the branch, he nearly fell, but he clutched the tree with his right arm and hung on for dear life as he stared in horror at his left arm. Or, rather, what used to be his left arm. Now, it was a wing from the shoulder down.

Sour bile rose in his throat, and he rested his forehead against the rough bark and tried not to be sick. All sense of urgency left him as he pondered this new problem. It scarcely mattered now if he got back to his clothes before he was found. There was no way of concealing for long the fact that he had a wing instead of an arm.

Mika's mind raced as he tried to think back over what he might have done wrong, but since the spell was gone from his memory, it was difficult to reconstruct. Obviously, he had fouled up some crucial part of the spell that channeled the return from one body to the other.

He tried to recall what would happen in such an instance, but he could not remember anything except the story of Grizzard, the shaman of a clan of Wolf Nomads that spent much of their time deep in the Burneal Forest.

During a convocation of shamans, which had taken place at their camp, Grizzard had attempted to polymorph himself into something, exactly what, Mika had never determined. But in the middle of the spell, Grizzard's young son, six years of age and old enough to know better, had interrupted his father with some childish tale of woe. Grizzard's wife had appeared and dragged the child away instantly, but the damage was done.

Grizzard changed right before their eyes. Or at least part of him did. His head, to be precise, changed into that of a goose. He was a man from the shoulders down and a goose from the neck up. An angry goose.

The goose-man chased the woman and child around the entire camp, honking its irritation, and when it finally caught up with the unfortunate child, it pecked him black and blue.

Three days later the spell came undone and Grizzard returned to his human form. But ever after, he was called Gizzard, in spite of his objections, and the child was afraid to come near him for several moon-turns. Grizzard also developed a fondness for worms.

Mika could not wait three days. He needed to be normal now. He considered staying up in the tree until the change took place, but it was chilly and the mosquitos had found him and were humming their approval. Then too, he would certainly be seen in the morning light even if he escaped detection now.

Mika could think of nothing worse than being gaped at by a crowd of curious nomads and drivers while he huddled naked in a tree trying to hide his wing.

A short bark sounded at the foot of the tree. Tam! Mika felt his spirits rise. Peering down over the edge of the branch he could just make out Tam's figure at the foot of the tree.

"Good boy," whispered Mika. "Tam, go get my clothes and the pouch," he directed. But Tam merely sat there wagging his tail from side to side. Mika hurled small branches at the wolf, but Tam just ignored them and continued barking.

"Stupid wolf," Mika muttered angrily, knowing that he had to get down immediately, before Tam's barking brought the searchers. He pushed himself up carefully and edged over to the trunk of the tree.

Getting down was easier than he had thought it would be. Mika had been climbing roanwood trees since he was a toddler, and his hand and feet found the correct placement without even thinking about it.

"Did I ever tell you that your mother was a dog?" Mika whispered nastily as he ran through the woods, deftly ducking branches and other obstacles. Tam loped alongside, tongue lolling, laughing in his wolf fashion.

Cries were echoing all around Mika, torches flashing like giant fireflies as he dove into the thicket and squirmed into his clothes, dragging his cloak over the offending wing.

He had no more than emerged from the thicket when he was met by a crowd of drivers.

"No one in there," he cried, pointing to the thicket from which he had just emerged. "Spread out and keep your eyes open. Don't let anything slip past you!" and he plunged off to the right before anyone could speak.

He kept up the charade for another hour, questioning men as he encountered them and sending them off in new directions with fresh instructions, receiving, in return, their impression of what they had seen.

It were turrible, Captain," said one of the drivers with a look of distaste as he brushed at his jerkin that was now stained a peculiar whitish-green. "It were as big as a cow an' had long horns stickin' out o' its head. An' it breathed fire, an' acid dripped out o' its mouth. Why, I were almos' killed!"

"A real horror," one of the nomads said somberly as he confided in Mika. "Some kind of feathered dragon, I think. It swooped down low, right in front of my face and tried to claw out my eyes with its claws, but I frightened it away with my sword."

The other stories were equally outrageous. None agreed with any other, and almost all of the men claimed some personal encounter with the mythic beast. Only one man told the truth.

"It was an owl," said the Guildsman after Mika had rounded up the last of the men and sent them back to their bedrolls.

"A most peculiar owl. It had human feet. I think now that you must have been correct," said the Guildsman as he fixed Mika with a speculative gaze. "I agree that we are being plagued by a magic-user. But I do not think that we have much to fear, if this is any indication of his ability. What say you, Master Wolf?"

"I always say that it is a mistake to underestimate one's enemies," Mika said stiffly.

"Perhaps," said the Guildsman. Then, yawning broadly, he turned to go. Dropping his hand he placed it on Mika's cloak, on the place where his shoulder would be, had he one, and squeezed lightly.

Mika's heart sank. He knew there was no way that the man could fail to realize that it was a wing, not an arm hidden beneath the cloak. He held his breath, waiting for whatever would come next.

But the Guildsman merely smiled enigmatically. "Good night," he said pleasantly. "Get to bed. It's been a busy night, but I'm sure that things will look different in the morning."

Puzzled, Mika watched him turn and walk away. Damn! What game was the man playing at? He had been certain that the Guildsman was his enemy and would expose him. Perhaps he would yet, but for now, Mika was more than willing to find his bed and call it a night. Maybe things *would* be different in the morning. Twitching his wing, he hoped so with all his heart.

Things *were* different in the morning. They were worse. His arm was still a wing and it was necessary to keep his cloak draped around him to hide it.

Further, his head and neck ached horribly from the pounding he had taken from the giant's sword and where the cursed man had pulled his feathers.

And if that were not enough, a large patch of the curly black hair that covered his chest was gone, ripped out by the roots where the giant had gripped him as he flew away.

One foot was badly swollen and throbbed constantly. He knew that he would have trouble getting it into his boot, much less fitting it in the stirrup. He could only hope that the giant felt worse than he did.

The grey was in a feisty mood that morning and began rearing as soon as he saw Mika. Rather than fool with the animal, Mika picked up a fallen yarpick that fairly bristled with sharp, inch-long spines and waved it under the grey's nose.

"You give me one minute of trouble today and you're a gelding. Got it?" he growled. A group of drivers laughed, but the animal must have heard something in Mika's tone, for he quieted instantly and gave him no reason to complain throughout the whole long day.

The day seemed to last forever, helped not one bit by a miserable breakfast of coffee brewed from scorched grounds and mealybread so old it had crystalized. Mika felt like taking the yarpick to the cook.

His mosquito bites itched miserably, and chafed by the saddle, his flanks were red and inflamed by evening. He dismounted with a groan, wondering what new horror the cook would produce for dinner. He had not seen so much as one rabbit all day.

He tossed the reins to a young nomad and asked

him to take care of the horse. The resulting howl, seconds later, assured him that the horse had not mellowed. He lowered himself gently to the ground and groaned, content to let Hornsbuck and the others set up camp.

They had found no forest this evening and were camped on the open prairie with nothing to see for miles in any direction. It was a bleak and lonely place that promised nothing hopeful.

It seemed to Mika that he had no more than closed his eyes than someone was shaking him by the shoulder.

"Here, eat this," said a voice. "You'll feel better."

Mika opened his eyes and saw the Guildsman holding out a steaming mug. Mika sat up groggily and took the offering. The steam that rose from the surface of the mug smelled very good indeed.

"Rabbit stew," said the Guildsman. "I have a pouch, too. Mine contains a mixture of dried meat and vegetables. That way, no matter where I am, all I have to do is mix it with hot water and I have a meal. You might find such a pouch more useful than the one you possess."

"Perhaps," Mika said noncommittally, wondering what the man was up to and why he was being friendly.

"I had thought to keep you out of our hair until we reached Eru-Tovar," the Guildsman said in a straightforward manner. "You see, your reputation as a connoisseur of beautiful women is as well known as your skill with weapons. I did not think that I could risk your knowing about the princess."

Mika gave a start and met the Guildsman's level

gaze. "So the messenger told the truth after all," he said. "I think you'd better tell me the whole story."

"Yes," said the Guildsman. "It's time. Come to the wagon with me. No, no, don't worry, Recknass won't harm you if you are with me. Besides, he has problems of his own at the moment."

Tam accompanied them to the wagon, the roof of which, Mika noticed, had been repaired. But Tam placed himself between Mika and the Guildsman and could not be dissuaded, growling whenever the man attempted to move closer to Mika.

"Quite an animal you have there," said the Guildsman. "Why don't you tell him that we're friends now, so he'll quit growling at me?"

"Wouldn't do any good," Mika said with a cold smile. "Tam makes up his own mind about people. I guess he just doesn't like you. Besides, I don't know that we *are* friends. It takes more than *words* to make it a fact."

The Guildsman looked at Mika with cold blue eyes and then nodded. "Just so," he said. "But sometimes friendships are born of need rather than the passage of time. Please suspend your decision until you have heard my explanation."

Reaching the back of the wagon, the Guildsman unlaced the covering and climbed inside, ignoring the curious looks of drivers and nomads alike. Tam tried to follow, but there was not enough room in the tiny wagon and Mika told him to stay outside. Tam complied. Neither Mika nor the Guildsman noticed when Tam snapped angrily at a small black fly that soared past the entrance flap into the wagon and hovered attentively in the shadows.

168

The scene was almost identical to that of the previous night. The princess lay on the bed looking much the same as she had the night before. Her diaphanous gown outlined her magnificent form, luscious bosom, tiny waist, flared hips, and long flowing legs, accenting her bodily charms, yet cloaking the princess in silky folds.

Her hair was thick and lustrous. Mika yearned to push his hands, well, *hand*, through the lush mass and twine the tiny curls around his fingers.

He could almost feel her soft warm lips against his own.

His breath came in quick spurts as he gazed on her amazing beauty. Only at length did he realize that she was still asleep and did not appear to have wakened since he saw her last. She was unchanged.

The same could not be said for the giant, Recknass. He glared at Mika out of the tiny slit that was his left eye. His right eye was swollen completely shut and was puffed up to an enormous size. It was also an ugly mixture of black and purple, or at least Mika thought it was. It was hard to tell because of the layer of dried blood that had scabbed over the entire mess.

The man's nose, or what used to be his nose, was also rather unpleasant to look at, flattened and smeared as it was over his cheeks and mashed upper lip.

Recknass flexed his massive fists and clenched his thick fingers spasmodically. Unfortunately, there was absolutely nothing wrong with his hands.

Mika suddenly changed his mind about wanting to see the princess again and began to edge backward.

"No, Recknass. It's all right," the Guildsman said,

enunciating both clearly and slowly while facing the giant. "The wolfman is our friend now. He wants to help the princess. You are not to hurt him. Sit down."

Breathing harshly and making unpleasant wet sounds through his damaged lips, the giant hesitated for another minute, then sat down heavily as he was bid, though he never took his gaze, impaired as it was, off Mika.

"I'm afraid you have to forgive Recknass if he seems to be taking this a bit personally. You see, if anything happens to the princess, he's a dead man."

"What a pity," said Mika as he started to sit on the edge of the bed next to the princess's delectable thigh. A guttural growl of warning changed his mind.

"Here, sit down on this chest," said the Guildsman, eyeing Recknass. "It's safer." And seating himself on an immense chest on the other side of the giant, next to the princess's head, he spared her a long lingering glance before he began to talk.

"I'd like to introduce you to Princess Julia," he said in a soft tone as he ran his hand lightly over the princess's hair. "I'd like to, but I can't, for as you can see, she's asleep. She's been that way for the last four moons." He sighed heavily, and Mika could see the pain in the man's eyes as he gathered himself and continued.

"The princess is the only child of the King and late Queen of Dramidja, an island principality in the Dramidj Ocean, many sea leagues distant from Yecha.

"Dramidja is a rich and powerful island, the port of call for ships of all nations. Our boat builders, navigators, and sailors are famous over all the seas. Our island is also the only known source for a rare gem known as dramadine.

"Dramadine is a crystalline formation that reflects both blue and green and has the unusual ability to heighten one's powers and abilities. In the case of a normal human it would mean that he could see better, jump farther, walk longer, hit harder, run more swiftly. . . ."

"I get the idea," said Mika staring at the fly that now hung suspended above them on the cowhide ceiling. It was a most unusual fly, he was thinking, before he was distracted . . .

"So you can see that, in the wrong hands, the crystal could be extremely dangerous," the Guildsman continued earnestly.

"The king and his forebears have always been most cautious in the use of the few gems that exist, keeping them hidden away from the temptation of man and forbidding their mining.

"There was great hope for a male son to carry on the royal line, but in this, the king and queen were disappointed, blessed as they were with only the one daughter.

"It was further hoped that the princess would marry well and continue the line and the protection of the gems with her husband. But that has not happened." It seemed to Mika that there was tremendous loss and regret in the man's voice.

"Why not?" asked Mika, looking at the exquisite beauty lying beside him. "I should have imagined that she would have her pick of thousands. She's very beautiful."

"True," sighed the Guildsman. "But she's also

very headstrong. The princess has found no one she chooses to marry."

"What do you mean, 'chooses?' " asked Mika. "In a matter this important, you simply tell the wench what she must do and see to it that it happens!"

The Guildsman looked at him with wry amusement, and it seemed to Mika that the giant's shoulders actually heaved with silent laughter.

"One does not 'tell' Princess Julia anything," said the Guildsman as though he were proud of his princess's willfulness.

"But that is not the point. One morning, the princess's maid attempted to waken her and could not do so. She summoned the royal doctor and he examined her and proclaimed that he could find nothing wrong with her.

"Eventually, he realized that it must be a spell and sent for the royal magic-user. He agreed with the doctor's diagnosis, but was unable to remove the spell.

"The king was frantic, of course, and gave the man a dramadine to heighten his powers so that he might try again. But the man was mysteriously killed and the crystal was found ground to powder beneath his foot."

"Sounds as though another magic-user wanted the crystal and put the spell on the princess, hoping that a dramadine would be used," mused Mika.

"Exactly," said the Guildsman. "That was my conclusion, as well. Fortunately, our magic-user was able to destroy the gem before it was taken from him." Interpreting Mika's cocked eyebrow correctly, he bowed low and said, "Hary Mubarik, head of

Dramidja security."

"You're no Guildsman. I should have known," said Mika.

"I have served in that capacity before," said Hary. "But I have served the king for many years longer and I would settle this business, for Julia is dear to his heart and I fear it may kill him."

And dear to your heart, as well, I wager, Mika thought to himself.

"So, if that's the story, why are we on the way to Eru-Tovar with the princess hidden away in a wagon like a sack of grain?" asked Mika.

"After the magic-user was killed, the king let it be known that we were in need of someone to take his place," continued Hary. "All manner of people showed up: wizards, warlocks, magic-users, magicians, healers, herbalists, shamans, and even an illusionist. Some of them were good, but most were frauds, and none were able to remove the spell which was the test that the king put to them.

"One day a message came, a scroll to be exact. It took form out of thin air, appeared right before the king's eyes on top of his breakfast plate. The scroll unrolled itself and a voice read aloud. It said that the man the king sought could be found in Eru-Tovar and commanded the king to send his daughter there and the spell would be lifted. Once the message was delivered, the scroll disappeared back into the air."

"And the price of this cure?" asked Mika.

"All the dramadine crystals that are known to exist."

"Didn't want much, did he?" noted Mika with a low whistle. "Where are they?"

173

"Not here," answered Hary. "The king is not such a fool that he would send his two greatest treasures, his daughter and the crystals.

"Julia is going alone except for Recknass, the driver, Cob, who is one of my best men—and myself, of course."

"Then you're a fool," said Mika. "What's to prevent this mage in Eru-Tovar from turning you both into pigs on the spot and then sending another message saying, 'I have your daughter now. Send the jewels, or else.' And then keeping them both?"

"That is a very real possibility," admitted Hary. "But Recknass and I have learned more than a few tricks in our years. We will see to it that such a thing does not happen," Hary said with a small smile. And something in his tone of voice told Mika that perhaps they would succeed.

The fly buzzed angrily in front of Hary's face as though disliking his words. Hary grabbed at the fly, but the insect evaded him easily and lighted on a strut, high out of reach, to feast on a dried spatter of Recknass's blood. Then they made the mistake of paying it no further mind.

"How does Jumbo here, fit into the story?" asked Mika intently.

"Recknass was Julia's personal guard," said Hary. "He was there the night the mage was killed. Unfortunately, he hasn't been able to tell us what happened, as his memory and speech were erased by whomever fought the battle. The king has threatened to remove Recknass's heart as well, if he fails. So you see, he has great motivation to succeed."

"How do you propose to find this magic-user?"

asked Mika. "You can't just stand in the center of Eru-Tovar and say, 'Yoo-hoo, we're here.'"

"I suspect that he already knows we're coming," said Hary. "I think that's what the attack at the river was all about as well as your encounter with the old man.

"You missed the real crux of the battle. Before you and your clan arrived, the kobolds attacked in full strength. The main thrust was aimed directly at this wagon. Only by clustering all of our forces around it were we able to beat them off. Then you arrived and the battle turned.

"It was my thought that whoever hopes to seize the jewels, thought to obtain them then. We were certainly more accessible once we were off the island.

"As to whether or not they would have taken Julia, I don't know. I can only guess. And worry." And once more, the man gazed at the princess with love in his eyes. He reached out a hand to stroke her hair, but a warning growl from the giant stopped him.

"You say you have seen this old man twice," said Hary. "Please tell me about it. Everything you can remember. Please, for her sake."

Studying the man, Mika found that he almost liked him. Gone was the irritating manner that had so annoyed him throughout the trip. Deciding, he told him all he knew.

" . . . so I don't think he's too powerful," concluded Mika, after the story was told. "Even though he froze me and Tam solid as logs. He's maybe fourth level, fifth at most. My father was far more advanced than that.

"All you need to do is find yourself a higher level

mage when you reach Eru-Tovar. It'll cost you a few grushnicks, but I assume the king can afford them.

"This fellow is probably just some little nobody, who's tired of being ignored," Mika elaborated, enjoying the look on Hary's face as he leaned forward, listening intently.

"He heard about the jewels and decided he'd try for them. Make something of himself—a name to be remembered before he died. He looked pretty old to me. I'll bet that Princess Julia and her magic jewels are his last chance."

"What you say makes sense," agreed Hary. "But there is one aspect of this whole business that you have not considered."

"What's that?" asked Mika with a frown.

"Any spell, as you know, must be renewed from time to time, if it is to remain active. That is why the man is hovering about, dogging our trail. He must do so if he is to keep the sleep spell in force.

"He doesn't care if we reach Eru-Tovar or not. He wants us out here on the prairie by ourselves. All he wants is to get inside the wagon and steal the gems that he thinks are hidden here. Since we've prevented him from doing that, all he's been able to do is keep renewing the spell on Julia!"

Mika brushed away the fly that chose that moment to buzz between them.

"Possibly," admitted Mika. "But may I remind you that this mage does not actually have to be close to Julia to extend the spell. It can be done from a distance."

"Not all that distant!" gloated Hary. "He must be within a certain radius and he must be in human form, for if he is in another guise, say that of an animal, he would not be able to apply the spell.

"Now, here is what I propose. We will travel back to the Bubbling Springs as fast as we are able and use that as our base, since it provides water, shelter, and firewood.

"We can ride the perimeter and make certain that the fellow does not get through! Then, once the spell is broken, we can return to Dramidja.

"Oh, it will take some extra precautions, but I am certain that it can be done. You see, these drivers are not really drivers, but men from my command."

The fly buzzed loudly, the rapid fluttering of its wings vibrating against the cowhide covering and resonating throughout the small interior of the wagon.

"I'm not sure we can keep the fellow away from her," Mika said slowly. "But it's a plan. A place to start and better than anything I can think of at the moment." And all the while he was thinking of ways to rid himself of Hary, Recknass, and the drivers, not to mention the mysterious old man, before Julia was taken back to her island kingdom. He was quite certain that once she wakened he would find favor in her eyes.

"Then we have your promise of cooperation?" asked Hary. "You understand what is at stake here? Julia is beyond your paltry triflings. She is no common plaything. Come, man, say that you will help us."

"You have my promise," said Mika. But he did not say what it was that he promised.

177

Chapter 11

THEY CAME AT DAWN, out of the east with the rising sun. Mika had been asleep, camped underneath the princess's wagon, much to the disgust of the driver, the man named Cob, when Tam began to growl and paw at his arm. Mika was so totally tuned to Tam, that he knew, even in the depths of sleep that this was no casual warning. Something was very wrong.

He opened his eyes, instantly alert, and reached for his sword, only half cognizant of the fact that his wing had finally turned back into an arm.

Tam was standing above him, head up, ears twitching forward, ruff fully extended, staring into the rising sun. He whined shrilly with each exhalation.

Mika rolled swiftly to his feet, snaking out from under the confining wagon. All around him, wolves, some twenty of them, were standing in postures identical to Tam's. Some, more highly strung than others, were yipping nervously and wheeling in small circles as though anxious to run.

All of the nomads, too, were on their feet, buckling on their weapons, straining to see what had so alarmed their animals.

A soft wind was blowing from the north, its cool currents carrying the scent of green things growing on the prairie, the legacy of the storm. Birds were twittering their morning songs and the eastern horizon was stained a brilliant crimson, promising a beautiful day to come.

At first, Mika could see nothing wrong, nothing that would so alarm the wolves. But it was difficult to see anything at all; the bright ball of sun brought tears to his eyes and caused him to see spots of yellow. Something was surely wrong, though. Tam was now growling deep in his chest, and his dewlaps were raised, exposing his canines.

Mika looked away from the bright glare, and shielding his eyes with his hand, he looked again, this time, focusing low on the horizon. And then he saw them, the dark outlines tramping toward them, shoulder to shoulder. With a sinking heart he recognized them for what they were and realized that they were badly outnumbered.

He turned and was surprised to find Hary at his side. The man moved so silently that Mika wondered briefly if he were part elf.

"What is it?" asked Hary.

"Gnolls," Mika replied grimly. "Sort of a cross between a human and a hyena. Seven feet tall and strong. Green-grey skin covered with fur, but they wear armor and use weapons as well as any human."

A quavering howl split the calm morning and hung shivering on the sweet air.

"Hyenas," added Mika. "You'll find them wherever you find gnolls and their larger cousins, spawn of Hades, hyenadons. And there'll usually be a couple of trolls, trailing in the rear to pick up the scraps."

"Sweet God of the Sea," whispered Hary. "How? Where? What shall we do? Can we fight them?"

"No way," said Mika, swiftly gathering his few possessions and throwing them onto the seat of the wagon.

"There're too many of them and we're not talking about kobolds this time. Gnolls are twice as big as kobolds and ten times as tough. Not to mention trolls. You can't kill them. Even if you cut them into cubes, they just regenerate, and even the pieces can kill you."

"Then what should we do?" asked Hary, gripping Mika by the shoulder.

Tam's head swiveled toward them and instantly he was between the two men, his long white teeth inches away from Hary, a harsh growl thick with menace rumbling from his twitching black lips. Hary dropped his hand immediately—and Mika made a slashing gesture to force the wolf back.

"Run. It's our only hope," said Mika, knowing that it would not be enough. "We cannot hope to stand and fight. They would have us in no time. Since they are afoot, we must try to lose them."

Hary lost no time in argument. Hurrying away, he roused his drivers with shouts and kicks, commanding them to harness their mules as quickly as possible. The men did as they were told and Mika had scarcely finished saddling the grey before Hornsbuck rode up and he was surrounded by wagons and no-mads, ready to follow his lead.

The mules had scented the rank aroma of the hyenas and hyenadons and their nostrils were flared and blowing, their eyes wide with terror. Unlike other mornings, it took no encouragement to get them started.

"Which way? What is the plan?" shouted Hornsbuck from astride his huge, thick-necked bay stallion.

"Ride for Eru-Tovar, it's our only chance," said Mika. "It cannot be more than six days distant."

"I say we should return to the Springs," argued Hary. "We'll never make it to Eru-Tovar. It's too far."

"Don't be a fool, man. There's no point in going back to the Springs," said Mika. "They'd just wait until we starved or the Springs dried up."

"But . . ." began Hary.

"No time for buts," growled Hornsbuck. "Mika's right. No sense in getting ourselves trapped."

"I've no use for running," snapped Hary.

"I've no use for dying," Mika replied coldly. "You and your wagons can do anything you want, I'm riding for the city as fast as this horse can take me. If you're smart, you'll come, too. If not, that's your decision."

"I thought you agreed to join us," hissed Hary. "To help."

"I made no agreement to die needlessly to salve your silly pride," said Mika as he turned the grey. "I've given you my counsel. If you choose to follow me, I will see to it that the nomads form a line of defense between the wagons and the gnolls. If you choose to ignore me, then say your prayers."

Glaring at the man, Mika gave the grey a sharp kick in the ribs and it leaped away, only too willing, for once, to do as it was told.

Then, before the driver of the princess's wagon could react, Mika ripped the traces from his hands, flipped them over the heads of the mules and dragged them after him, forcing the mule-team to race at his heels.

Cob let out a yell but could do little more than cling to the seat with both hands to avoid being bounced off.

Recknass stuck his head outside to see what was happening, but other than glare at Mika, there was nothing he could do.

Hary stared after the runaway wagon in fury, then glanced back toward the rapidly advancing army of gnolls and trolls as though calculating his chances. They were close enough to see now, the sun glinting off their sharp pointed pikes, and the howls of the hyenas were loud and terrifying.

All around him, frightened drivers, yelling and cursing loudly, were whipping their teams into a gallop, the great mule muscles straining against the traces, the huge wheels thundering across the stony soil.

Nomads and wolves streamed past him on either side, raising clouds of dust under their frantic feet. Fear and urgency were a disease transmitted by mere proximity.

Hary felt panic rising in his own breast and as the dust settled he saw that he stood alone, surrounded by the few pathetic remains of their camp, bedrolls, cooking utensils and clothing left behind in the commotion. His own horse whickered in terror and ran, after a moment's hesitation. Hary followed in the wake of the flight of nomads and drivers alike who were already well on their way.

The advancing army was now close enough to see the telltale banner of dust rising from the wagons. The gnolls, trolls, and hyenas began screaming and yowling eerie caterwauls that sent shivers of fear up and down Hary's back.

Only at that moment did Hary comprehend how great was their danger and that, perhaps, Mika had made the right decision.

Kobolds were not unfamiliar to him, along with many monsters of other sorts. But never before had he encountered either trolls or gnolls in any great numbers, and as a result, he had indeed underestimated the enemy. He whipped his horse harder until, at a breakneck gallop, he caught up with the front line of retreat.

They drove the mules as fast as they could go, and soon the distance between themselves and the trailing army of horrors was increased to approximately five miles.

"What do you think, Mika?" shouted Hornsbuck as his bay matched strides with the grey stallion.

"Got to increase our lead," Mika replied.

"The men are tiring fast," Hornsbuck replied, yelling to be heard over the thundering hooves.

"The mules can eat on the run or go without, but the horses will need a feed. And rest—or they'll founder," added Mika.

"Cursed gnolls! Blasted trolls! They never stop. It ain't human."

Mika smiled, amused at Hornsbuck's unintentional joke. "I have a plan. But it will have to wait for nightfall. Keep an even pace—and keep together—for now."

"Gnolls can see just as good at night, if not better. What's your plan?" asked Hornsbuck.

When Mika gave no answer, Hornsbuck stared at Mika curiously, trying to fathom his silence. Mika's face was hard and his eyes distant, giving no clues to his thinking, so Hornsbuck had to content himself with dropping back to pass the word.

The mules were exhausted by nightfall, their backs covered with a thick layer of foam and their long ears drooping in front of their eyes. The horses and men were tired, too, but less so than the mules, which had been pulling the heavy wagons rapidly over the rough terrain.

Night came on fast, but barely fast enough to suit Mika, who had been riding wide circles around the wagon train all day, keeping a nervous eye on the trailing army, hoping that they would fall further behind. Their progress was also constant, but neither could maintain the grueling pace forever.

As night fell, Mika rode up to each wagon and gave the signal. Without wasting a moment, the drivers turned their wagons into a circle, then freed the mules from the wagons.

Breaking their normal pattern, they loaded a ready-packed sack of provisions, weapons, food, and water atop one mule's back, threw a saddle blanket across the back of the second, and rode the startled animal out into the dark prairie on the far side of the wagons.

While the drivers were dealing with the mules, Mika, Hornsbuck, and several of the nomads rode toward the army and observed it under the cover of darkness.

"I count nearly two hundred," grunted Hornsbuck, "give or take a few hyenas."

"I agree," said Mika. "I wish it were fewer. We might stand a chance if they catch up with us."

"No chance," said Hornsbuck. "No chance at all, not with the likes of them."

"There has to be a leader somewhere among them," said Hary, who had rejoined them noiselessly. "Perhaps one of us could go talk to them, make a bargain of some sort."

"Ha!" Hornsbuck snorted, his immense leather-girded bulk heaving up and down as he shook with laughter. "You do that, son, and let me know what they have to say!" Still laughing, he wheeled the bay and rode back toward the wagons.

"You would be dead in a heartbeat if you were lucky—or praying for death if they let you live," Mika said contemptuously.

"Kobolds are sweet little kittens compared to gnolls. Gnolls lie awake nights dreaming up new ideas for torture. We are their dreams come true. Believe me, you do not want to fall into their hands. And trolls are worse. They do not reason, they exist for just one purpose—to kill. Trust me, Hary."

"What is your plan?" asked Hary.

"We will leave the wagons," said Mika, holding up his hand to forestall Hary's objections. "There is no other way. We will draw them in a circle and start a few fires. The gnolls will think that we are making a stand.

"They are not stupid, and even though they out-number us, they will not rush us directly. They will take their time and advance carefully.

"If they were sent by the mage, they will not want to risk harming the princess. They will take the time to surround us and then attack. By the time they discover that we are gone, we will have gained valuable distance and time."

"Your reasoning is sound," said Hary. "We will sacrifice the wagons."

They rode swiftly back to the wagons and found that the princess's wagon had been separated from the others, and stood waiting, surrounded by the no-mads and the mounted drivers.

Six mules, those weakest and deemed least able to keep up the exhausting pace, had been staked out along the edges of the circle of wagons. They stood with heads down, too tired to even crop the meager grass.

"Move out," Mika whispered, circulating among the men. "And stay together. Your lives depend on it." Slowly, quietly, they stole away, leaving the firelit wagons and the mules behind them.

"How long have we got?" asked Hornsbuck, keep-ing pace with the grey.

"I don't know," answered Mika. "But not long enough."

At that moment, realizing that they were being left to the hyenas, the stranded mules began to bray, harsh terrified cries that echoed across the plains.

Even the nomads, those hardened warriors, were touched by the animals' plaintive cries, and more than one of the drivers turned their heads to look back toward the wagons. The lucky mules that had not been abandoned dug in their heels and tried to turn back, bawling out their own confusion.

"Muzzle the mules!" cried Mika, fearful that the keen-eared gnolls would discern the distance between the two sets of sounds. His instructions were quickly followed; strips of leather, shirts, whatever was handy, were wrapped around the mules' jaws, muffling and finally stopping their cries. Harsh blows got them moving again, and the small party crept on, trying to close their ears to the piteous cries behind them.

They had positioned the wagons so as to block themselves from the view of the monster horde. With the cacophony of the mules covering the sound of their retreat, they increased their pace steadily until they were out of sight of the wagons.

Unfortunately, they were not out of hearing. An hour later, the abandoned mules began to scream. Even though they should have continued, nomads, drivers, horses, and mules alike stood riveted as though imagining tooth and fang on their own bodies. The screams, which rang loud and traveled far in the thin night air, were mercifully short. A shrill outbreak of frenzied cries signaled the end of the mules' misery.

"I don't see that it gained us much time," said Hary. "Those mules would barely make a mouthful among that horde."

"The mules will keep the hyenas and the hyenadons busy," Mika explained patiently as they spurred their horses into motion.

"The gnolls don't care about eating, but the contents of the wagons will occupy them for a while. With any luck at all, greed will cause them to fight among themselves. And we need all the luck we can get right now."

The sharp snarling yowls erupted once again from the direction of the wagons even as he spoke, evidence that the hyenas and their foul cousins had disagreed over the division of the mules.

Mika prayed that the gnolls would find the wagons likewise irresistible.

They stopped in the hour of deepest darkness, too exhausted to continue. They watered the mules and horses and fed them small amounts of grain to augment the sparse grass. Then, wrapping themselves in their blankets, men and wolves collapsed wherever they found themselves and were asleep within seconds.

Mika, although as tired as the rest, stayed awake for the next two hours, watching the darkness intently for any sign of the inhuman army. Then he wakened Hornsbuck to take the watch, and he and Tam curled themselves under the wagon and fell asleep instantly.

Chapter 12

IT WAS A NIGHTMARE that went on seemingly forever, whether waking or sleeping, not that there was much of the latter. The army followed them with single-minded determination. Sacrificing the mules had not bought much time, as Hary took every opportunity to remind Mika.

They had extended their lead to nearly ten miles by the continuous movement. They ate and even slept in the saddle. They were doing better than Mika had any reason to hope or expect, but he knew that the constant activity, plus the lack of adequate food and sleep, would soon begin to take its toll. And those that fell behind, whether human or animal, would be left to their own fate.

"I don't see why we have to drag that cursed wagon along with us," growled Hornsbuck as he and Mika rode apart from the men and rested their horses on a slight rise where they could view their pursuers. "The damn wagon just slows us down. We could ride all the faster without it. Dump it, Mika!"

"All right," said Mika, through teeth that were gritted with prairie sand. He pictured the princess, asleep, held in Recknass's thick arms, her beautiful slender form pressed close to his ugly body. He shuddered and forced the picture from his mind. He knew that Hornsbuck was right; the heavy wagon was a luxury they could not afford.

"Mika, the men want to know what's in the wagon," said Hornsbuck. "They've been grumbling and complaining about the mystery ever since we left the other wagons behind. And I do, too. It's our right to know.

"I'm as brave as the next man. I've fought my share of orcs and kobolds and even a few goblins when I was younger, but never anything like this army of fiends behind us. And I don't even know why they're after us. I think you do, Mika, and before I get myself killed fighting for the Great She Wolf knows what, I think you should tell me what's going on."

Mika hesitated, glancing at the older man, noticing for the first time, the white lines thick at the corner of each eye, the scars that marked his dark tanned arms, corded with muscles from years wielding a heavy sword, and the steady green eyes that appraised him coolly. He knew that no lie would suffice. In spite of his bluff manner, Hornsbuck was no fool. Yet still Mika hesitated. What would Hornsuck do when he learned of the princess?

"Tell me, lad, and none of your fancy stories," Hornsbuck said softly, as though guessing Mika's thoughts. I will have the whole truth or I will leave, and the nomads will go with me. We'll separate and ride off in twenty different directions. Yon army will not follow us. They will follow you and your stupid wagon, and they will catch you. So tell me the truth, lad, and do it now."

Mika bit his lip and nodded, knowing that the older warrior had spoken his true intent. Mika knew that while many of the nomads liked him, if the knucklebones were thrown, the men would follow Hornsbuck.

Slowly, hesitatingly, Mika told Hornsbuck the whole story, including his encounters at the hands of the old magic-user. When he was done, Hornsbuck stared off into the distance without speaking.

"You should have told me this sooner," he said at last, his voice curiously flat. "I can't believe that you have been such a fool. If you thought with your head instead of your balls, you might turn out to be a halfway decent warrior.

"Enor begged me to take you in hand, allow you to lead the caravan, give you a chance to prove yourself. I did it for the sake of your father who was a good man. And because you remind me of myself at your age. I should have known it would never work.

"I thought I could prevent any damage you did and give you a chance to redeem yourself. I see that I was wrong. Your folly will be the death of twenty good men, including myself. They will curse you with their last dying breath."

Hornsbuck stared at Mika with empty, stony eyes, his big calloused hands holding the reins. Mika saw the intelligence behind the brusque manner and realized for the first time how badly he had misjudged the man, taking his easygoing, casual attitude for stupidity rather than the kindness it was meant to be.

"I, I did not mean . . ." he stammered, at a loss for words.

"Oh, you meant all right, lad," Hornsbuck said levelly. "You just didn't think of anyone, save yourself."

And Mika knew it to be true.

"Well, what do you intend to do now, Master Wolf?" Hornsbuck asked in a cool, mocking tone. "What is the plan?"

"Ride fast," Mika muttered softly.

"Oh, ride fast. Yes. That's a wonderful clever plan. Would never have thought of it myself. We'll certainly shake those monstrosities off our tails in no time."

"Well, what would you do?" asked Mika.

"I'd cut that wagon loose, for starters," said Hornsbuck. "Then I'd ride for the hills. We'll never lose them out here on the plains; we're too easy to see. We might stand a chance in the hills."

"What hills?" asked Mika.

"The hills outside Eru-Tovar along the southern march," replied Hornsbuck pointing out the landmarks on an oiled leather map. "We are here," he said, stabbing the map with a thick finger. "The hills are there, two days hence."

"Do you think we can make it?" asked Mika, his heart giving a leap within his chest."

"Aye, probably, if we abandon the wagon and ride for all we are worth," Hornsbuck said slowly, turning the situation over in his mind, weighing their chances.

"Gnolls are lazy bastards. They would not venture

from their lairs and stick to us like this unless there was some extra kicker, like this magic-user fellow, pushing 'em on. They like blood and killing and torture, but how much work are they willing to do to get a chance to enjoy them?"

"Seems like a lot," said Mika, glancing behind him to see how close they were.

"Nah! This is simple stuff, following," said Hornsbuck. "Anyone can follow in a straight line. But will they follow us if we make it difficult for them? That's the question."

"We can try!" said Mika.

"You understand, though, that it could work against us."

"Why?" cried Mika.

"They are creatures of darkness," answered Hornsbuck. "They can see better at night and might lay traps for us. We will have to be on our guard at all times."

"Right," agreed Mika, relieved that Hornsbuck was still an ally.

"And Mika," said the older man, gripping Mika's arm tightly. "Try to remember that we might have avoided this, had you been straight with me from the first. No more secrets. We must work together if we are to survive."

"No more secrets," Mika assured. "You have my word."

They turned their horses and galloped swiftly back to the wagon where Mika called a brief halt.

Weary men slid from their saddles and poured out a small amount of water for their mounts and themselves, barely enough to wet their parched mouths.

"We must abandon the wagon," Mika told Hary. "There is no other way. I have told Hornsbuck everything. We have imperiled the lives of him and his men. They have the right to know what it is they die for."

Hary's blue eyes blazed for a moment and it looked as though he might argue, but he nodded briefly and bit back the words that rose to his lips.

"I can see that it is necessary," he said. "I appreciate all that you are doing for us. I will go and tell Recknass." Dismounting from his horse, he climbed into the wagon.

While Hary was making his arrangements, Mika called the nomads together.

The air was cool and fragrant with the smell of grease bushes in bloom. The sun was beginning to set, bathing the prairie in crimson like a shroud of warm blood. Night hunting birds came awake slowly, twittering and chirping quarrelsomely.

The nomads trotted up, one at a time, on horses whose necks drooped with fatigue. Wolves sat on their haunches alongside their humans, their tongues lolling, too tired to visit among themselves.

The nomads stared at Mika, waiting for him to speak, knowing that the words he spoke would affect their lives.

Mika looked into their weary eyes and felt as though he were the enemy. And, in a sense, he would have to admit that he was, since his actions, and the lack of them, had helped place them in this dangerous position. Waiting would accomplish nothing. He prayed to the Great Wolf Mother to give him the right words.

"I know you're all wondering what this is all about—who this army belongs to and why they are following us," he began. A loud murmur assured him that this was true.

"There is a lady in yon wagon," Mika continued. "A lady who lies in a magical sleep from which she cannot be wakened. We have been charged with taking her to Eru-Tovar where there is said to be one who can break the spell.

"It would seem that someone would like to prevent us from reaching the city, but I am pledged to see that she reaches it in safety."

The nomads leaned from their horses and conversed among themselves with angry murmurs and much gesturing. Mika continued, speaking more loudly to draw their attention.

"We are abandoning the wagon so that we may travel more quickly. We are making for the hills along the southern march. It should take us two days to reach them. We hope to lose the army in the hills and enter the city unharmed."

"Abandon the woman!" called one of the eastern nomads, a dark, hawk-nosed man unfamiliar to Mika. "Give her to those who follow and spare us a needless death."

"I have given my word," said Mika. "I will not leave her."

The man spat contemptuously on the ground, his comment on the value of Mika's word.

Mika was spared from answering the silent challenge by the appearance of Hary and Recknass as they emerged from the wagon.

Hary descended first, jumping down lightly, then held his arms out as though willing to take the princess from the giant. But Recknass ignored him, standing tall and straight atop the wagon, staring each of the nomads in the eye, challenging them to deny him and his fragile charge their right to life. None spoke.

Only when he had stared them all down, even the eastern nomad, did he step down, cradling the princess in his arms like a tiny waif.

It would have taken a very brave or a very foolish man to have challenged Recknass, for the giant appeared even larger and more frightening than he had inside the wagon.

His face was now a mass of purple, yellow, and black bruises, and his nose was still flattened against his cheek. He stared at the men with his one good eye. They drew their horses back a step and lowered their eyes, unwilling to aggravate the brute.

Mika had eyes for the princess alone, having seen more than enough of Recknass. But she was completely swaddled in the soft pink coverlet and all that could be seen of her was a few glossy curls.

Hary and the driver Cob passed almost unnoticed in the small drama, fastening bulky trunks and bits of luggage to the sides of the mules that were being unfastened from the wagon.

"What are you doing?" asked Hornsbuck.

"It is the princess's luggage," replied Hary. "We cannot leave it behind. She will need it when she wakens."

"If she wakens," growled Hornsbuck, striding up to the mules and unceremoniously stripping the luggage from their backs.

"This is no garden party, no pleasure outing. The gnolls and trolls back there will grind your precious princess between their teeth and not appreciate the difference between her sweet flesh and your stringy meat. Mount up and leave this foolishness behind."

Hary stepped back, dropping the trunk on the ground as though it had burned his fingers. Mika smiled sympathetically, glad that it was not he who was the object of Hornsbuck's anger.

Recknass strode over to the largest of the mules and, without shifting the princess or even stepping on a stone, threw his leg over the animal's back and seated himself carefully. The mule sagged beneath the man's great weight and its legs wobbled as though they might give way.

"That will never do," muttered Hornsbuck and ordered Marek, who rode a huge roan stallion, to give the animal to the giant. Marek frowned and looked as though he might argue, but at that moment, the wolves began to howl, their tails curled high above their backs. A quick glance behind them told them that the gnolls were gaining rapidly.

The time for talk was done. Marek handed the reins of the roan over to Recknass who mounted and settled the princess across his legs. In a rare mood of concern, Mika rode up next to the giant and handed him the fragile gold chain with the crystal bead that always hung from his neck.

"Take it," he said, after looking around to see that no one noted the unusual gesture. "Put it around her neck. It has been lucky for me. Perhaps it will bring her luck as well."

The giant stared suspiciously at Mika. Then, seeing nothing other than honest goodwill, he nodded curtly and slipped the gold chain over the princess's head.

All around them, men were whipping their mounts into hasty retreat, with the exception of Marek who crawled with ill-concealed bad grace onto the back of the mule. They rode off swiftly, leaving nothing but the empty wagon and a pile of baggage behind.

There was a loud outcry when the army of monsters reached the wagon a short time later. Shrill cries pierced the air, along with furious barking yaps as though the hyenas were fighting over some delectable prize. But it didn't hold them long.

Mika and Hornsbuck positioned themselves atop a ridge a short time later and looked down on the entire horde.

They were spread out over the plains in a ragtag smear without any sign of order or organization. The hyenas and the larger hyenadons loped at the fringes of the mob, and the shambling figures of the trolls brought up the rear.

A multitude of weapons ranging from great bows to pole arms, long two-handed swords, battle axes, and morning stars were clearly visible.

Here and there, soft pastel bits of silk—the tattered remnants of Julia's finery—rippled from the tops of barbed pikes or swathed the necks and heads of hairy, slope-browed gnolls. Scarcely three miles separated the vile army from Mika and the others.

"Got to do something," muttered Mika. "Hornsbuck, do you think we could fire the prairie? It worked on the kobolds, it might work here."

"Maybe," said Hornsbuck. "Wind's coming from the west. It would blow in their direction. It's worth a try."

Dismounting, Mika and Hornsbuck struck their firestones and lit a grease bush which instantly burst into flames.

"Remount!" cried Hornsbuck as he yanked another bush out of the ground. "We'll have to do it from horseback; they're spread out too widely!"

Leaping on his bay in a single bound, Hornsbuck stabbed the point of his sword into the base of the grease bush and then lit it. It flamed instantly, and he kicked his nervous horse into a trot, passing from one bush to the next, lighting them.

Mika followed suit and soon a whole line of grease bushes sputtered and raged, throwing thick black clouds of acrid smoke into the air. They sputtered and popped as the flames devoured them, tossing fiery sparks up to fall on other bushes. The sparse dry grasses and soon the entire prairie behind them were being consumed by the ravenous flames.

"That should keep them for a while," yelled Mika as he watched the flames being swept toward the gnolls by the intermittent west wind.

"Hah!" yelled Hornsubuck, wearing a wide grin on his bearded face. Shaking loose the flaming remains of their torches, they wheeled their mounts and raced after their fleeing comrades.

They rode as hard and as fast as they could for the remainder of that long evening, leaving the gnolls behind them hidden by a stinking curtain of black smoke. Finally, mules and horses nearly dropping with exhaustion, they were forced to stop.

The land had begun to change. Not that it was any less empty; if anything it had fewer grease bushes and little or no forage for the animals. But there were slight hills now and then, folds in the land and empty stream beds that told of water in other, happier seasons. For now, they were empty and dry and the waterskins were falling dangerously low.

Hoping to escape the sharp night vision of the gnolls, Mika led the party into one of the deepest of the arroyos.

Hornsbuck instructed the men to water the horses and mules and then feed them. Once this was done, they were hobbled and muzzled so that no careless whicker would give them away.

The men themselves sprawled against the banks, enervated by their fatigue. Few spoke. Hornsbuck gestured to Mika and led him a short distance away from the temporary camp, peering intently at the ground.

Soon, a slow smile spread over his broad bearded face, and he pointed at the ground. Mika looked down but saw nothing. Tam, however, had no such problem. Shoulder to shoulder, he and RedTail, Hornsbuck's big male wolf, pawed at the earth beneath the rocky overhang. Earth flew in all directions. Then, ceasing their activities, they crouched low and Mika heard the sound of lapping tongues. The wolves drank their fill and then moved aside and began grooming themselves.

"Water," said Hornsbuck. Noting the puzzled look on Mika's face, he laughed. "There's usually water in places such as this; you just have to know how to look for it. See there—footprints of mice and lizards."

Looking more closely, Mika could see the tiny footprints in the sand, the curved sign of a dragging tail converging on the hidden water.

"It could save your life sometime," said Hornsbuck.

"I'll remember," said Mika as he knelt to drink.

The water was warm and brackish and thick with sand, but they drank their fill and wiped their wet hands over faces that were tight and cracked from harsh exposure to sun and wind. And it spared them from drawing on their own meager supply of water. When they finished, there was naught left but a hole filled with damp sand. This, Hornsbuck filled with sand and rocks.

"No sense leaving them beasts anything if we can help it," said Hornsbuck. "They need water same as us. I hope they're suffering."

But if they were suffering, it was not apparent. During the night, the army of monsters had circled around the line of fire and could now be clearly seen on the lower slopes.

Drawing strength from the brief respite, the small party mounted and began climbing the steep incline as swiftly as their tired mounts could carry them.

Chapter 13

AND SO BEGAN A LONG PERIOD of hurried flights interspersed with short periods of rest. Eru-Tovar, while only a few days distant, might as well have been on another world, for it seemed that the army of monsters never slept.

They dogged the nomads' footsteps, following whatever path they chose, whether by night or by day, and they were not deceived by false trails or the most clever of traps.

The nomads tried all of Hornsbuck's tricks—from deadfalls to sweeping the trail behind them—and they even used one of Mika's spells of illusion, creating an exceedingly realistic chasm where none had previously existed. But nothing worked.

The gnolls showed an uncanny amount of intelligence for creatures that were not known for their ability to think. It was almost as though they knew what the nomads were planning and were taking steps to anticipate their tactics.

They were well into the hills now and all were glad

to see the last of the empty prairies. The hills were barren, mostly stone and hard-packed earth, but here and there were soft green patches of grass and these the mules and horses cropped greedily.

There were also small pools of water to be found, and the nomads did their best to see that these were either emptied or concealed before they moved on.

Everyone was tired. Horses and mules showed their exhaustion in the curved bend of their necks and their slow, shambling gaits. The men rode loosely, often slumbering in the saddle. Even Mika and Hornsbuck felt the lack of sleep in their muscles, which were stiff and slow to respond, and in their eyes, which felt as though sand scraped beneath their swollen lids.

Only Recknass seemed untouched by the lack of sleep and food. His back remained straight and his eyes alert. His arms still held the swaddled princess in a tight embrace, and he glared forbiddingly at any who rode near.

The wolves themselves were showing signs of exhaustion—their tails dragged the ground and their tongues lolled from their mouths dispiritedly. They flung themselves on the ground and panted whenever they stopped, licking their footpads, which were sore and cracked from the rough terrain.

In spite of his promise to Hornsbuck, Mika still thought about Princess Julia. The giant was an abomination. Nothing that ugly should hold someone that beautiful.

Mika thought of Julia as he rode throughout the long endless night. Her delicate beauty filled his mind and the subtle scent of her body lingered in his nostrils. He craved her as he had never craved another woman, even Celia. And the thought of her was the cause of his every action. Just thinking of her dowry filled him with a warm glow. He was determined that he would have her yet.

A sliver of a moon, cold and white, shedding no warmth, rose above the stony hills, allowing them to continue their journey that night. The tramp of many feet could be heard behind them as the gnolls and their foul companions trudged along, following in their still-warm footprints.

Mika dozed fitfully, his hands gripping the reins without feeling, his knees numbly clenching the big barreled chest of the grey, moving automatically in rhythm with its movements. The grey was too tired for tricks. Its head bobbed listlessly at the end of its long neck as it sought out and followed the easiest path.

Mika slipped in and out of slumber, his sluggish brain flickering back and forth between the happy illusion of dreams and the pain of wakefulness. Not surprisingly, his mind chose to rest in the warm pleasantness of the dream state more often than the physical and mental traumas of wakefulness.

Wrapped in his cocoon of illusion, Mika felt the whispery patter of tiny feet on his neck. To his exhausted mind, it seemed the soft caress of Julia's tiny hand.

Some small corner of his mind which had not surrendered itself to sleep recognized it for what it was. A fly. A tiny black fly . . .

Annoyance flared briefly and Mika thought to raise his hand. To sweep it away. But exhaustion was

207

greater than the effort required, and the moment passed and was gone.

Mika fell into a deep sleep, an ongoing dream of Julia which was far more pleasant to contemplate than the fly.

So deeply immersed was he in the dream, that he barely even noticed when the fly bit him on the neck. His exhausted mind imagined it to be a love bite from Julia, a small hint of what was to come. Her way of showing gratitude for his bravery in single-handedly saving her from the spell and the horrible army of monsters.

The black fly crouched low over the puncture it had made on Mika's neck, tensing itself for the blow that might fall, readying its tattered black wings for flight, but it had chosen its moment well, and the man did not move.

Soon the fly began pumping a thick, black noxious fluid out of its mouth and down between its hooked mandibles. Directing the flow of the spittle, the fly channeled the awful stuff directly into the open wound.

The spittle entered the wound, thinning the blood on contact, and it quickly entered the man's bloodstream, where it spread throughout his system until it pervaded every inch of his body, even the heart and mind, with its evil poison.

Mika slept on, dreamed on, unknowing. Satisfied, the fly left the site of the wound and flew off, abandoning the man to his fate.

The tenor of Mika's dreams changed. He saw Julia in his arms, waiting for him with a sultry, knowing look in her eyes. This was no demure maid bestowing soft kisses, this was a woman using a woman's body, taking greedily as well as giving freely of her favors. Mika felt her hot flesh roll beneath him, the scorch of breath on his chest and the rake of sharp nails down his back.

Then he wakened, cold and chilled, racked with more than fatigue, and as the grey stumbled up yet another hill, Mika knew with a fevered intensity that whatever the cost, he would have Julia for his own.

Julia controlled his every thought from that point on. The slender sleeping girl locked in Recknass's arms had little or nothing to do with the woman he saw in his mind's eye. They were the same, but somehow different.

He had changed. This was obvious to everyone from Hornsbuck to Recknass. He was quick to follow Hornsbuck's every suggestion. He encouraged the men and rode point, scouting out the lay of the land ahead, pushing his tired mount and himself to the very limits of endurance.

The giant had little to complain about for it seemed that Mika had found fewer excuses to ride at his side, and he ceased offering to hold the princess should Recknass grow tired. Even Hary noticed the change and mentioned it to Hornsbuck.

"Aye, I have eyes. I can see what is happening," said Hornsbuck. "Sometimes it happens that way. Trouble can do that to a man, be the making of him. I've seen it happen before—a boy growing up before your eyes, becoming a man."

"More frequently it happens the other way," said Hary. "Trouble, hard times will reduce a man to jelly, make him useless. Frankly, that is the path I would have expected Mika to take. I did not figure him for leadership."

"I am surprised as well," said Hornsbuck, "but glad. I always knew he had it in him. Whether he chose to use it or not was the question."

"What bothers me," continued Hary, "is why the gnolls haven't overtaken us yet. It almost seems as though they're content to remain behind us. Sort of like they're driving us forward, herding us."

"Don't imagine things that are not there," replied Hornsbuck. "We've just been smarter than they, and we've chosen our course. They're not herding us anywhere."

As though in reply, the gnolls began to chant. Their voices could be clearly heard even though they themselves were not in sight. The words were indistinguishable. Their tongue was not one spoken by man, but the meaning was obvious.

"HUNhunhun! HUNhunhun! HUNhunhun!" they intoned over and over in deep bass tones, a shrill chorus of hyena and hyenadon wails providing an eerie contralto counterpoint. After a short time, the sound thrummed in the ears of the listener, striking over and over, maddening in its insistent repetition.

The horses and mules tossed their heads and hurried their pace unbidden, breaking out in nervous sweats. The wolves turned and faced the unhuman horde, whimpering softly, their dark eyes darting in all directions as though searching for an escape.

It was then that Mika made his move. Riding up alongside Hornsbuck, he spoke.

"You remember when you said that if I did not tell you what was happening, you would take the men and ride away?" he asked. Hornsbuck nodded.

"Well, I think that the time has come to do just that," said Mika. "I think it is our only chance."

"What do you mean?" asked Hornsbuck.

"Look ahead," said Mika, gesturing toward the series of peaks that rose before them.

"We are entering some sort of watershed, a place where the hills form a series of ridges like the spread fingers of a hand. I suggest that we split up into many different parties, each of us choosing one of the fingers to climb.

"The gnolls will be unable to decide what to do, which path to follow, or how to divide themselves. They will not likely fight among themselves while trying to come to some agreement.

"Eventually, of course, they will follow. But we are bound to gain some time through their confusion. Once over the top, we will regroup at some place that we decide in advance and then make our way to the city in safety."

Hornsbuck looked at Mika in admiration, while examining the plan for some flaw. He could not find anything wrong with Mika's logic, although there was something odd, something he could not place, in the man's attitude.

"There should be no more than two or three of us to each group," said Mika. "I will go with Hary or some of the drivers."

"No," said Hornsbuck, convinced by Mika's demeanor. "Go with the giant. He should have someone to protect his back since he has his hands full."

"If you insist," Mika said quietly, turning his head aside so that Hornsbuck could not see the smile of triumph that flitted across his face. As he wheeled his horse around, the grey nearly trampled on TamTur, who was inexplicably skulking behind.

Tam whined low in his throat and backed up a few steps. Hornsbuck stopped and looked at the wolf. RedTail touched noses with Tam and looked at Mika with uncertainty.

"What's the matter with Tam?" asked Hornsbuck, recognizing the disturbed tone in the wolf's voice.

"Nothing to be concerned about," Mika said smoothly. "He's highstrung. Gets this way once in a while."

Hornsbuck stared at Tam with narrowed eyes. He had never thought Tam to be highstrung, but still, a man knew his own wolf better than anyone else, and it was considered a serious breach of nomad etiquette to meddle between another nomad and his wolf. Hornsbuck held his tongue.

A council was quickly called and instructions given. Mika listened intently to Hornsbuck as he carefully described the point where they should reconvene. For the first time since the gnolls appeared, a feeling of elation swept over the men as they grasped the possibility of escape.

Hary and Recknass looked as though they might choose to disagree with Hornsbuck's directions, which paired Mika with Recknass and separated him from the company of the others. But as Hornsbuck spoke, delineating the reasons for the small parties, they remained silent, for his stature had risen among the men.

Mika conducted himself in a cool, detached manner, speaking politely to the giant and expressing concern for his imperiled mission. Recknass eyed him suspiciously but could find no fault with Mika's words. Still, Mika knew by the way that the man watched him that he was far from being a trusted friend. But as he led the giant into the dark hills, he smiled to himself; friendship wasn't what he was after.

TamTur trotted after the two men, then wagging his tail slowly, he looked back at Hary, Hornsbuck and the rapidly dispersing riders and whined unhappily. His dark eyes rested on Mika's back as the man rode into the shadows, and he whined again. Then, head hanging dejectedly, knowing that something was terribly wrong, he hurried after the man who was his bond companion.

Chapter 14

MIKA HAD CHOSEN HIS ROUTE carefully. He led
the giant up the spine of the low ridge. Deeply eroded
rock fell away steeply on either side and it was necessary to pick their footing with great caution.

After a time, the ridge flattened out and then disappeared completely as it merged with the flanks of
the higher slopes. Here there were trees, and the
heady scent of the short, wind-battered firs glad-
dened Mika's heart. He increased their pace, feeling
safer. Here, a man could do many things and not be
seen. The forest was a good place for secrets.

Once he heard a noise, the rattling of a rock falling,
and he turned swiftly but saw nothing. He began to
suspect that they were being followed, but no matter
how closely he watched, he saw nothing to confirm
his suspicions. Even Recknass was uneasy, turning
his big head from side to side as though anticipating
an ambush at every turn.

"Seek, Tam," whispered Mika, directing the wolf's
attention back down the trail. But Tam merely looked

at him with sorrowful eyes and whined plaintively, refusing to obey.

"Damn wolf!" cursed Mika, and striking out with his booted foot, kicked Tam squarely in the ribs. "Seek, Tam! Seek!" he commanded, and Tam slunk off into the brush with his tail curled beneath his belly, ears flattened against his skull.

Recknass looked at Mika with a curious, calculating gaze. His arms tightened around the princess protectively, as though any lingering doubts had just been erased, and he steered the roan stallion several paces farther to one side, widening the gap between Mika and himself.

Mika sneered at the giant and began planning just how he would separate him from the princess.

Tam slunk along behind him, his mind numb. Nothing in his world had prepared him for the change in the man who was half his being, half his reason for existence. He could not understand why Mika was angry with him.

It was Mika; of that he was certain. At least the body was Mika's. It looked and smelled the same, but everything else was different.

Tam had bonded with Mika at an early age. It was a bond that would take them through life and, if necessary, death. For it was not uncommon for a wolf or a nomad to give up his life to protect his companion. But the unhappy and confused wolf did not understand why his bond companion was acting so strangely.

There it was again! The faint scraping, the soft sibilance of foliage whispering across clothing. Mika stopped, listened, held up a hand gesturing for Recknass to wait. The giant obeyed, pulling up the roan and halting under the shelter of a large pine.

Mika slipped back down the trail, creeping from one tree to the next, crouching in the darkest of shadows, searching for signs of gnolls. How could they be so close? There was nothing to be seen other than a swaying tree branch. Funny. There was no breeze . . .

Mika was perplexed. Gnolls were not clever creatures, nor were they given to slinking and hiding; straightforward bashing and battering was more their style. Perhaps he was just paranoid, suspecting entrapment where there was none. If only that damn wolf had done something besides stare at him with stricken eyes!

Mika crouched in the shadow of a large spruce tree, watching the trail until he became convinced that no one was following them.

So intent was he on looking down the slope, that he failed to notice the figure standing behind him until it was too late. A heavy branch lashed out. Sensing the movement at the last second, Mika turned his head and so received a glancing blow on the thick of his braid rather than a direct hit on his temple, but he crumpled wordlessly in a silent heap at the foot of the tree.

Tam was crouched some distance away where a scornful Mika had left him, commanding him to stay. His ears pricked forward at the sound of the blow and the soft grunt that followed. He hesitated for a brief moment and then went to investigate.

That brief moment was all that was needed for the attacker to escape from sight. Tam saw only Mika lying at the base of the tree, slumped and unconscious. Tam sank down beside him and began licking the blood that welled up through his Master's hair. Tam would not leave Mika's side until the man either recovered or died.

This was what Hary had hoped for, if he even spared a thought for the nomad who stood between him and all that he desired.

Hary had labored loyally in the service of his king, first admiring and then adoring the beautiful child who was his daughter. As she grew into young maidenhood, his adoration had turned to love and then to longing as he yearned for that which could never be his. He had sought out the most dangerous of missions, hoping to subdue his rising obsession. Then, when that failed, he had hoped to gain the princess's admiration through his daring exploits. She barely noticed.

When the princess first fell into the magic-induced coma, Hary had viewed the journey to barter her recovery as his last chance. He would find the person responsible and force him to remove the spell. It was Hary's hope that the princess would then see him for the person he truly was and appreciate the skill and effort that had freed her. Her appreciation might then grow into love and she would accept him as her mate. Such dreams had driven Hary on, and as Eru-Tovar drew closer, allowed him to believe that he might succeed. Until Mika appeared.

As the nomad showed more and more interest in the princess's wagon and ultimately discovered her presence, Hary came to fear that it would be Mika she would come to appreciate once she wakened.

Mika was tall, handsome, and full of life. He projected a carefree, reckless attitude that promised laughter and good times and more. Hary felt dull and boring in comparison. He was afraid, no, he was *certain*, that Mika's dashing personality would appeal to his beloved princess. Hary would cease to exist in her eyes.

The more Hary thought about it, the more obvious it became that he would have to do away with Mika before they reached Eru-Tovar.

But the storm and the army of gnolls had set his plans awry, forcing him to depend on the nomad rather than kill him. Now, at last, his opportunity had come.

Even if the nomad were still alive, the gnolls would soon take care of that. Hary and the princess would be gone long before they arrived. He hurried up the ridge, anxious to be with the princess once again.

But as he burst out of the trees and entered the little clearing, Recknass the giant looked at him with surprise, his arms tightening around the princess as though he suspected that something was wrong.

Hary slowed his pace. He had forgotten Recknass. Now he searched for the words that would reassure the immense brute.

Recknass was not one of Hary's minions. The princess herself, as a small child, had chosen the giant, pointing prettily with one tiny finger at the hulking brute as he paraded past the throne with a hundred other brutes of similar size and qualifications. The fellow had been her creature and obeyed her every wish with blind devotion since that day.

Hary knew that Recknass had always viewed him

with suspicion, but then, Recknass viewed all men that way, all men who dared to even look at his young charge.

Not content to glower, the giant had killed several men who had ventured too close to the princess after being warned away. Patience was not his long suit. One fellow had had his head wrenched off his shoulders. Two others had merely had their backs broken over the giant's huge thigh. Hary knew that he had to be very careful.

Recknass took a step toward Hary, peering behind him into the dense cover of trees.

"Mika thought he heard some gnolls following," Hary explained. "He wants us to go on. Hornsbuck changed his mind and told me to join you in case you needed help with the princess."

The excuse sounded logical to Hary, but Recknass seemed to doubt him, staring out of his one good eye with disbelief.

Shouldering Hary aside, Recknass dismounted from the roan and, still holding the princess, began walking down the slope in the direction that Mika lay.

The blood rushed to Hary's head and throbbed in his temples. A red veil fell before his eyes and his breath grew strangled and harsh.

It was not fair! Even the giant, a huge stupid brute whom the princess treated like a large dumb dog, chose to doubt his word in favor of the nomad, a man who had injured him cruelly while openly plotting to steal the princess!

A blind fury rose up in Hary's mind, a mindless madness fed by long years of frustration and unhappiness. Seizing a fallen branch from the ground, he struck the giant a mighty blow on the back of his head. Recknass staggered. Hary struck again and again and at last the giant fell, toppling to the ground like some massive, lightning-struck tree, burying the princess beneath him.

Hary dropped the branch and steadied himself against a tree, his breath rasping in his throat. Slowly, his mind cleared and he looked down at his handiwork.

Recknass lay sprawled on the stony ground at the base of a small tree on the steep slope. He lay face downward, the back of his head a soggy mass of blood and purpling skin. Here and there, bits of white bone poked through the skin. Yet still, he clutched the princess safely in his arms.

Closing his mind to the unspeakable act, the violation of all the codes he had lived by, Hary bent down and tried to turn the man over so that he might free the princess from his grasp. Then, as he touched the giant's arm, he felt a faint pulse beating beneath his fingers, and he realized with a shock that the man was still alive!

Hary was overcome with a terrible irrational fear that Recknass might revive at any moment, reach up and grab him around the throat and strangle him!

He began to tug at the giant, pulling and pushing, struggling to turn him over, terrified of the stentorian breathing sounds the giant made. At last the princess came free, and Hary sprawled in the dirt holding her in his arms.

Time seemed to come to a halt as he gazed down on the face of the woman he worshipped. He tenderly brushed a wayward curl aside from her brow and then noticed a smear of the giant's blood staining her bodice. It seemed sacrilege.

He ripped his scarf from his neck, and daubed at the blood. As he did so, he felt something move under the soft silk. It was a hard object. Bewildered, he noticed a thin gold chain and drew it forth from between the cleft of her breasts. Dangling at the end of the chain was a crystal bead which he recognized as belonging to Mika!

Hary sat back, shaken to the marrow of his being. He felt his heart break within him and he was overcome with grief. The wolfman had been there before him. The princess was no longer the pure innocent he had adored.

It seemed apparent that somehow the nomad had persuaded the giant to let him have his way with her, although such a thing seemed unlikely, for the giant loved her too and would never have let another man touch her, unless . . .! No! It all seemed too terrible to consider. Mika *AND* the giant?

Hary's mind whirled. Yet think as he might, his thoughts kept returning to the same conclusion. To his jealousy-ridden mind, there seemed no other explanation.

He sat there for a long time, cradling the princess in his arms, grieving for what had been and what would never be. In his bitter and lonely misery, Hary now admitted to himself the folly of his love and realized that the princess would never love him. It had all been but a foolish dream. She would never be his.

Then a strange coldness came over him and he looked at the sleeping princess in a different manner. Why not? Who would ever know? Not Recknass.

Not Mika. It was only fair. They had had her and so would he.

Some time later, some thirty yards down the slope, Mika wakened with a terrible, pounding headache. TamTur was pawing at him, whining and licking him full in the face as he dragged himself to a seated position.

"Stop," Mika said with a groan, turning his head to avoid the wet endearment. Mika loved his wolf as much as the next man, but he drew the line at slobbery kisses.

There was some terrible commotion going on somewhere close. The noise echoed and thundered in his ears and he put a hand to his aching head. To his surprise, it came away sticky with blood.

Mika stared at his hand stupidly and tried to remember what had happened. But nothing came to mind.

He could remember climbing the slope with the princess and the giant, but his memories of that period were wrapped in a strange fuzziness as though he had been sick.

His mind was clear now, free of whatever sickness had gripped it, but still he couldn't seem to remember anything that would account for his presence under the tree. What was he doing here? Who had hit him and why?

It hurt to think. Mika would have liked to lie down, to rest. But there was all that noise. A man couldn't possibly rest with all that racket. Sounded like fighting.

Mika groaned. Maybe he had better go and see

what was happening. He struggled to his feet, fighting the waves of dizziness and nausea that washed over him. He planted one foot resolutely in front of the other and staggered uphill, gripping the trunks of trees and overhanging branches to pull himself along. Tam was close at his side, whining happily and giving little leaps, trying to lick Mika's face.

"Down, Tam. Behave yourself," growled Mika, fending off the wolf. "Go see what all that noise is about and leave me alone." But Tam ignored his orders, his concern for Mika far greater than his interest in outside events.

As Mika dragged himself up the rocky, tree-covered slope, there was a terrible pain-filled shriek and then there was silence. Muttering to himself, holding his pounding head, Mika tottered into the small clearing and stopped in open-mouthed amazement.

The two horses, the roan and his own irritable grey stood tethered to tree limbs, contentedly browsing on the tender tips of branches.

To the left of the horses, lying on the downhill edge of the clearing was the giant, Recknass, flat on his back, his skull a bloody ruin.

Mika gawked at Recknass in total disbelief, his headache totally forgotten. Someone had actually killed the huge brute! Mika could scarcely comprehend it. His mouth flopped open and he stared at the man thickly as though something would change or understanding would dawn if he only looked long enough.

But nothing changed and understanding did not dawn, no matter how long he stared. Closing his mouth, Mika blinked, gulped, and then gazed on the rest of the strange scene.

Sprawled on the ground next to the giant was the princess, her pink silk gown in disarray, exposing her slender, delicate legs from the knees down. Her hair was charmingly mussed, framing her beautiful face with clouds of shimmering black curls that cascaded down her chest, modestly covering her bosom, which rose and fell in a most provocative manner.

Mika would have liked to have examined her longer, and closer for that matter, but she appeared to be alive and well, albeit still asleep, so he reluctantly turned his eyes toward the third figure in the strange tableaux.

Lying on the ground furthest from Mika, on the far side of the princess, was Hary, who lay with his arms and legs akimbo. His bright blue eyes were staring up at the sky, unseeing, glazed with that terrible vague opacity that belongs only to death. A long-handled knife, which Mika easily identified as belonging to the giant, was buried to the hilt in the center of his chest. Clutched in his right hand was a heavy tree limb covered with gore.

It was too much to take in. Especially for a man with a headache that he didn't even know how he got. Mika's knees wobbled and he put a shaky hand out and sat down on the ground, staring at the bizarre trio, still trying to make some sense out of the situation.

"Well, they must have killed each other," he said, slowly. "That much is obvious."

Tam looked at him sideways as though thinking that even he could have deduced as much.

"But why?" asked Mika. "Why would they fight? I thought they were friends. The only one they disliked was me! I don't understand this at all. I don't even know what happened to me, much less them. Hornsbuck will never believe me!" groaned Mika.

Suddenly a series of sharp yapping barks burst on them, followed by a shrill ululation of victory. The gnolls!

So wrapped up had he been in the pain of his head and then the terrible discovery of the bodies, that he had actually forgotten why they were alone on the ridge and what they were supposed to be doing.

Sounds carried well in the cold clear air, and he sat there on the dank ground and hugged his knees as he listened in sick horror to the ravening cries of hyenas and gnolls running their luckless prey to earth.

There was a clash of steel on steel, a short fight, then desperate screams, both human and horse. Finally, there was only the sound of hyenas fighting over the scraps of flesh.

There was no way of telling how close the creatures were, but it was obvious that they were on the mountainside.

"Close, Tam," whispered Mika. "Too close. Maybe the next ridge over. We'd better get out of here before they find us, too." And all the while he wondered who the gnolls had gotten, whether it was Hornsbuck or one of the others he had known and liked.

It hurt his head to bend over, but fear of the gnolls drove him on. He leaned over and slid his arms under the princess. He straightened up and the princess hung from his arms like a sack of stones. A pretty sack of stones.

"By the Great She Wolf, she's heavy," grunted Mika as he began dragging the princess over to the horses. He tried to lift her up onto the roan, but she hung from his arms limply, without any stiffness in her backbone.

He took a deep breath and tried to heave her up over the saddle. She slid back down and lay in a heap at his feet.

Muttering more loudly now, Mika got down on his hands and knees and positioned the princess until she was sitting on his shoulder. He grabbed her wrists and held on tight. Then, slowly, he got to his knees with the princess wobbling on his shoulder like a drunken parrot. A heavy drunken parrot. He got to his feet and stood up slowly. Slowly, slowly, he allowed the princess to fall over the saddle. He placed a hand on her back to hold her steady. Then, just as he was reaching for his belt to tie her in place, she began to slide. Forward.

Mika made a grab, but the slippery silk just whispered through his fingers like wind through trees and the princess slid over the saddle and landed on the ground on the far side of the horse with a meaty thump.

Mika winced. "I'm not the only one who's going to have a headache," he said to Tam. "She certainly will, too, if she ever wakes up. She's pretty, all right, but is she worth all this fuss? Damn, she's heavy!"

With gnolls and hyenas wailing inspirational music in the background, Mika was stirred to brilliance. Using his belt, he lashed the princess's wrists together and then tied Hary's scarf around the belt. Positioning himself on one side of the horse and the princess on the other side, he laboriously hauled her over the saddle and then, passing the scarf under the horse's belly, tied it round her ankles.

Mika stepped back, breathing hard, and examined his handiwork. The princess was secure, even if she did look like a pink silk sack of wheat. Tam began to whine nervously, his ears twitched forward, and he danced from one foot to the other.

"Gnolls, eh?" Mika asked, looking down the flank of the hill, following the direction of Tam's gaze.

"Then we'd best be going," he said as he leaped onto the grey. "We've been lucky to escape them this long. At least these two will buy us some time."

The horses were nervous too. The whites of their eyes rolled and their ears were pasted flat to their heads. The grey tried to rear and, showing some of his old spunk, swung his head around and tried to bite Mika's leg. Mika yanked the reins hard, sawing the grey's head in the other direction. He slashed him hard on the flanks. Then he dug his heels into the horse's ribs and the grey bounded forward as though shot by an arrow.

Mika held the roan's reins in his hand, forcing it to follow his lead. Together they plunged up the steep hill, into the shadow of the trees, and with the cries of gnolls and hyenas echoing in their ears, raced for safety.

Chapter 15

THE SLOPES RANG with the screeching yowls of the gnolls and the horrible yapping of the hyenas. Mika could tell when they succeeded in cornering and ultimately dragging down some hapless human by the terrible cries of the victims. Wolf howls cascaded down the slopes periodically before they too ended abruptly, and Mika knew that wolves and nomads were dying.

He tried to close his ears to the horrible cries, knowing that people he knew and cared about were being killed. He said a prayer to the Great Wolf Mother that Hornsbuck was not among them and asked for guidance in setting his own course.

Several times, unable to bear the anguished cries, he had pulled the grey up hard, on the point of turning and riding to help, only to realize that it was useless. There was no way of telling where the battle was being fought, and by the time he found it, it would be too late. His misguided chivalry would only serve to endanger the princess, as well as himself. His mouth was set in grim concentration as he raced into the on-coming night, shying from every dark shadow as though it sheltered the enemy.

There seemed to be safety in no direction; the gnolls were closing in on him rapidly. Their ominous tramping could now be heard flanking him on either side.

Now the earth rose steeply on Mika's right, forcing him lower on the steep ridge. Mika knew that it would be death should they descend farther, and he pushed the horses on, fighting them at every turn, causing them to skitter and plunge across dangerous slopes they would never have attempted of their own volition in daylight.

The moon, tiny sliver that it was, rose over a cruel landscape. The trees were below them now, and a cold wind keened harshly across a barren vista of sharp rocks and sheer drops.

They rode along a narrow path, no real trail, but an eroded watercourse that flowed from the crest of the peak. The land was steeply pitched on either side, bare stone that caused the horses' hooves to clatter loudly, reverberating in the confines of the narrow defile.

Mika cursed to himself, wishing he had time to dismount and muffle the horses' hooves with cloth, fearful that the enemy would hear them. As though in answer to his fears, there came a demonic laugh, followed by the familiar cackling yap. Hyenas!

Looking behind him, Mika saw large round eyes glowing yellow in the cold moonlight. Their long sharp canines, so well adapted for ripping and tearing, gleamed white through the froth of spittle that

230

drooled from their open mouths. Their backs humped forward between their shoulder blades, and their backsides sloped away into insignificant hind-quarters that were shorter and far less powerful than their front legs.

The lead hyena spotted its quarry and stopped short. Lowering its massive bear-like head till it nearly touched the ground, it uttered a low mournful howl that was echoed by its three foul companions. The howling grew louder and louder as the pitch rose till it seemed to fill the narrow defile, bouncing from one side to the other. Then it broke off and became a demented cackle that caused the hair to rise all over Mika's body.

The grey reared, neighing hysterically, and lunged forward, nearly toppling Mika from the saddle. Mika gripped the pommel and hung on as the grey thundered up the trail, dragging the roan behind him.

The hyenas broke into their strange gait, moving the legs on one side of their bodies in opposition to the legs on the other side. Strange it might have been, and reminiscent of the gnolls' own shambling gait, but it got them where they wanted to go, and fast.

If it had been a matter of speed only, the hyenas might have caught them, but ironically their fearful din spurred the horses on. Mika added his cries to those of the hyenas and beat both horses with the flat of his sword. He had no desire to die in the jaws of such low creatures. Even Tam ran like the wind beside the horses; there was no honor in fighting carrion-eaters such as these.

The horses were breathing hard now, froth blowing from their nostrils, but they were breaking from the hyenas, pulling away steadily.

The peak was before them now, the saddle clearly outlined against the star-filled sky. Mika urged the horses on, driving them cruelly. Later, there would be time to rest. Later.

Then, clearly outlined against the starry sky, two hump-backed figures appeared on the ridge and stood waiting, one swinging a sharp-edged, double-headed axe and the other a four-foot-long two-handed sword. Gnolls.

Mika's heart sank like a plummeting rock as he pulled the grey up hard. But the grey wasn't having any of it. Head down, driven beyond fear into a fear-induced madness, he seized the bit between his large yellow teeth and, ignoring Mika's command, galloped on.

It didn't matter in the slightest that two large gnolls, each standing seven foot tall and weighing at least three hundred pounds, stood directly in his path. The grey did not discern that they were covered with shaggy hair and had low jutting brows. Nor did he care that they had massive jaws filled with sharp teeth that inspired fear in the most reckless of men. None of that mattered to the grey, for they were dressed in leather tunics and had man-like shapes. To the grey, they appeared as humans. Big humans.

What did matter was that the grey was being pursued by hyenas. The grey understood hyenas and still bore scars on one flank from a hyena attack suffered when he was a mere colt still running free on the plains. He had survived, but many of his band had not. The stink of urine, blood, and carrion clung to the hyenas and filled the grey's nostrils, reminding him of that day of death so long ago. He ran from them with the fear of madness, and it mattered not that man-things stood in his way.

Screaming his fear of the hyenas and his hatred of humans, the grey put down his head and charged.

The gnolls were startled. Clearly, they did not expect such a thing to happen. Nothing ever attacked them by choice! The gnoll on the left narrowed its eyes and lowered its sword, bracing the hilt against its body. The gnoll on the right appeared slightly less certain, but following its companion's lead, planted its feet firmly on the rocky trail and raised its battle axe above its head.

"No! No! Stop!" screamed Mika, yanking on the reins in desperation. But the grey ignored him and barreled into the gnolls at full speed.

The gnoll that stood directly in front of them was crushed beneath the grey's hooves, its hard skull splitting like an overripe yarpick fruit, its squat body mangled beyond gnoll-mother recognition. But not before it had driven its sword into the grey's chest.

Even now, impaled on the awful blade, the grey wreaked death, unleashing his old hatred of man on the second man-thing that stood there, still holding the battle axe overhead, too stunned to move. That small hesitation was the gnoll's undoing, for the grey lashed out with one sharp-edged unshod hoof and opened the leather-clad figure from breastbone to navel.

The gnoll looked down, unbelieving, as its intestines slid out of its belly in slow, sinuous, slimy loops. It dropped its arms, the axe forgotten, and tried to replace its guts, stuffing them back into a cavity that now seemed too small to hold them.

The gnoll stared down, its eyes wide with pain and disbelief, and for a second, its eyes met Mika's. Mika almost felt sorry for the creature, but then it no longer mattered, for the grey, feeling the cold steel twisting in his vitals, stumbled and went down, driving the sword still further into his body. But as he did, he carried the gnoll with him, its face crushed between his strong square teeth.

Mika had no time to be thankful for the death of the gnolls, for hard on his heels came the pursuing hyenas. The roan reared and screamed, and the salty stink of blood, both horse and gnoll, lay pungent on the cold night air.

Mika clung to the reins that dangled from the roan's bridle as he disengaged himself from the dying grey. He was thankful that the grey had not fallen on his side and pinned him beneath his great weight. He was certain that the grey would have done so, had he thought of it, carrying his diabolic hatred of man beyond him into death.

Mika scrambled to his feet and tugged the roan's head down as he attempted to mount, but the roan reared hysterically, screaming in fear and clawing out with his sharp hooves, refusing to be calmed as the hyenas slunk closer. The princess was dangling securely, still asleep, blithely ignorant of what was going on around her. Mika shoved her forward and swung behind her on the roan's back. He gave the horse a vicious kick. Still he reared and bucked but did not move forward.

Tam leaped in front of the hyenas, positioning

himself in front of Mika, shielding the roan from the hyenas. Mika fought to bring the horse under control, hoping that the four predators would not be too much for Tam to handle.

Tam dropped his head and raised his dewlaps, exposing his black gums lined with sharp teeth, capable of killing even a hyena. He stalked forward on stiff legs, emitting a harsh, deep, guttural growl full of menace that would have sent a lesser creature running in fear for its life.

But hyenas feared little and certainly not a lone wolf. Spitting out their own eerie cries that prefaced a clash, their short bear-like faces with upturned blunt noses seemed to grin in appreciation of the feast to come. Their ungainly bodies leaned forward in hump-backed anticipation. Their spotted, mangy fur and leering expression gave them a comedic look, but as they spread out around Tam and began to circle, Mika was in no way inclined to laughter.

Their actions caused Tam to circle as well, but no matter which way he turned, one of them was always at his back. If he advanced, jaws snapping ferociously, the hyena behind him slashed out with razor-sharp teeth.

They harried Tam back and forth between them, cutting, slashing, nipping, biting. And always when he attacked, they were not there, sliding away from him like ghosts. Had he been able to grasp one, he would have found himself holding nothing but loose folds of skin that swung loosely in his jaws. This worked to the hyenas' advantage, for while the wolf was futily biting excess skin, the hyena would twist around and seize the wolf in its powerful jaws. This was the beginning of the end, for the hyena's jaws were extremely strong, and once they bit down, they seldom let go. While he held on, his companions would rip the victim to shreds before it even realized its desperate plight.

Tam was bleeding from a dozen wounds before Mika succeeded in bullying the roan through the circle of vicious hyenas. "Go, Tam, go!" he hollered, leaning down and lashing his sword at the hyenas.

Tam turned and ran, leaping over the carcass of the grey and the mangled gnolls. Mika skewered one of the hyenas on his sword, then flung it, still yapping, into the midst of its companions.

Another of the hyenas leaped for the soft unprotected swell of the roan's belly, but Mika swung and sliced its head off neatly. Hot blood spurted from the stump of the thick neck, drenching his leg and the roan's side. The two remaining hyenas were momentarily distracted by their fallen comrades, which they tore into with ravenous hunger. Mika kicked the roan harder as they plummeted over the peak, the shrill shrieking of the hyenas loud in his ears, as he caromed down the opposite side of the ridge. The hyenas were left behind, feasting on their own dead and wounded.

Mika gulped as the pale moonlight illuminated the sheer slopes below them, throwing the sharp upthrust boulders, the smooth sliding scree, and abrupt cliffs into contrasts of black and white. Tam, torn and bleeding profusely, teetered on the edge and looked up at Mika with stricken eyes before plunging downward.

The roan quivered beneath Mika as he tried to

steer him across a deceptively smooth expanse of gravel that appeared safer than the alternative, a rocky stretch of ground strewn with fist-sized stones. A sudden nameless intuition caused him to drop the reins, allowing the roan his head, allowing him to make his own choices.

The roan swerved at the last moment, avoiding the smooth talus, choosing instead, the rocky ledge above it. As he jumped, the weight of his impact dislodged a small stone which fell onto the gravel below. Instantly, the whole mass started to slide, moving faster and faster, picking up speed and sweeping everything in its path before it as it thundered down the dark slope.

Mika had only a moment to view the catastrophe before the roan leaped again, plunging down the ridge from one tenuous bit of safe footing to the next. Had Mika not given the roan its head, they too would now be at the foot of the slope, buried beneath tons of rock and gravel.

Mika shuddered and held onto the pommel tightly. Tam raced to keep up with them, blood streaming darkly from a multitude of wounds. Mika could see that Tam was tiring, but there was nothing he could do. Their only hope was to keep going until they reached the bottom.

Because of their great speed and the extreme steepness of the incline, they reached the bottom in a fraction of the time that it had taken them to climb its opposite side.

The bottom was a wide ravine that held a goodly amount of water and was shielded by a dense overhang of spruce trees.

The roan came to a stop on the far bank and stood, all four legs outstretched, braced stiff-kneed, head down, and blew great sobbing breaths, flecked with white foam. His sides heaved with effort, and his body was drenched with sweat.

Mika dismounted and leaned against the exhausted horse, his own legs and thighs quivering with the tension of having gripped the horse so tightly. Together they slowly brought their breathing and their emotions under control. Mika patted the horse and rested his forehead against his neck. He stroked him and murmured softly, "Good horse. You're the best."

Still moving slowly on rubbery legs that scarcely felt capable of supporting him, Mika searched for something to use to rub the horse down. Time was valuable and danger was still near, but the horse would surely founder unless he took the time to cool him down.

But he could find nothing. His cloak was gone, ripped from his shoulders somehow, somewhere. His leather clothing was too hard and too stiff to be of use, and his bedroll was still tied behind the grey's saddle.

Sighing deeply and shrugging philosophically, Mika ripped the princess's silk gown off at the knee. "Excuse me, Your Highness, I need part of your gown to wipe the horse down. You don't mind, do you?" he asked as an afterthought, his hand resting casually on her upturned buttock. She was oblivious, of course.

"There, Tam. You're a witness," Mika said to the wolf curled up on the ground, licking his wounds. "I asked her and she didn't say anything, so I guess it's all right."

The silk made a fine horse-cloth, and Mika stroked and wiped the weary animal clean with handfuls of moss, then dried it thoroughly with the soft silk cloth.

The roan nodded his head up and down, contented and reassured by the gentle rhythmic movements, then rested his head on Mika's shoulder and groaned deeply. Mika was taken aback, used as he was to the ornery nastiness of the grey. Startled, he stroked the velvety smoothness of the roan's muzzle, and he breathed softly in his ear.

Once the roan had cooled off, Mika led him to the stream and allowed him to drink briefly. Then he tied him to a low branch and left him to rest.

He thought about removing the princess from the horse's back, but decided that since she was still under a spell, and evidently not aware of any discomfort, he had best tend to Tam's and his own needs first.

Fortunately, the medicine bag still hung from his shoulder. He was glad that he had decided to keep it on his person. Opening the mouth of the bag, he carefully placed the contents on the edge of the mossy bank and studied them.

There was the book, bound in leather, its thick pages frayed and worn, a small bone pipe, and a dried twist of wolfsbane. There were a number of vials filled with healing potions and unguents, and several horns stoppered with wax plugs that contained medicinal salves. There was his father's ceremonial wolf cloak, a variety of other useful items, and a small sack of the dried meats and vegetables that Hary had given to him.

Mika picked up the antelope horn of healing salve and the sweat-stained silk cloth and turned his attention to Tam.

Tam whined plaintively as Mika examined his wounds. Though none of the wounds were immediately life threatening, Tam's thick pelt was ripped and torn in at least a dozen places from his head to his tail, and a number of the wounds extended deep into the flesh itself. Infection, if not loss of blood, could cause the wolf a slow, lingering death. The wounds had bled freely and that was good, for the dead flesh that gathered in the jaws and teeth of the hyenas was rotting and putrid and could cause disease and death even if the bites healed over.

Mika knew that he needed to clean the wounds thoroughly and then dress them with healing salve or Tam could sicken and die.

First, it was necessary to find shelter, for even though there were no gnolls in sight, it was best to remain hidden.

As their hiding place Mika chose an ancient blue spruce that towered high above him. He crawled under the broad skirt of the tree and found that, as he had hoped, there was ample room beneath its branches. Over the years, the lowest limbs had died and broken off, leaving a comfortable cavern. The fragrant branches draped around him like a living tent.

As he was moving the wolf, who allowed himself to be picked up like a small cub, Mika noted a stout witch hazel bush and remembered that the leaves made a fine cleansing lotion. After he built a small fire next to the base of the trunk, he stripped several handfuls of leaves from the bush, then looked around for something that would function as a container. There was nothing. Nothing at all.

Determined, his gaze fell on his own leather boot, not exactly the best recourse, but one did with what one had. He quickly crushed the leaves between two rocks and dumped the pungent grey-green mess into his boot, then filled it to the ankle with water from the stream, allowing the leather to remain in the stream until it was saturated both inside and out.

When the boot had absorbed as much water as it could, Mika propped it over the fire with a tripod of green sticks. While he waited for the water to heat, he washed the strip of sweat-stained silk in the stream.

The water soon came to a rolling boil, and Mika let it stew until the air was thick with the sharp fragrance of the medicinal leaves before he removed the boot from the fire.

"Well, old boy, this won't do much for my boot. I just hope you don't suffer any ill effects. My brother always said my feet could be used as lethal weapons. Phew! It certainly smells strong enough."

Mika's tone was jovial and confident, but inside, he was aching. Thoughts of Veltran-oba suddenly filled his mind. He remembered their friendly banter with a sense of acute loss and wished that his brother were here with him now.

Tam looked away and growled, licking his lips constantly, nervously, as the sharp aroma filled his nostrils. He looked at Mika out of the corner of his eye and his head moved stiffly, his dewlaps twitching.

"Calm down, boy," Mika said soothingly as he stroked the wolf between his ears and scratched his throat. "You know I wouldn't do anything to upset you unless it were necessary. You have to trust me. We've been together too long for you to start doubting me now."

The words, the tone, or both seemed to soothe the wolf, but Mika wanted to be certain he wouldn't snap in fear or pain. He rummaged about in his supplies and filled the tiny bone pipe with crushed wolfsbane and lit it. Trying not to inhale, he cupped his hand behind the wolf's head and blew the smoke directly into Tam's nostrils. After several puffs, Tam's agitated heartbeat slowed and his pupils dilated. He was as ready as he would ever be.

Dipping the silk cloth in the hot liquid, Mika began swabbing out the wolf's wounds with the hot herbal brew. Soon Tam's pelt was streaming with the fragrant fluid which pooled beneath him on the needle-strewn ground.

Mika worked quickly, packing the clean wounds with the thick healing salves and stitching the jagged edges of skin together in the worst instances, while keeping the wolf calm with his voice.

Tam began to move restlessly, showing signs of recovering from the effects of the wolfsbane. Mika hastily filled the pipe again and, taking a deep pull of the narcotic smoke, blew it into the wolf's nostrils. Unfortunately, he had forgotten to hold the smoke in his mouth and had no sooner exhaled the last of the smoke than he felt the familiar warm lassitude spread throughout his own body. Shrugging mentally, he took another pull on the pipe and blew it more or less in Tam's general direction. Just to make sure the wolf was really out, he loaded the pipe again. However,

Tam seemed to be sleeping, so he was forced to smoke it all himself.

It took him a minute to think of what he was supposed to be doing. Then he remembered. Sighing heavily, he turned the wolf over and began cleaning the wounds on the other side. One of the hyenas had seized Tam's tail in its teeth and in the struggle had pulled the flesh as well as the skin away from the vertebrae for the length of a finger joint. The flesh on either side was already swollen and discolored.

Tam was still sleeping, but Mika felt nauseous looking at the mangled flesh and felt the need to fortify himself. "Only a puff," he murmured as he relit the pipe.

Eyes blinking dreamily, he put down the pipe with exaggerated caution and once more bent to the onerous task.

"Ugh!" he said with a shudder as he rinsed the horrible wound with the cleansing liquid. "Now I know why I didn't want to do this for the rest of my life!" But still, he felt grateful that he had learned the skill, for without it, his friend would surely have died.

At last the awful injury was cleaned and the worst of the mutilated flesh trimmed away with his knife. Mika packed the remainder of the salve around the wound. There was a great deal of flesh still exposed, and Mika knew that it had to be covered or it would attract insects that would lay their eggs in the flesh. Mika sighed and smiled, then wrapped the pink silk cloth round and round the wolf's tail and tied it in a knot. Tam would not be pleased and would do his best to remove it, but with luck it would stay until a scab had formed.

Mika leaned against the rough trunk of the spruce, the branches coming down on all sides of them like a living wall, shutting out the outside world. The small fire had warmed the space, and he was tired and his head still ached. He stared into the fire and blinked. His eyelids drooped, then closed, and he drifted off into a deep and dreamless sleep.

Chapter 16

MIKA WAKENED SLOWLY. Everything hurt. His head throbbed and his eyelids were thick and swollen. His throat was dry and his stomach was cramped. Every single joint was stiff and sore. And he was cold. He groaned in misery.

Tam added groans and whimpers of his own. Mika sat up and rubbed his head, which was now scabbed over with dry blood. His hands and arms were covered with Tam's blood and his body was rank with old sweat. He could feel a line of blisters beginning to rise under the edges of his tunic at neck and shoulders.

Mika flexed his arms and rolled his head cautiously, feeling the muscles complain at the smallest movement.

Tam lay still, barely lifting his head from the ground. He tried to wag his tail, but even that small effort was too much, and he stopped after one feeble wave.

"By the Great She Wolf, if we feel this terrible after such a little encounter, pray the gods we never have to go into a real battle," muttered Mika.

The roan, hearing Mika's voice, whickered softly.

Mika crawled out from under the overhanging branches and looked around carefully. The day was dark and grey. A dense rain-swollen cloud cover hung over the ridge, obscuring its upper reaches from sight. Mika stared up at the almost vertical drop, frankly astonished that they had descended it safely. No sane person would purposely choose that route unless he had a death wish.

The roan was tossing his head impatiently, and as Mika untied him from the tree limb, he butted him gently in the chest with the flat of his head. Mika shook his own head in quiet amusement.

He had been riding for almost as long as he had been walking and never had he viewed a horse as anything but an uncomfortable but necessary means of transportation. He had known of nomads who had an almost mystical relationship with their horses, but he had never felt such warmth for a horse until now.

After leading the roan to the stream and allowing him to drink his fill, Mika tethered him in a patch of grass. Then he tended to the princess.

She was beginning to look a little shopworn, Mika reflected as he untied her from the horse. He supposed that it was partially his fault for leaving her draped over the horse overnight. After all, there were limits to what one could expect from magic spells. Even one cast by the best of magic-users. For instance, her need for food and water was magically suspended. But even the best spell didn't extend to clothes and dirt.

The princess's hair hung down over her head, all

dusty and dirty with muddy drops where the horse had splashed water. Her dress was filthy and wrinkled and had torn in several places. Maybe she would look better right side up, Mika mused.

But she didn't. The princess was definitely a mess, and of course, she was still sound asleep.

"This is getting tiresome," Mika said between gritted teeth as he slung her over his shoulder and tottered toward the stream. "The least she could do is carry her own weight."

Mika sat the princess down at the edge of the stream and propped her up against the trunk of a tree. Ripping yet another strip off her gown, he dipped it in the cold water and rubbed it over her face. The water ran in muddy rivulets down her bosom, which no longer looked quite so attractive.

In fact, the whole princess thing was beginning to pall. She was about as much fun as listening to a lecture on the medicinal properties of goldenwort.

Other questions now presented themselves. Now that Recknass and Hary were dead, what about the mission to ransom the princess?

And where would Mika take her if they ever got to Eru-Tovar? How would he locate the mysterious magician? And what should Mika do if the magician demanded payment in advance? Mika sighed and shook his head. All of these new problems made his head ache just thinking about them.

He finally abandoned the cleaning of the princess as a lost cause and turned his attention to his own needs. Stripping off the sweat-stiffened leather tunic, his single remaining boot, and his loincloth, he waded into the stream.

The water was cold but invigorating. Mika found a sinkhole near the edge of a greenery-hung bank and submerged until only his head stuck out, staying there until he felt the last of the tension ease from his body, as well as the multitude of aches and pains.

After a while, he moved to a more shallow location where a layer of white sand lay thick on the floor of the stream. This he scooped up by the handful and rubbed over his body till his skin tingled and squeaked beneath his palms.

Next he unbraided his hair and floated spread-eagle on his back, letting the current wash away the blood and the grime. Then he scrubbed his hair with sand, gingerly avoiding the still painful bruise.

His skin was puckered and blue by the time he finished rinsing his few bits of leather clothing, knowing that they would dry stiff and unbending.

Naked, his dripping clothes tucked under his arm, he returned to the spruce and crawled inside. He hung his clothes over several of the lower branches, restarted the fire, and added small bits of dry wood, enough to take the chill out of the air, but not enough to cause smoke which could be seen through the trees.

Tam stood shakily and nosed his way out from under the tree, his pink bandaged tail looking very odd in the cold light of the morning. As Tam drank at the stream Mika dragged the princess under the shelter of the spruce and took stock of their situation.

It seemed reasonable to expect that some of the drivers and nomads had escaped the predations of the gnoll army. It also seemed logical to assume that the entire area was probably crawling with a large assort-

ment of gnolls, hyenas, trolls, hyenadons, and nomads and drivers, all trying to either escape or kill
each other.

With any luck at all, most of them would leave the
area soon, running and pursuing each other westward. Mika was concerned about Hornsbuck and
Marek and Klaren and a few of the others, but not
enough to join the fray. It made sense to stay right
where he was, under the tree, until all danger had
passed and he and Tam were in better shape.

The more Mika thought about it, the more unusual it seemed that such an army of creatures would
appear in the middle of the desolate plains. It was obvious they must have had some connection with the
magic-user. Who in Hades was that man, and when
would he turn up again?

Tam crawled back under the tree, collapsed next to
the fire, and began licking himself, his every movement a visible effort.

Mika took his second boot, now washed by the
stream, and scooped some water up. Mixing in a
large amount of the dried vegetables and meat, he set
it to simmer over the fire.

It began to rain before the stew was done, big fat
drops of water that splatted against the ground. But
under the tree it was warm and dry. No rain squeezed
through the densely matted branches. He was feeling
safe for the first time in days.

Tam wasn't too interested in eating the stew, so
Mika ate alone. He offered some to the princess out
of politeness, but of course, she didn't want any either.

Dinner finished, Mika rinsed out his boot and

hung it up to dry. His breechclout was dry, so he put it on, then busied himself with combing the tangles out of his hair. His head still ached so he left his hair dangling loosely about his shoulders. Then he rubbed some of the herbal ointment into his blisters and over a number of other cuts and scratches that covered his body.

The unguent was soothing, spreading an icy cool across the skin, and Mika felt good, knowing that he owned the recipe for the mixture and had the knowledge necessary for making it. Once again, he felt grateful to his father for persevering in the face of his disinterest and said a quiet prayer of thanks.

His quiet ruminations were set aside abruptly, for at that moment, the roan neighed and Mika felt more than heard the tread of heavy feet nearby.

Gripping his sword, he crouched low, ready should anyone or anything attempt to invade his area.

Tam raised himself up and growled once, his ears stiffly erect. Then, his posture eased, his ears lowered and his injured tail thumped softly on the ground. Mika knew that whoever was nearby was no enemy.

Pushing the branches aside cautiously, Mika looked out and saw Hornsbuck and RedTail crashing through the underbrush, both sodden and miserable looking. They had not spotted him. For a moment Mika was tempted to let them pass by, but they looked so wretched that he relented.

"Hornsbuck!" he called in a low tone. Hornsbuck whirled, drawing his sword in a harsh clang of steel.

"Mika!" he said in wonderment, then a scowl creased his face and he frowned at Mika suspiciously.

"What be you doing here, hiding under this big

tree like a rabbit?"

"Come out of the rain, Hornsbuck. We can talk in here. Come on!" he urged as rain pelted down his face.

Mika pulled his head in and added several sticks to the fire. He was glad to see that Hornsbuck was still alive, but he was in no mood for the man's militaristic drivel. Personally, Mika saw no sense in wandering around a wet forest thick with gnolls when it was possible to be dry and safe.

"Where are you?" Hornsbuck roared in a loud whisper as he plowed straight into the dense foliage, showering those inside with moisture and causing the fire to hiss and sputter.

"Hornsbuck! Down!" Mika commanded, tugging on the man's soggy breechclout, forcing him to his knees.

"Eh? Oh!" said Hornsbuck as he parted the branches and looked down into the warm dry interior of the tree. "Tree, eh?" he said with great insight. "Pretty smart. Dry too. Smelled the smoke. Couldn't see it, but smelled it. Knew someone was around. Have you seen any gnolls?"

"Come inside, Hornsbuck," Mika said impatiently as wind gusted through the open branches, spread wide by Hornsbuck's broad bulk. RedTail needed no further urging. He entered, touched noses with TamTur, and was immediately busy sniffing Tam's wounds.

"Glad there's a fire," grunted Hornsbuck as he squeezed through and walked in to where Mika sat at the base of the trunk.

He sank to a seated position in front of the small

blaze and sat there steaming like some giant semi-tamed bear, his great bulk seeming to fill the interior, making the space small with his huge presence.

"Where's Recknass?" he asked suddenly, peering around him as though he might somehow have overlooked the giant.

"Dead," said Mika, and he quickly told Hornsbuck all that had transpired since they had parted. Hornsbuck looked puzzled.

"Why would they have killed each other?" pondered Hornsbuck. "Did you have anything to do with it?"

"Me? I've told you everything," Mika said indignantly. "In fact, I expect it was one of them who hit me on the head. And now I'm stuck nursemaiding the princess all day!"

"Oh, so that's why you're not out hunting gnolls. Wondered about that," muttered Hornsbuck. "But I can see as how you'd have to stay here with her. I hate gnolls!" And he spat a stream of brown tobacco juice toward the princess as though to add emphasis to his hatred.

"Uh, Hornsbuck, not in here," Mika said with distaste.

"Women," sighed Hornsbuck. "They're a problem even when they ain't yapping." And he leaned over and wiped the ugly brown stain that was spreading across what remained of the princess's dress with his ham-sized fist. He only made it worse.

"Well, maybe she won't notice," he said, wiping his hand on the front of his tunic. "Maybe she won't ever wake up!" he added, the idea obviously much to his liking. "Then we could just leave her here and be on our way."

"Neither Enor nor the Guild would approve," said Mika. "And besides, Tam is injured and needs to rest."

"You're right," said Hornsbuck. "What's a nomad without his wolf? But Tam should be up and about in a day or so, nothing to really fuss about, just a few hyena bites. It's just that I get crazy sitting around doing nothing. Don't suppose you've got anything to eat? I'm starved. Damn gnolls got my horse and all my provisions, too."

Mika poured a generous portion of the dried mixture into his boot, added water, and set it over the fire once more. If Hornsbuck saw anything strange about cooking in the boot, he said nothing about it while gobbling the hot concoction.

"Not half bad, this," he said, gesturing at the stew with his food-smeared fingers. "Be better with beans, though." Then, spraying food in all directions, he told his tale.

"Separated from the rest of the men, just like we decided. Took Klaren and Meno with me. They both got themselves killed.

"Klaren got pulled from his horse by a troll and Meno took a gnoll's pikestaff in the chest. Their wolves stuck by 'em till the end, then they got cornered by a pack of hyenadons. RedTail and I tried to help, but it was hopeless. The only thing we could do was try to save ourselves. Damn shame about Klaren. He was a good man.

"We got to the rendezvous point and waited, but nobody showed up, 'cept some gnolls. So we left. My guess is that everyone is scattered from here to Eru-

Tovar and gone. We'll just have to make it on our own."

"But how are we going to do that if the woods are crawling with gnolls and trolls and hyenas?" asked Mika. Then, seeing Hornsbuck casting a critical eye on him, he hastened to explain.

"I mean, I'd like nothing more than the chance to kill some more of those filthy creatures, that's for sure, but there is the princess to think of. She's still my first concern. I know that Enor will expect me to deliver her safely to the city, so I mustn't think about myself and what I'd do if I were alone. Too bad, really. The two of us could see to it that there were fewer gnolls in the world," Mika said with a sad sigh.

"I know, lad," said Hornsbuck, patting Mika on the back. "I don't like seeing them murder my men and get away with it, but you're right about the princess. We've got to see to her first. Once she's taken care of, we can find a few gnolls and show them how we feel about their kind."

Not if I can help it, thought Mika as he tried to look as though he agreed with the older man.

"But how do we get her to Eru-Tovar safely?" asked Mika. "The gnolls will surely find us before we reach the city."

"I know a way," said Hornsbuck. "But we'll need some food. We'll have to kill the roan."

"No!" blurted Mika, unwilling to sacrifice the horse to Hornsbuck's great undiscriminating belly. "We'll find something else. What is your plan?"

Hornsbuck's green eyes pierced Mika and stared at him intently. "I'll show you when the time comes," he said slowly. "It's a lost way, a path I have kept secret these many years. You must promise me not to tell anyone once I show you."

"All right," agreed Mika, not really caring, so long as it was safe and free of gnolls.

The next few days passed slowly. Very slowly. Hornsbuck ate what little wild stuff they were able to gather, tossed knucklebones, hawked, spat, cursed, belched, farted, and made other obnoxious and rude noises. Smart and wily he might be in the ways of survival, but the man's social graces were all but nonexistent. Mika had never quite noticed before what a coarse brute Hornsbuck was, but then he had never been thrown so intimately into his company before.

The man was addled from war-lust and if insufferable when awake, he was only slightly less noisy when asleep. Never had Mika so missed or so appreciated Celia and the company of women. Wedged in one small corner between Tam and the princess, Mika read his book of spells out of sheer despair, in an attempt to separate himself from Hornsbuck's endless, mindless commentary.

As he read, a plan began to take shape in Mika's mind, a dangerous, yet wonderful plan.

Chapter 17

TWO DAYS HAD PASSED, and Tam was well, or nearly so. His wounds had healed enough so that he was able to walk and run without difficulty or pain.

The princess lay across one side of the tree space, and most of Mika and Hornsbuck's possessions were hung from various portions of her anatomy. In her inert state, she had taken on the air of a seldom used and rather unnecessary piece of furniture.

Hornsbuck fretted about food. He and RedTail had ventured out the previous night, hoping to return with a deer or, at the least, rabbits. But they had found nothing but gnolls, which they had killed.

Mika rose and, holding his book casually, said, "Tam and I will go out and look for deer. It will do Tam good to stretch his legs."

"Be careful," growled Hornsbuck. "Take my bow and arrows."

"No. I have everything I need," said Mika, leaving quickly before Hornsbuck could question him.

The night was cool and the air fresh and heavy

with the aroma of wet evergreens. He checked on the roan, watering him and moving him to yet another small patch of grass, grateful the horse had escaped the notice of the gnolls.

Standing in the center of the small clearing, Mika shed his few bits of clothing and stood full in the light of the moon. Opening his book of spells he turned to the appropriate page and thanked the dullness that Hornsbuck had brought into his life, which had forced him to study the spells.

He wedged the book firmly into the notch of a tree and then, confident of his skills, sank into a cross-legged position and faced Tam.

Slowly, deliberately, with great precision and careful enunciation, he stared into Tam's eyes, while holding the end of his tail, and recited the words of the spell. There would be no mistake this time.

Once again he felt the strange, whirling dizziness, the nausea, and the sour taste of bile at the back of his throat. Tam's eyes blurred and multiplied, and in spite of himself, Mika closed his eyes. When he opened them, everything was different. It had worked. He was a wolf!

Joy spread throughout his body. His new, strange body. He had done it! He had succeeded! He stood erect, his sensitive nostrils quivering. He realized now for the first time how very little man knew compared to wolves. He smelled the clear, sharp, wet smell of water, the green growing scent of trees and grass, the hot, sweet aroma of horse flesh. He lifted his head and drew in the foul distant stink of gnolls and the carrion stench of the hyenas. He threw back his head and howled for the sheer ecstasy of it, the sound issuing from his throat in tight rippling waves. Tam threw back his own head and they sang together of the joy of brotherhood and the goodness of life.

They looked at each other out of wolf eyes, now well and truly brothers. Their long tongues lolled from the corners of their mouths, and Mika knew that such a gesture was indeed a laughing grin as he had always suspected.

Standing, the two wolves sniffed each other from head to tail, spending much time scenting each others genitals, for as Mika discovered, there was much information to be learned there. In some indescribable way, it told of the personal strength of the animal and his position among others of his kind. Mika learned that Tam was a wolf of power and high standing among others.

Mika wagged his tail, feeling it beat back and forth through the air. Curling it high above his back, he turned and trotted off into the forest, knowing without looking that Tam was close behind.

The woods were alive with sound. Tiny squeaks told of frightened mice leaping for the safety of their burrows, rabbits bounding swiftly away, their broad flat feet pounding against the soft debris of the forest floor, and even the smooth slither of a night-hunting snake. Mika's ears swiveled back and forth as he ran, catching the most subtle of sounds.

Mika's muscles moved smoothly under his thick black pelt, his heart pumped strongly, and he ran more swiftly than he had ever imagined possible with little or no effort. And he felt pity in his wolf heart for the weakling that was man.

Later, as the moon rose higher in the dark starry sky, they scented a roanbuck, the rank bitter smell declaring that it was a full-grown stag. They paused and looked at each other, staring deep into each other's golden eyes, silently reading the challenge, considering, deciding.

They lifted their muzzles and drank in the bitter odor, finding the specific thread of it in the air, separating it from the myriad of others and reading it like a map. Absorbing the knowledge, they turned and followed the musk deeper into the forest.

The partial moon had nearly reached its zenith before they tracked the scent to its source. The stag loomed large before them, full-grown, immense, powerful and wise. Its wide, sharp-tipped rack of antlers, capable of disemboweling an incautious wolf, were silhouetted against the night sky.

The stag pranced lightly, shaking its head up and down, snorting its contempt, brandishing its horns in their faces. Its dark eyes reflected no fear, only hatred, as it faced the ancient enemy.

The stag picked his ground carefully, a high knoll that rose improbably inside a tall circle of sablewood trees. The grassy mound was twined with intermeshing circles of mushrooms, their earthy redolence filling the air as the stag crushed them underfoot with its sharp hooves.

Mika lowered his head and slunk forward, circling the stag and forcing it to turn to keep him in sight. He felt his dewlaps twitch as he drew his lips back in a snarling grin, exposing his long, sharp canines. He inhaled the thick muskiness of the stag through mouth and nostrils, drawing it across his tongue, tasting the essence of it. He salivated and felt the thick moisture roll off his tongue.

The grass was cool and slick beneath his paws, and he circled steadily, rushing in, in false feints, forcing the stag to respond, to thunder down from its knoll, waving its antlers in Mika's face.

Mika leaped aside with ease, feeling the strength of his new body and the power in his legs. He dodged in under the great tines and nipped at the soft underbelly, causing the stag to swing its hindquarters downhill. Instantly, Mika leaped up, high on the stag's neck, behind the threatening horns, and slashed down with his teeth. The stag bellowed, more in anger than pain, and whirled about to menace the wolf that was no longer there.

Mika, bold with daring, dashed forward and ripped at the fat belly again, sinking his teeth into the smooth hide and using his weight to pull down, opening the wound. Letting go, he dropped to the ground and rolled, rising to his feet unharmed.

Mika and TamTur worked the stag between them, inflicting small wounds that bled, till the proud animal stood with its head bowed, its hide streaming with dark blood, and its breath coming in wheezing gasps. They allowed it no chance to rest.

Now, the element of fun vanished, the wolves filled with deadly intent. The salty iron tang of blood tainted the air and coated the wolves' tongues, acting as a powerful stimulant. A primitive compulsion thrummed in Mika's brain, entreating, urging, demanding blood.

Messages, all unspoken, but yet heard and obeyed, flooded into Mika's subconscious, telling him what to do. He darted, he feinted, he baited, he bit.

Then, the moment was at hand, the moment when all the right elements came together. Tam leaped, flinging himself directly at the stag, and sank his teeth into the fleshy lips, curling his body up into a tight ball to present no target for the plunging horns and slashing hooves.

The stag bellowed in pain, shaking its head from side to side and up and down in an attempt to dislodge the wolf. Tam clung ever tighter, using his weight to inflict as much damage and pain as possible.

The stag screamed, a high-pitched strangled sound, and lifted its head high, trying to shake Tam loose. Mika, who had been waiting for just such a moment, flung himself upward, seized the stag's throat between his jaws, and bit down with all his strength.

The stag shrieked, blood burbling thickly in its throat, even as it flowed into Mika's. Mika clung until he felt the great beast shudder and stumble off balance. Only then did he release his hold.

The stag foundered, its knees buckling beneath it as the blood poured from its mangled mouth and spurted from the ruptured arteries in thick gouts. It attempted to rise and failed.

Tam and Mika were on the stag before it crashed to the ground, ripping, slashing, tearing into the still-living flesh.

They ate their fill of the sweet, hot meat, wrenching off great chunks and gulping them down whole till their sides bulged and they could hold no more.

They lapped the thick, salty blood and lay swollen and sated in the middle of the bloody carnage.

Mika was exhausted but filled with a sense of satisfaction. He and Tam looked at each other, and Mika felt love swell in his breast for the creature who was now his brother in truth. He knew that they were truly kin after this night, their bond greater than any shared by wolf and man. Tam looked into his eyes and laughed, tongue lolling, as though to say, "You see what you have missed all these years?" And Mika could not but agree.

They were cleaning the blood off their pelts when they heard the first yapping hyena howl. They leaped to their feet and listened carefully, pinpointing both the direction and the distance.

Taking hold of the stag, they began to drag it back toward camp, hoping that they could reach it in time, knowing that there were too many of the dangerous enemy to fight them off.

They were better than halfway back when Mika felt the peculiar tingling which he now recognized as the onset of the end of the spell. He sat down on his haunches and waited, realizing that it might be easier to carry the stag in his human form, and glad that he was on the ground and not in mid-air.

The transformation was less traumatic than the first time, since he now knew what to expect. He shivered and rubbed his hands over his arms as the cold night air raised bumps on his chilled flesh.

Tam stared at him with amusement and perhaps just a touch of pity.

"All right, all right," said Mika, "but at least I can carry the damn thing instead of dragging it in my teeth. So be quiet and let's get out of here!"

He heaved the stag to his shoulder, staggering under the great weight. Blood dripped down his chest and back, no longer raising the same emotions it had evoked when he was still a wolf.

Mika also regretted loss of the ease with which he had traversed the forest earlier, trudging along heavily over ground he had covered so effortlessly only a short time before.

They reached the spot where he had left his clothes and he changed into them quickly, also retrieving the precious book. The howls of the hyenas had faded into the distance and he wondered if they had perhaps found some other prey.

Shouldering the stag once more, he and Tam made their way back to the spruce. He paused outside, inhaling the cold night air, more than a little reluctant to enter, to rejoin the race of man, to let go of what he had been privileged to share with Tam if only for a short time.

Tam pawed his leg. Placing the stag on the ground, Mika pushed aside the branches of the spruce and entered.

Chapter 18

HORNSBUCK AND REDTAIL greeted the arrival of the stag with much happiness. RedTail gobbled the numerous scraps greedily as Mika and Hornsbuck butchered the animal quickly and efficiently at the edge of the stream.

"By the Great She Wolf, you look as though you've bathed in the blood," Hornsbuck said with a laugh. "You'd best wash off. Anyone seeing you would think you'd rolled in the thing before you brought it back." Mika just smiled and did as he was told.

Hornsbuck could not understand Mika's refusal to partake of the stag, but lost no time in worrying about it, stuffing himself with great quantities of meat, barely waiting for it to sear over the tiny flame before he choked it down.

"Now that we have meat, can we leave?" Mika asked.

"Aye, we'll leave tomorrow," said Hornsbuck.

"And the gnolls . . ." began Mika.

"They'll never find us. You'll see!" said Hornsbuck, and then there was no more talking as he addressed himself to his food in a serious fashion that precluded speech.

RedTail slobbered and growled over a leg bone, bits of flesh and gristle dotting his thick red pelt, and Mika could not help but observe that man and beast bore a strong resemblance to each other.

Tam and Mika lay down together and tried to ignore the sounds of crunching and slurping.

Mika looked at the princess, his eyelids heavy with fatigue, and in that foggy state, she looked quite lovely, almost as beautiful as she had when he first laid eyes on her. His half-closed lids filtered out the dirt and the smudges and the torn clothes and the snarled hair. In his mind's eye, she was fresh and clean and lovely.

He yearned to see her awake, with her eyes open, staring at him with love. He tried to picture what form her gratitude might take, for now it was he alone who would win that reward when the spell was lifted—now that the others were dead.

Of course, there was the small matter of finding out who had placed the spell, persuading him to lift it, and emerging alive in the bargain. But that was another matter . . . and one that he would think about later. Still thinking of the princess and his reward, he closed his eyes and slept.

"Time to go, Mika. Best be awakening," said a loud voice, rupturing the pleasant dream into splinters.

Mika opened his eyes and stared up blearily. Hornsbuck leaned over him, shaking his shoulder, a smile splitting the great beard.

Mika groaned and closed his eyes, trying to recapture his dreams. The princess had been just about to take off her dress.

"Go away, Hornsbuck. It's the middle of the night."

"Pah!" snorted Hornsbuck. "Get up lad, get up. Time's a wasting, the sun will be up any minute now. It's time to go!"

Mika opened his eyes and glowered at the ceiling of branches. The dream was gone and would not return. He turned his head and looked at the princess who lay scant inches from him, then closed his eyes and sighed. Sometimes dreams were far more preferable than reality.

He sat up and groaned. Mornings were not his favorite time of day. Hornsbuck handed him a stick, layered with grilled chunks of deer meat, singed and covered with a fine layer of ash. "Eat up," he advised. "We won't be eating for a while to come."

Mika closed his eyes and did as he was told, finding it strange indeed to compare this meal with his last and declare it far inferior. Being a wolf had its advantages.

They packed the meat in two bundles made from the hide of the deer. The meat, unsmoked, would last no more than two days without going bad. But Hornsbuck said that it would be more than adequate, although he still refused to give any explanation of where they were going.

Other than the meat, which they loaded on the roan at Hornsbuck's insistence, they took as much grass as they could gather. They cut the grass off at the roots and bound it in sheaves, and Mika was thankful that it was both lush and abundant or Hornsbuck would have left the roan behind. Lastly, they heaved the princess up into the saddle and tied her in place in front of the pile of pitch-soaked limbs Hornsbuck likewise deemed vital for some reason.

Mika took the opportunity to try and clean the princess up a bit, smoothing down her tangled hair and trying to wipe some of the dirt off her dress.

"Leave off," growled Hornsbuck. "It won't do any good, and the damn female probably won't approve no matter what you do. You can't ever please a woman. Why, once I brought back a whole bagful of hydra eyes for a woman . . . thought she could string 'em on a necklace, do something pretty with 'em. Almost got myself turned to stone getting 'em for her. And did she appreciate 'em? No, she did not! Threw them away! Said they made her sick! Can you imagine? Women. Pahhh!"

Hornsbuck eyed Mika critically. "If you need to do something, braid your own hair. You look like a damned woman with it down on your shoulder like that!"

Mika sighed, refraining from mentioning the painful bruise that still covered much of his scalp, and he scraped his hair into a loose braid to appease the older nomad who had definite ideas of what was appropriate.

Hornsbuck grunted with approval, then, taking one last look to make certain that nothing was being forgotten, turned and began leading them in a north-westerly direction.

They walked for several hours, leading the horse

by the reins. They met nothing living, although they found a number of gnoll and hyena corpses, all of which had been chewed upon by hyenas or hyena-dons, most forest dwellers being too choosy to eat such foul offerings.

Only once did they find humans, a driver and a no-mad, or what little remained of them, made unrecognizable by the severity of their wounds and the teeth of predators. They quickly buried the pitiful remains, said a few words, and hurried on their way.

The forest was thinning now, the sablewood and roanwood trees giving way to smaller softwoods—white-barked birch and quaking leafed aspen. The soil underfoot was changing from soft loam to hard-packed earth and stone. Periodically they were forced to skirt large boulders that stood alone like giant monoliths.

Hornsbuck called a halt and turned to look at Mika, his brow furrowed in deep thought. He studied Mika wordlessly for some moments as though filled with uncertainty. Then, coming to some decision, he sighed and shook his head.

"Look, Mika," he said gruffly. "No man alive knows what you are about to see, excepting me an' RedTail here. I learned it from someone else, and he's dead now. It's secret. You *can't* tell. You've got to promise. Give me your solemn vow."

"All right," said Mika, puzzled as to what could possibly be so important.

"Don't promise unless you really mean it," growled Hornsbuck. "I mean, even if they pull your toes out with their teeth, you can't tell. It's that kind of promise I'm asking for."

"All right," Mika said slowly. "Even if they pull my toes out with their teeth, I promise not to tell," he vowed, wondering all the while who "they" were and why they should want to do such a thing. Surely Hornsbuck was exaggerating.

"By the spirit of the Great She Wolf, Mother of us all, Guide of our spirits and protector of our souls, I Mika, son of Veltran, do promise never to tell this path to any man, not even if he pulls off my toes with his teeth and other horrible things," intoned Hornsbuck, holding up his hand and nodding at Mika, commanding him to repeat the words.

Mika held up his own hand and repeated the words word for word, feeling foolish all the while. Tam sat on his haunches and looked up, tongue lolling, laughing. Mika refused to meet his eyes.

Satisfied, Hornsbuck lowered his hand and resumed walking. The ground began to rise underfoot. The trees grew sparse and then disappeared completely, giving way to a dense mat of coarse and prickly bushes. They shoved their way through them with difficulty. Once again, they began to encounter the strange boulders, although now there were more and more of them, the ground more rock than dirt. The land began to rise in a series of low, jagged hills, stretching away to the far horizon. Mika was not pleased at the thought of traveling across such harsh open land and started to speak.

Hornsbuck chopped off his speech with one slash of his hand and held it up as though forbidding Mika to speak while he stared in all directions with sharp eyes, scanning the forest behind him intently.

Seeing nothing and receiving unspoken confirmation of some sort from RedTail who had been busily snuffling the air with upturned muzzle, Hornsbuck led the roan to a large boulder that stood nearby, a boulder seemingly no different from any of the hundreds that surrounded it. He then gestured for Mika to follow.

Mika did so, thinking that they might be taking a brief break, but Hornsbuck dropped to the ground and began moving stones at the base of the boulder. Mika stared down at the grizzled nomad, totally bemused. What was the man doing?

Hornsbuck moved to the opposite side of the boulder, making certain that the roan was out of the way, and then leaned his shoulder against the rock.

"Get over here and help," he growled, looking up from his efforts and seeing Mika staring at him strangely. Mika joined him, putting his own weight against the rock, although he had absolutely no idea what on Oerth they were doing or why.

Suddenly, the rock began to move. It shivered under their palms and trembled with the anticipation of movement.

"Push!" commanded Hornsbuck, straining against the rock, his face suffused with dark blood and his neck corded with effort. Mika obeyed, pushing harder now that it seemed that something was actually happening.

There was a loud rumbling groan, and the boulder rolled to one side, exposing a yawning black cavity at their feet that Mika barely avoided falling into.

He stared into the dark hole with disbelief. He looked up at Hornsbuck who grinned at him broadly. "What is this? Where does it go and how does it come to be here?" Mika stammered. "And how did you come to know of it?"

"Hah!" exclaimed Hornsbuck, slapping his hands on his thighs. "That is for me to know. There are still a few things left in the world that you have not discovered.

"Hornsbuck has had more than a few adventures in his day," he said, green eyes glittering. "I am not just some dusty old nomad who knows nought but wolves and killing. Dainty manners ain't everything. I, too, have my secrets, and they may save your life yet, young pup, so save your laughter and sneers for someone other than I."

Mika felt the blood rush to his face and he sneaked a look at Tam who also appeared somewhat chastened.

"My apologies, Hornsbuck. I did not mean to give offense. I'm sure TamTur and I can learn much from you and RedTail."

Their eyes met and held, then Hornsbuck turned away. "Too much talking," he said gruffly. "You've even got me doing it. Let's go." Sweeping the area with one last look, he grabbed the reins and dragged the roan into the dark hole.

The roan was not pleased at the prospect and attempted to rear, his nostrils filled with the scent of damp earth. But Hornsbuck allowed no such opportunity, holding the reins tight in his huge fist right below the horse's muzzle. He had no choice but to follow where he was led.

Mika was more than a little reluctant himself, having never liked close, dark places. But he followed hard on the heels of the roan with Tam close behind.

The earth sloped gently for the first few feet, and as his head dipped below the surface of the ground, Mika felt a hand grip his arm and pull him aside.

Hornsbuck pulled two of the pitch-stained limbs from the roan's back and, striking his flint, lit them. They burst into flame immediately and began to burn with a bright flame, trailing tails of dark smoke.

Hornsbuck handed both limbs to Mika and then reached up and started pulling on what appeared to be the roots of bushes, that dangled from the earthen ceiling. There was a low, rending groan, and the boulder began to move. Mika's chest grew tight and a feeling of panic came over him as the boulder rolled back into place, blotting out the blue sky above. It settled into place with a solid, final-sounding thump. Mika wondered with a panic if it would ever move again.

"Don't mind," Hornsbuck said roughly, clamping a callused hand on Mika's shoulder, "it ain't so bad, after a bit. You'll get used to it. Come on, we'd best get going. Keep your mind busy so you don't have time to think."

Mika was not too sure about Hornsbuck's logic, but he agreed in principle, so he handed one torch back to the older man and then followed behind the roan, concentrating on his immediate surroundings rather than the thought of where he was.

Their heads and shoulders brushed occasionally against the earth walls and ceiling. Roots poked through the ceiling, flaring briefly as they were touched by the torches. The roan filled the narrow corridor completely and scraped dirt from the walls which fell in Mika's path.

Quite soon, however, the path dropped abruptly in a series of gigantic steps. It gradually widened until it was broad enough for both he and Hornsbuck to walk comfortably abreast, the wolves in the lead and the horse bringing up the rear.

The ceiling rose higher and higher until it was more than three man-heights above their heads, and Mika's feeling of oppression lifted somewhat.

He looked about him curiously, noting the smooth blocks of stone underfoot that had obviously been worked by man or dwarf. Metal torch brackets were fixed to the walls at regular intervals, although the wooden stubs that filled them were draped with cobwebs, sad testament to the passage of long dark years since they had last known the heat of fire.

"What is this place?" Mika asked in a whisper that rustled about them in ghostly echoes.

"Don't know for certain," rumbled Hornsbuck. "I think it was a mine of some sort, although it seems too fancy for that. There's all kinds of other passages coming in here and there. You've got to be careful not to stray."

"Why? What's down the side passages? Where do they go?" asked Mika, his voice filled with concern.

"Don't know," said Hornsbuck with a shrug. "Main path takes me where I want to go, so I never tried exploring. I figured it was safer sticking to the main trail."

"Where does the main trail go?" persisted Mika.

"Straight into Eru-Tovar," said Hornsbuck with a broad grin, looking at Mika, anticipating his surprise. He was not disappointed.

"Eru-Tovar?" questioned Mika, his eyes wide

with surprise. "You mean this tunnel goes straight into the city itself?"

"That's right," nodded Hornsbuck. "Ends up right under an old abandoned temple. Discovered it one night when I was looking for a place to go with a friend. Quiet like, if you get my meaning."

"I know," said Mika with a smile, although it was hard to imagine Hornsbuck snuggling up to any woman. Still, the man did have his positive qualities, and once again he had surprised Mika with his ingenuity.

The passage of time was strange and different without the light of day. Mika grew disoriented and he could not tell if he was hungry or tired or how long they had been traveling by the time Hornsbuck called the first halt.

The ceiling and walls had turned from dirt to stone some time ago and now rose in vaulted arches above their heads. The walls were regularly spaced with rounded pillars of stone that flowed into the ceiling, more ornamental than functional. The passage had taken a sharp turn to the right when Mika became aware of a sound, more felt than heard, that reverberated through the tunnel.

A current of cold damp air struck them full in the face as they intersected a new passage. The sound was louder now.

Hornsbuck hesitated for a moment, then turned to enter the new tunnel which was lower still than the corridor they traveled. It was reached by means of a narrow ramp. As they descended, the cold rush of wind grew stronger and their torches flickered wildly and threatened to extinguish. However, once they reached the floor of the new corridor, the draft gentled and the flames steadied.

Now Mika could see the cause of the noise and the damp draft, for on the far left edge of the passageway, which now yawned wide enough for twenty men to walk abreast, there ran a fast-flowing torrent of water that rushed by at a pace more rapid than a man could walk. It flowed in the same direction as they traveled.

Mika approached the water cautiously. It was black and oily in appearance and barely reflected the light of his torch. Mika shuddered, not anxious to draw closer nor tempted to slake his thirst from such a concourse. It looked as though it could suck a man under.

"Nasty, eh?" said Hornsbuck. "Don't like the looks of it myself. That's why I filled my waterskins from the stream before we left. Don't want to wet my gullet from the likes of that. Don't trust water at the best of times, and this," he said, nodding his shaggy head toward the black water, "ain't exactly the best of places."

Mika nodded his total agreement.

They halted briefly beside the rushing water and built a small fire against the far wall, roasting chunks of meat on the ends of their knives. They sliced off generous portions of raw meat for the wolves and then fed and watered the roan.

"Well, at least she doesn't cost too much to feed," said Hornsbuck as he whacked the princess on the buttocks with casual familiarity. "And I've got to admit that she doesn't talk too much. This spell certainly has its good points!"

Somehow, Mika felt offended on the princess's behalf and spoke up, drawing Hornsbuck back to the fire.

"Why are we eating here? It's so cold and drafty."

"Figured the draft might wash away the smell of the food," said Hornsbuck. "I've always figured that there must be some critters living down here. I don't know what they are, and I've never seen any, but it doesn't hurt to take precautions."

"Critters? Like what?" asked Mika, the meat suddenly lying heavy in his stomach.

"Don't know," Hornsbuck said with a shrug. "Could be almost anything. All sorts of critters like the dark better than the light. Could be kobolds or gnolls or bugbears or trolls or gnomes, dwarves, goblins, or even orcs, for all I know. I can't say for sure. I just keep my eyes open when I'm down here, and I don't dally."

"How long will it take to get to the city?" Mika asked, looking around uneasily at the mention of all the horrible possibilities.

"Two days, two nights," said Hornsbuck. "If we don't run into any trouble. I figure that with two of us, it'll be easier to keep watch, although RedTail and Tam should let us know if anything's on our trail. Leastwise, I hope so."

So did Mika. They packed up and set out again after their brief respite, following a long, confusing set of tunnels. Mika had only admiration for Hornsbuck's amazing memory, for as far as he could tell, the older man consulted no map other than that which he held in his mind.

They had descended to a passage that lay even fur

ther below ground than the water tunnel when Mika noticed that it was becoming harder and harder to stay on his feet.

The path was rougher here, the walls and ceiling far less refined than the upper levels, and he stumbled often. It grew more and more tiring, just walking. He stopped for a minute, resting against the wall and felt the fatigue in his legs. Even Tam's tail lay limp between his legs, and he walked with his head hung low.

"Hornsbuck," Mika called. "Let us stop for the night. I am weary and would rest."

"Pah!" spat Hornsbuck. "You young pups have no endurance. Why, I could walk for many an hour more and never even feel it!" But Mika noticed that he did not argue the point further but set up camp in a matter of moments.

Camp was a rude affair with the roan tethered on one side and the wolves resting on the other. They ate their meat cold and raw and washed it down with water.

Mika lowered the princess to the ground, although Hornsbuck thought it a waste of time, and arranged her neatly along the wall, wiping her hands, wrists, and face with a dampened square of silk, ripped once again from the bottom of her dress.

The closer they got to their destination, the more Mika imagined what she might be like if she wakened.

"I've taken care of her well, under the circumstances," Mika assured himself, under his breath. "After all, what do I know about taking care of princesses? It's not like I asked for the job! That damn fool giant went and got himself killed; it's all his fault!"

Tam's dark eyes reflected laughter in the light of the torches, and after a moment, Mika grinned too. Then, lying down on the cold earth, he closed his eyes and slept.

Chapter 19

SOMETHING WAKENED MIKA, although he was not sure what. A soft sound perhaps, a whisper of movement, or maybe just intuition. Whatever it was, it caused the short hairs on the back of his neck to rise up in prickles.

He lay there in the dark, for the torch had gone out while they slept. He strained against the darkness, trying to see, but it was hopeless; the dark was impenetrable.

Then it came, the softest sibilance of movement, yet he could not tell where it was coming from. Off to his left, or maybe even behind him.

His hand inched toward his sword, and he hoped that Hornsbuck was awake, too. Yet he could not call out to his comrade without letting whatever was lurking know he was awake . . .

He closed his hand round the handle of his sword, the metal cold and reassuring, but now there was no sound, no hint that he was not alone. Doubt swept over him and he wondered if he had been mistaken.

Perhaps it had been but a dream. Perhaps, it had been . . . Pain, excruciating pain, pierced his ankle like two red hot pincers, and shot up his leg, twisting and coursing through his body like fire through dry tinder.

Mika screamed aloud, all thought of silence abandoned as the agony continued to chew its way through his ankle. Lifting his sword, he slashed down at the unseen assailant, once, twice, three times, feeling his blade cut through little or nothing.

Light flooded the tunnel and a rough hand covered his mouth, choking off his screams. Mika thrashed about wildly, fighting the hand, and raised his sword to strike.

"Don't be barmy," Hornsbuck whispered harshly. "What's the matter with you? Are you tryin' to call every monster in the place down on us? Quit your noise!"

"My ankle! My ankle!" Mika gasped, doubling over and gripping his booted ankle with both hands, his sword dropping uselessly to the ground with a dull clang.

"Ain't nothin' but a measly centipede," growled Hornsbuck in disgust, wrenching the pincers of the creature open with his bare hands and thrusting it head first into the flame of the torch. It shrilled a brief high-pitched scream, then crumpled as the fire shriveled and blackened its segmented carapace.

Mika groaned with pain and bent nearly double, clutching his bloody ankle, for while the thing was dead, the awful pain continued.

"I don't understand why you're carrying on like this," said Hornsbuck, as he stared at Mika with disgust. "It was just a little one, barely even two feet long. Why, once when I was traveling—"

"Hornsbuck, I don't care if you eat them ten feet long for breakfast every morning," Mika said through clenched teeth. "The damn thing bit me, and it hurts like the devil. Aren't they poisonous?"

"Poisonous? Well, yes, I suppose they could be," mused Hornsbuck, stroking his beard as he tried to remember. "Maybe so, but not a lot," he finally concluded.

"Hornsbuck, a little bit dead works just the same as very dead," gasped Mika, propping himself up against the wall next to the princess. Steeling himself, he withdrew his bloodstained hand, pulled off his mutilated boot and examined the wound.

The skin was already turning purplish-blue on either side of the twin gashes, each of which extended the full width of the ankle and appeared relatively deep. The flesh was sore, and the lips of the wound had swollen shut, sealing inside whatever poison had been injected into his body.

Mika sighed deeply, noting the two crimson lines that were already inching their way up the calf of his leg, leaving a deep throbbing pain in their wake that seemed to increase as he watched.

Mika hated pain and blood, especially when it was his own, and even more so when he had to inflict it on himself on purpose. Yet there was nothing else to be done; if he did not treat the poison, it would only get worse. Much worse.

Under Hornsbuck's amused eye, Mika seared the blade of his knife in the flame of the torch, then, without pausing, slashed the flesh above the ankle, cutting across the two lines of poison. Blood flowed freely, pouring down his foot in dark streams. To his surprise, he felt immediate relief from the awful pain. Soon, the blood turned bright again and the flow diminished and then slowed to a trickle.

Acting nonchalantly, Mika rummaged in his pouch and found a horn of healing salve that he thought appropriate. Its principal ingredients were borage, bittersweet, red clover, golden seal, and mullein, all of which were used in cases of blood poisoning. To that he added a handful of cobwebs scooped from the walls, to aid in clotting.

He smeared the wounds with the thick salve and webs and ripped yet another strip from the remains of the beautiful silk dress to wrap around his ankle.

"Done?" Hornsbuck asked politely, although laughter still twinkled in his eyes.

"Done," replied Mika.

"Then let us be on our way," said Hornsbuck, gesturing with a broad sweeping movement of his hand, indicating the path beyond.

"But isn't it still the middle of the night?" asked Mika.

"Who can tell and what does it matter down here where there ain't no light?" said Hornsbuck with a grin. "We're up, so we'd best be going."

There was no arguing with the man's logic, so with a shake of his head, Mika got to his feet and put his boot back on, which, he noticed, still smelled slightly of rabbit stew.

He was astonished to find that there was little or no pain in the ankle and congratulated himself on his fine healing skills, choosing not to remember that he had made the salve months ago under his father's explicit direction.

The wolves were all too glad to leave the tunnel, skirting the blackened remains of the centipede with obvious aversion.

"Thanks a lot," muttered Mika as he limped along next to Tam. "I thought you were supposed to sleep with one eye open. My faithful companion, always alert, never surprised. Hah! That centipede could just as easily have gotten me by the neck, you know. Then where would you be?"

Tam licked his lips and, meeting Mika's eyes only briefly, looked away.

"All right, all right. I'm not too wild about centipedes either. I forgive you . . . this time," Mika said grudgingly, and they walked along the dark passage in companionable silence.

It seemed that Hornsbuck also spoke to RedTail, conferring with him quietly when they came to junctures that the older man seemed unsure of. In those instances, Hornsbuck seemed to talk to the wolf and then listen to a reply that Mika could not discern. It puzzled him, but he was certainly not going to ask. A nomad's relationship with his wolf was sacrosanct. Twice, Hornsbuck and his wolf seemed to disagree. Once, Hornsbuck did not take RedTail's advice and they turned left rather than right. RedTail remained at the juncture, allowing Hornsbuck, Mika, Tam, and the horse to go off without him. Quite soon, however, Hornsbuck had to admit that the wolf had been right, and the entire party was forced to return to the juncture and follow a smirking RedTail along the route the wolf had preferred.

This corridor led them to a wide hall that stretched in all directions as far as the eye could see, the dark shadows hiding much from their view.

The ceiling was brightly colored and appeared to be made up of tiny pieces of mosaic tile. Closer examination revealed the tiles to be semi-precious gems struck square and unfaceted, reflecting the light dully.

The pictures they comprised were of nothing that Mika could recognize. Joyous swirls of bright primary colors clashed and conflicted with heavy threatening slashes of darkness—ebony opals and black sapphires. Somehow the riot of colors was disturbing in a way that Mika could not even begin to articulate, but he experienced a shiver of foreboding.

"What is this place?" he asked in a whisper.

"I don't know," replied Hornsbuck. "Creepy, ain't it? Over the center, there's this throne-like thing. Big. Bigger than any human would need. I don't know what sat there. I certainly don't want to meet it. Come over here and look at these pillars."

Hornsbuck held his torch up close to one of the hundreds of pillars that supported the roof. Mika cringed back.

Flames shot up the rounded sides of the pillars, reaching for the ceiling. Flames that were made of blood red rubies embedded in the stone and outlined in a dried rusty brown medium that looked suspiciously like blood. Circling the base and the top of the pillar, also embedded in the stone, were skulls, human skulls. Their empty eyes stared out at Mika, their jaws gaped wide in silent anguish.

"They're all like that," whispered Hornsbuck.

"Every one."

"Let's get out of here," said Mika, chills running down his back. "I don't like this place."

"I don't either," said Hornsbuck. "But at least no one seems to come here any more. There's that to be glad for."

As though waiting only for his words, the wolves began to growl, low ominous sounds rumbling deep in their chests. Their ears lay flat against their skulls, and their hackles rose thickly about their necks.

"What is it, Tam?" asked Mika holding out his torch and reaching nervously for his sword. But Tam never shifted his gaze and continued to stare into the darkness and growl. Slowly, RedTail began to move, gingerly stalking forward on stiff legs as though treading on eggshells. Tam followed reluctantly, his thick silver-plumed tail curled tightly over his black furred back. He seemed uncertain, cautious and perhaps even afraid, but his gold eyes blazed with hatred, and Mika knew that a blood lust was building in him.

Then Mika heard it, the rapid shuffling of a heavy body moving over the gritty floor. It was coming from his right. He held the torch up high, but there was nothing to be seen. The roan began to back and sidestep, yanking at his reins and whickering anxiously.

"What is it, Hornsbuck?" Mika asked, growing more and more anxious himself.

"I don't know," said Hornsbuck, unsheathing his sword. "But you'd best get ready. Tie that horse to one of those pillars. I suspect you might need both hands; the wolves say trouble's coming."

Mika tied the roan to the nearest pillar and unsheathed his sword.

They heard the breathing before they saw the creature, a heavy, stentorian sound that rasped on Mika's nerves like a sword striking bone.

Mika's hands grew sweaty and his sword drooped. A terrible roar cut through the darkness, and Mika stiffened, his sword springing to attention, quivering upright!

A darker shadow hovered in the shadows at the edge of the torchlight. Mika's spirit wilted. He could see that it was immense, over eight feet tall and more than five feet wide.

TamTur and RedTail were barking at the unseen enemy—short, harsh, staccato yaps—and their dewlaps were drawn back over their white slavering teeth.

"What is it, Hornsbuck?" asked Mika again, attempting to conceal the fear in his voice.

"I don't know!" growled Hornsbuck and, reaching over, wrenched a skull loose from the base of the pillar nearest him and threw it at the shadowy creature. There was an immediate roar of anger, and the thing lumbered into the circle of torchlight.

Mika wished with all his heart that it had stayed hidden in the dark. For now he could see the whole of the horrible thing. Never in his entire life had he faced anything more frightening. It was like the worst of nightmares come true.

Its head, if it could be called that, was merely a rounded extension of the whole. It had no neck. Its eyes were like four opaque stones, showing no glint of intelligence, clustered together and buried deep in the rolls of flesh in the center of its forehead. Its mouth was nearly as wide as its body and was lined with rows of gleaming, jagged teeth. Two great long teeth sprouted from the corners of the gaping maw and pointed toward the center. Curving out from the base of the two fangs for a distance of some two feet were two sharp-tipped, razor-edged, mandible-like devices that probed the air in front of the monster's face as though searching for prey.

Two massive arms were attached to the huge, ponderous, bulbous grey body and ended in four clawed fingers each. Its massive legs were similarly powerful yet primitive, resting on three-toed, clawed feet that advanced slowly, yet all too surely.

Its body reminded Mika of that of a giant tick, the grey skin stretched swollen and taut over the immense bulbous body.

"What is it!" shrilled Mika, backing up until he felt the warm bulk of the roan quivering fearfully behind him.

"Umber hulk," said Hornsbuck, backing up quickly and covering his eyes with his hand. "Don't look into its eyes, it'll stun you. Confuse you till you don't know your own name."

"What's it want?" asked Mika, wondering if the thing liked jewels or treasure or even horse meat!

"You, you dummy!" roared Hornsbuck. "What else? It eats anything and everything it can catch, but it likes folks best! We've got to make a run for it. There's no fighting it!"

This was the best news Mika had heard since before the cursed messenger had stumbled into camp with word of the kobold attack. He did not stop to argue but put his foot in the stirrup and swung himself into the saddle behind the princess. He was leaning forward to jerk the reins loose from the pillar when he heard a noise behind him. A chill ran down his spine.

He ripped the reins free and kicked the roan in the ribs. It shot forward, then dashed to the right, away from the awful umber hulk, which was still advancing slowly but steadily.

"RedTail! Tam! To me, wolves, to me!" screamed Hornsbuck, as the wolves barked and danced nimbly at the feet of the monster.

"Mika, call Tam. They don't know! They've never met one before! They think they can kill it!" yelled Hornsbuck, fear apparent in his voice for the first time, fear not for himself, but for his wolf.

"TAM! To me!" hollered Mika, equally terrified that Tam might be caught up in that horrible clawed hand and shoveled into the gaping mouth. But neither wolf obeyed the command.

The hulk was within three feet of the wolves now, swinging its arms before it like trees swaying in the wind, its teeth clacking audibly as the awful mouth opened and shut, opened and shut.

Mika was torn, afraid for his own safety, yet panic-stricken over Tam, who did not seem to realize his own danger. The barking, yapping, and slavering of the wolves was causing so much noise that Mika almost failed to hear the heavy, stentorian breathing of a second umber hulk! But the roan did not mistake it and reared, nearly tossing Mika from his back, and bleated in abject terror. Mika looked behind him and saw the other umber hulk, even larger than the first, ponderously making its way toward the wolves.

"Hornsbuck!" cried Mika just as the grizzled nomad darted forward and scooped a snarling RedTail up in his arms, wrestling him away from the approaching monster.

Hornsbuck turned and looked at the spot where Mika had stood only seconds before, but Mika had already mounted the roan and moved away. Hornsbuck found himself staring directly in the face of the second umber hulk, catching the full impact of its hypnotic gaze.

Hornsbuck stood there like a statue, holding a torch in one hand and his wolf and his sword in the other, mouth open, eyes wide, sensibilities gone, as the umber hulks moved toward him on their stumpy, clawed feet.

Mika cursed, knowing that he had to do something or the man was as good as dead, and there was no way that he would ever find his way out of the tunnels by himself. It was this thought more than any other that decided his course of action.

Kicking the roan hard, he drove him forward between the two hulks, now separated by no more than ten feet. As he came up to the stunned nomad, Mika threw his torch into the mouth of the nearest hulk and grabbed Hornsbuck by the hair, turning him about roughly and propelling him forward as fast as his feet could carry him. Mika prayed that Hornsbuck would not drop the torch or the wolf and would keep his footing.

"Tam! To me, Tam. Follow!" he screamed without looking back, praying that for once in his life, Tam would obey.

He heard the scamper of wolf claws on the floor behind him and, praying to deities long ignored, he

291

raced into the gloom of the ancient amphitheater with the agonized screams of the hulk echoing around them.

The deities must have been amused and taken pity on him, for when he finally brought the roan to a halt and loosened his desperate hold on Hornsbuck's hair, there was no sound of pursuit.

"Hornsbuck?" said Mika, dismounting and staring up into the older man's eyes. But there was no answer. Hornsbuck's eyes, always so quick to spot danger or foolery, were open wide and gazing straight ahead, all signs of intelligence gone. A thin line of spittle drooled from the corner of his open mouth.

RedTail squirmed in Hornsbuck's arms, struggling to free himself from the tight embrace that pinned him to the nomad's chest.

Mika crouched at Hornsbuck's feet and took Red-Tail's chunky head between his hands, staring into the wolf's gold eyes in the light of the torch.

"RedTail, have I ever told you what a wonderful beast you are?" said Mika. RedTail looked at him with the same kind of derisive gaze that Mika was accustomed to seeing on Hornsbuck's face.

"And a wonderful wolf like you could help us out of this mess. I'd be willing to bet that you know the way out of here just as well as Hornsbuck, if not better. In fact, I'd be willing to bet a nice, fat, juicy . . . NO! Make that TWO nice, fat, juicy bucks, which I personally will kill, that you can show us the way out.

"All of us are counting on you, RedTail: me, Hornsbuck, the princess, and your old pal, Tam. You wouldn't want us to die down here, would you?"

RedTail's tongue lolled out of his mouth and Mika

stifled an impulse to boot the beast. Calming himself, he continued.

"Look, RedTail, old pal, this is all your fault in a way. Yours and Tam's. If you'd come when we called you, Hornsbuck would be all right now and we'd be on our way. But you two wanted to stay and fight. So why don't you just cut out this nonsense and get us the hell out of here, 'cause if you don't I'm going to kick you from here to Sunsebb!"

RedTail gazed up at Mika as though calculating, then, twisting his head free, stood next to Hornsbuck and sniffed him thoroughly. Rising up on his hind legs, he poked his muzzle into Hornsbuck's chin and nudged the man hard several times. Hornsbuck rocked on his feet and Mika took the torch from his hand and steadied him so that he didn't fall over.

RedTail whined plaintively and dropped to the ground. He looked up at Mika, all humor gone from his eyes, then turned and set off at a steady lope.

Chapter 20

TIME PASSED. ENDLESSLY. Tunnels passed. To their left. To their right. Up. Down. And sometimes sideways. RedTail led and Mika followed.

The passage grew more and more elaborate once they left the great hall. The walls were smooth dressed stone or inlaid with mosaics that glittered in the torchlight. Intersecting passageways were cause for high vaulting ribbed ceilings and elaborate columns and pillars with delicate carvings that Mika did not care to examine.

It was an extraordinary, fascinating place, rich with the artifacts of some bygone culture. But Mika was not interested in architecture, nor in solving the mystery of the vanished inhabitants. All he cared about was getting out.

The meat was beginning to go rancid; grass, water, and wood for the torches were nearly depleted. Mika and TamTur were exhausted and frightened. Hornsbuck still drooled and the princess still slept, dirty and uncombed, her dress hanging about her in tattered disarray.

"Man the barricades!" shouted Hornsbuck, his mind obviously drifting back to some ancient battle. Mika ignored the outburst, plodding stolidly ahead through the dark corridor, trying to believe that the wolf really knew where he was going and that they would not die down here in the dark, surrounded by cold stone.

The first time Hornsbuck spoke after the encounter with the umber hulk, Mika had rushed to his side, thinking that perhaps the older man had shaken off the effects of the spell. But it had not been so. "Flay him alive! Boil the rascal in oil!" he commanded, ordering unseen underlings to do his bidding.

Since that moment, Hornsbuck was alternately silent and staring, or loudly vocal, reliving much of his life in disjointed bits and pieces. He raved and hollered, chuckled and cajoled, and gave orders that went unanswered. But the worst of it was that he mistook Mika for someone named Lotus Blossom and frequently sought to enfold him in his hairy embrace. After the first mustachioed kiss, Mika was careful not to be taken unawares and made certain that Hornsbuck walked behind the roan.

Perhaps it is true that the gods protect fools and small children because the party met nothing more fearful during the rest of their journey than one measly foot-long centipede which quickly scurried out of their way.

Mika thought his eyes or the torch were failing when everything suddenly paled to grey. Slowly he realized that the passage had been rising for some time and that it was daylight, blessed daylight, filtering down through the tunnel ahead.

Mika's step quickened as he hurried up the passage, while Hornsbuck bellowed out some fragment of a nightmare.

"Greed! Sloth! Envy! Avarice! Hatred! Deceit! War! Obsession!" roared Hornsbuck, a litany of all the evils of the world spewing from his mouth like stones from a sling.

"Keep it down, Hornsbuck," said Mika. "No telling what's waiting out there."

"Oppression! Wickedness! Pain!" hollered Hornsbuck, and Mika shook his head and gave up, concentrating on the growing light ahead of him.

The roan snorted happily and trotted up the last few feet of the passage, the light outlining his body in a shimmering aura. RedTail and TamTur followed, tails curled high above their backs.

Mika stood at the mouth of the passage and leaned against the marble pillar that flanked it. He rested his forehead against the cool stone, closing his eyes against the bright sunlight that filtered down in dust-filled beams from the narrow openings that circled the columned dome high above his head.

In his heart he gave thanks to the Great She Wolf for bringing him out of the dark passageways. Then he heard the roan neigh and stamp his feet in alarm and Tam growl low in his throat.

Danger! Mika lifted his head quickly and moved forward into the room, squinting his eyes against the bright light. He stepped over the hunks of broken stone that littered the floor, trying to focus. He drew his sword and blinked his watering eyes. Behind him, he heard Hornsbuck trudge into the room and stop.

"I thank you for bringing me the princess," said a creaky old voice, somewhere off to his left. Mika crouched low and whirled, facing the direction the voice had come from, holding his sword out in front of him and sweeping it back and forth.

"Put down the sword like a good lad," the voice said soothingly. "I know you don't want me to hurt you again."

Mika blinked his eyes furiously and things began to come into focus. Light and dark separated, flowed together, blurred, and then separated once again.

Outlined in the bright sunlight, dust motes raining softly on his shoulders, stood a small dark figure holding the horse's reins. The sunlight was so beautiful, the voice so gentle. And Mika was tired. Tired of danger. Tired of fighting. Tired of being afraid. All he wanted was for things to go back the way they had been, to be normal again. For one brief moment, his sword arm wavered, and he was sorely tempted to do as he was told.

But the roan had no such problems. His ears were plastered flat against his head and his eyes rolled wildly. His teeth were bared in a square-toothed grimace, and his breathing was harsh and rattled in his throat. His legs were stiff and braced hard against the pull of the bridle.

The wolves were in total agreement with the horse. Tam and RedTail circled the small dark figure, their tails curled above their backs and their ears twitched forward, alert, watchful.

Abruptly, Mika straightened up, alert now to the danger. He had no need to go closer. He knew who the old man was.

"I see you recognize me," said the little old man, his features slowly coming into focus. Mika shuddered and took a step backward.

"You have no reason to fear me," said the old man, his body still shrouded by the long, voluminous cape. "I have what I want now. Before, you made the mistake of coming between me and that which I sought. Now, thanks to your efforts, I have my prize."

"You mean the princess?" Mika blurted out in puzzlement. "Why would you want the princess?"

"It's a long story," said the old man with a dry chuckle. "A very long story. But since you've brought her to me, I suppose an explanation is the least I can offer."

"Lies! Oppression! Murder!" ranted Hornsbuck.

"Your friend understands," said the old man, nodding toward Hornsbuck, an amused look flitting across his withered face.

"This is my temple," he said, gesturing around him at the ruined building with a bony hand. "Or what little remains of it."

"There," he said, pointing at a massive block of marble that had broken in two and fallen on its side, "was the altar. Sacrifices were laid on its surface, and the floor ran deep with their blood.

"These walls," he said, waving around the apse with his bony hands, "were filled with those who worshipped me and did homage in my name in honor or in fear.

"Once, this land was nearly mine. I held it in thrall and squeezed it tight. Nearly, nearly, was it mine. Then, other forces rose up, conspired against me and broke my hold, but never, never have I forgotten. I pledged that I would return and take back what is mine. And you, lad, have given me, this day, the instrument of power," the old man said with a trembling voice as flecks of spittle sprayed from his mouth and fell to the dusty floor with a soft hiss.

"What are you talking about?" asked Mika, beginning to wonder if the little man had taken leave of his senses. Magic-user he might be, but the Great She Wolf knew that the cities were crawling with hundreds of old has-beens who bored passersby with imagined tales of their days of glory.

"You do not recognize me in this old and tired body," said the old man. "But perhaps you would know me by another name."

"And what would that be?" asked Mika, casually resting the point of his sword on the ground.

"Some know me as Iuz," said the old man, a harsh light glittering in his eyes.

Mika's blood ran cold.

"That is not a name one uses lightly in these parts," Mika said sharply.

"Well, I'm pleased to hear that," said the old man in a pleasant tone as though he were discussing the weather. Then, still smiling gently, he drew the roan closer and began to fumble with the bonds that held the princess.

"Death! Destruction! Pestilence!" thundered Hornsbuck as he turned round and round, holding up his arms and staring up at the broken dome.

"Leave her alone, old man!" cried Mika, lifting his sword once more. "Take your hands off her and stand back. I will listen to no more of your nonsense, and do not think to stun me again. I will slice you through with my blade before you can say the words."

"You do not believe me," the old man said sadly as he turned around and gazed at Mika. His expression was mournful as though Mika were a prize pupil who had suddenly fallen stupid.

"Perhaps you would recognize me if I looked different. Like this, perhaps." And the old man's body began to change. His back humped under the dark cape and then it seemed to fill out, bulging strangely in odd places.

Then the cape fell away from his head and the skull itself began to twist and move as though it were made of soft clay and being shaped by an unseen hand.

The skull lost what few threads of hair it possessed and swelled to three times greater in size. The forehead bulged grotesquely and eyebrows, great bushy red eyebrows, pushed through the skin and grew before Mika's startled eyes.

Red eyes. Red, the color of warm blood, with no pupils, looked out at Mika and seemed to gleam with an evil light.

The withered cheeks grew fat, the deep wrinkles smoothing away as though they had never been. The nose became bulbous and misshapen, and a gold stud was fixed in each nostril. The mouth formed wide and cruel and the lips fleshy and somehow obscene. The ears were mere slits in the sides of the skull.

The cape fell to the ground as the man-thing grew, revealing an immense broad-chested, round-bellied body, thick with layer upon layer of fat.

Its arms and legs were massive, smooth of skin and

301

hairless and red. The entire monstrous manifestation was red. The red of a lobster boiled in seawater.

The man-thing continued to grow, becoming taller and taller and wider and wider till it towered over Mika, more than seven feet tall and four times his weight. And it wore nothing but an evil smile.

The horrible thing stood before Mika clasping the princess against its ugly body like some tiny toy. Mika could hardly bear to look; it was a sacrilege just watching the foul thing touch her.

The dome of the temple seemed to whirl around Mika's head and he closed his eyes to stop the giddy sensation. His heart hammered against his ribs, and his fear was like the taste of cold iron in his mouth. He shivered and his hands could barely grip the handle of his sword. The roan screamed, wheeled, and ran from the frightful apparition. Mika heard Tam and RedTail whine and slink away and wished that he could do the same.

"Do you believe me now?" thundered the awful red demon.

"I believe," whispered Mika with his head bowed, daring to wonder if there was any hope of escape. Opening his eyes, he saw the demon's hand reaching out for him, its long fingers twitching as though they already held him in their grasp.

"Wait!" cried Mika, shrinking back out of reach, totally terrified. He knew that he would not survive if ever the creature touched him.

"Wait!" he croaked through his fear-clenched throat. "Don't kill me! You can't kill someone who's done you a favor. Can you?"

"Of course I can," chuckled the demon, smiling

widely, exposing his long sharp fangs. "I've done so many times. But perhaps it would be more fitting if we permitted the princess to reward you herself. Yes, I think I would enjoy that more." And gesturing with his long fingers, waving them over her head in strange arcane moves, the monster muttered soft words beneath his breath and Mika saw the princess stir. A lump filled his throat. He had envisioned this moment many times, but never had he pictured it happening like this.

One grubby slender hand trembled and lifted shakily to press against the tattered silk-clad breast. The magnificent bosom rose and fell, taking in great gulps of air, and her eyelids fluttered and then opened.

Mika recoiled in shock! Peering at him groggily through a dirty tangle of thick black curls was one brilliant blue eye and one as green as the grass of spring!

"I shall allow the princess herself to bestow your reward," said the demon. Then, before Mika's bewildered eyes, the monster began to shrink and whither, until it was once more the same wizened old ugly man in the voluminous black cape.

The princess leaned against him, seemingly too weak to stand alone and, as yet, totally uncomprehending.

The old man gestured with his frail, thickly veined hand, and the princess's hand rose and pointed at Mika.

Mike knew without a doubt that something terrible was about to happen.

"Wait! Wait! Stop!" he yelled. "I don't understand. What's happening? Who are you? All right, I saw some horrible apparition. Something big and red, but maybe it was all illusion, it doesn't prove that you're Iuz.

"Why would Iuz need to kidnap a princess? None of this makes sense. I don't believe you're Iuz at all. I think you're just some old has-been magic-user. You can do some illusion and some spells and you can kill me, but you're not Iuz."

Mike held his breath as he waited for the old man to respond. In his heart he was not at all certain that the old man was not exactly whom he claimed to be. But if he could get the old man talking, he might be able to think of a way to escape what now seemed to be certain death.

"You have touched on more of the truth than you know," sighed the old man and he seemed to stagger off balance for a minute as the princess leaned on him more heavily.

The old man fixed Mika with a baleful eye and his voice rose in cold fury. "I *am* Iuz! This, this old tired body is that which I have inhabited on this plane of existence for more years than I can number. It is a tired body, no longer strengthened by the blood and spirits of sacrifice. Soon, unless I take steps to prevent it, this body will die, and I will have no access to this material plane for more than a century.

"I have bided my time in the planes of other existence, in other forms of being, one of which you have just witnessed, searching for that which could return me to strength and power. And at last I found it.

"The answer is twofold. First there is the gem which you know as dramadine.

"Dramadine is a rare gem, occurring but seldom in nature, and it has never been replicated by man or mage. As you have heard, it heightens one's powers to the greatest potential. Such a gem would strengthen me and make me invincible.

"But it is not the gem alone I desire, for the princess herself is a conduit of power; her eyes, as you have no doubt noticed, give evidence of the strength hidden within."

"But how can you use her power?" asked Mika, noticing with a quickening of pulse and a thread of hope that the princess was standing on her own feet, no longer leaning against the old man, and her eyes seemed to be focusing more clearly. If only he could keep the old man talking until she regained her senses! If she heard what he was saying, she could not fail to recognize their danger. Maybe she would help Mika in some way, or at the very least, allow him the opportunity to escape.

"I will encapsulate her power," the old man said patiently, not seeming to notice that the princess was now erect and was staring down at her hands and arms, examining them in a puzzled manner as though she had never seen them before.

"The power of a virgin is very strong," said the old man. "It will rejuvenate this old tired body and make me young and strong enough to bring this world under my control. And I have you to thank for bringing her to me. Without your special brand of protection, she might never have reached me."

"How do you encapsulate a princess, and wouldn't just any old girl do? Does it have to be a princess?" Mika asked hurriedly, hoping to keep the magic-user from noticing the bright look of fury that Mika detected in the princess's eyes as she picked up the shredded remains of her filthy silk dress between her dirty fingers and stared at it in angry silence.

"It's really a simple process," said the old man, warming to the explanation. "I need only distill the essence of the virgin and place it in a crystal, or in this case, the gem.

"No ordinary virgin will do. This princess, despite her plain exterior, is the end result of several hundreds of years of breeding that have produced kings, queens, magic-users, and men of power. Although her potential is as yet unrealized, I shall bring it to greater heights than she would ever have realized as a mere human.

"But enough talking, let me show you what I mean." And with a gesture, he caused the princess's arm to rise above the filthy skirt and her grubby fingers pointed directly at Mika's chest.

Mika opened his mouth to yell and tensed his body to drop and roll, but before he could even move, a pale, sickly stream of ochre light shot from the princess's filthy fingernail and struck him full in the chest.

"I'm dead," he thought, and waited to die. But nothing happened. He looked at his fingers and wiggled them. He was still alive!

The old man looked as though he had swallowed a bitter potion. Thrusting the princess's hand out again, he seized her finger and pointed it at Mika a second time. He screamed out words that Mika could not understand, and a faint pink light wobbled from the princess's finger and then faded in mid-air before it even reached Mika.

Mika laughed out loud.

Iuz turned the princess around violently and shook her hard, staring into her eyes. She struggled in his tight grip and tried to break away. Iuz pulled her closer and scrutinized her intently as though reading a familiar text whose message had suddenly rearranged itself into strange and peculiar words.

A blank look came over his features, and his fingers loosened their hold. He looked old and lost for a moment and then, feeling Mika's gaze on him, lifted his eyes. Hatred leaped from the dark eyes, hatred so tangible that Mika felt as though he had been physically struck.

Iuz flung the girl away from him furiously, and she staggered for several feet before she gained her balance.

"She is no longer a virgin!" shrieked Iuz. "Not a virgin! And it is your fault! You've ruined everything! Now I shall be forced to depend on the gem alone!" And the edges of his cape began to shimmer. He began to grow taller, and his skin took on a rosy hue. Mika knew that he had waited too long. It was time to leave.

But the princess had other ideas.

She too seemed to have grown in stature. She was no longer asleep, and she marched angrily up to the magic-user.

"Forget it, old man," she said harshly as she shoved him aside, propelling him into the catatonic Hornsbuck. Hornsbuck swung his right arm in a reflex motion and caught Iuz under the chin, knocking him down into a dizzy heap.

"It's my turn, and I've got a few words of my own!" She stalked toward Mika, hatred blazing in her multi-colored eyes.

"You! You're to blame for this . . . this mess!" she screamed at Mika as Iuz wrapped his skinny hand around Hornsbuck's leg and began struggling to his feet.

"One minute, I'm at home safe in my castle where I belong. And the next minute I'm here! Wherever *here* is! And just look at me! I'm dirty! I'm filthy! My hair's a mess! My dress . . . my dress, or what little there is of it, is totally ruined! I even smell bad, if you can even imagine such a thing! And now! Now . . . thanks to you, whoever you even are! Certainly no one I would ever even talk to by choice! Look at you! You're . . . you're . . . YOU'RE NOBODY! I find out that I'm not even a virgin any more, and I don't even remember what happened!"

Iuz staggered up, clinging to Hornsbuck's tunic. He steadied himself and then turned and stumbled forward, his face a contorted mask of rage, his hands outstretched, reaching for Mika like claws.

The princess, never ceasing her litany of rage, batted him out of the way with the back of her hand. So accustomed was he to inspiring fear, the demon had no reason to expect an attack on his frail person. The princess dispatched Iuz with ease, knocking him to the floor at Hornsbuck's feet, where he lay stunned.

Mika almost felt sorry for Iuz. He could have told him that even a demon has something to fear from an angry woman.

The princess looked around with a stormy gaze as though searching for something to throw. Not finding it, she reached down the front of her dress and pulled out the tiny crystal bead that Mika had used for his spell of invulnerability. She gazed at it with a curled lip as though it were a slimy slug. She knotted her fist around it and yanked it hard, breaking the chain, then tossed it aside with distaste.

Her fingers sought and found a second chain, which Mika had never noticed, tucked at the edges of her dress. Dangling on the end of the chain was a gem the size of a goose egg that glittered a brilliant rainbow of green and blue.

"The stone. Dramadine!" Iuz muttered hoarsely as he tried to crawl to his feet. Mika stared at it with awe. So much death and anguish for one pretty stone and one unpleasant princess.

The unpleasant princess's nostrils were pinched and white, her brow was creased with a frown, and her eyes glittered with anger no less brightly than the gem. Her mouth was an angry slash in her dirty face.

She snapped the gem free of the chain and, drawing back her arm, she let fly. The shining stone flew through the air and struck Mika in the center of his forehead. Mika staggered off balance and the gem fell at his feet and bounced along the floor before coming to a halt several feet away.

Iuz scrambled to his feet, his eyes fastened on the stone. Then he halted and screamed a hoarse flow of words, pointing his own claw-like finger at Mika.

Just then, Hornsbuck, who had been staring upward, his face bathed in the warm sunlight, looked toward them, his attention captured, finally, by all the noise.

Blinded by the bright light that had been shining

directly in his eyes, he looked at the small dark figure in front of him and exclaimed joyously, "Lotus Blossom!" and wrapped his arms around the magic-user, interrupting him in the middle of his incantation.

A bright bolt of fiery red light shot out of the end of Iuz's finger and then, as Hornsbuck touched him, breaking his concentration and disturbing the elements of the spell, the red light doubled back upon itself and entered the magic-user's body.

Iuz shivered and stiffened as the red light spread throughout his being. His eyes turned up in his skull and his lips peeled back from his teeth in a terrible rictus. His body twitched and jerked as the red light pierced his skin, illuminating him from within like a cruel aura. The air about him seemed to resonate as though echoing to unheard music. Then, there was a thin curdled scream, and the demon disappeared completely, banished from the material plane.

"Lotus Blossom?" Hornsbuck said plaintively, looking at his huge hands as though she might somehow be concealed behind one of his immense fingers.

Mika gaped at the spot where the demon had stood, then at Hornsbuck, then at the gem at his feet. Then he stared at the princess. It was almost more than he could comprehend.

There was a faint whine. Mika looked down and saw Tam crouched at his feet, his eyes filled with bewilderment.

"I hate you!" cried the princess, as she stamped her foot on the dusty floor. Her strange eyes were huge and wild. She did not even seem to realize that she had just helped dispatch a major demon.

"I'll kill you," she screamed. "I'm royalty! I'm a

princess! You just can't treat me like this and live!"

"Now wait a minute," Mika said appeasingly as he took a step forward and picked up the stone, meaning to hand it back to her as a conciliatory gesture. Maybe something could be salvaged yet. After all, it was a long way back to her island.

"Give it back! Give me back my stone!" shrilled the princess, her hands curling into threatening claws.

"Now hold on!" said Mika, beginning to get angry. "I didn't exactly take it from you. You threw it at me, if you remember. And you've got this thing all wrong. I didn't do anything to you. It was Iuz, not me."

"Did you bring me here?" asked the princess, now deadly calm.

"Well, yes, in a matter of speaking," admitted Mika. "But . . ."

"Are you responsible for the way I look?"

"Well, yes. I guess you could say that. But there were a few things . . ."

"Am I still a virgin?" asked the princess, tight-lipped.

"Well, I guess not," Mika said diffidently, "but I didn't . . ."

"Shut up!" screamed the princess. "Just close your stupid mouth. There's nothing else to be said." And walking up to Mika, she seized his arm and tried to pull his sword free.

Mika looked down at her in disbelief, tempted to laugh as she flung her tiny self, scarcely taller than his chin, on his sword arm with intense fury.

"Oh, come on now," he said, tucking his sword behind his back and trying to put a calming hand on her shoulder.

"Leave off," he said with a laugh. But his laughter drove her further into her rage, and she turned her head and sank her teeth into his hand.

Mika yelled in pain and surprise.

Tam leaped for her, snarling. This! This was something he could understand! Demons were one thing, but no human threatened Mika and emerged unscathed!

"No, Tam!" shouted Mika as he stepped in front of the wolf and flung the princess from him with ease, scarcely believing her ferocity. He examined his bleeding hand, putting it to his mouth and sucking the blood. What had happened to the sweet gentle beauty he had believed her to be? If this was her true nature, it was no wonder she had never married!

The momentum of his push carried her back toward the entrance to the tunnel. Back toward Hornsbuck who was still standing in the beam of sunlight, gazing at his hands, still in the grip of confusion.

"Lotus Blossom," he said in wonderment as the princess careened into him, his face spreading in a beatific smile.

"Oh, Lotus Blossom your stupid fat self," screamed the princess, and ripping his knife from his belt, she turned and threw the knife at Mika with all her strength.

The knife flew through the air, straight as a sable-wood arrow. Tam, knowing only that she was still a threat, leaped into the air at the same moment and caught the knife square in the center of his chest.

Things seemed to go very, very slowly from that

moment on. Mika felt, saw, each and every separate movement around him as though it had been caught in a crystal and hung up to view at his leisure.

The princess bared her teeth in unreasoning hatred and came toward him again.

Hornsbuck sat down and began singing a raucous nomad drinking song.

RedTail crawled into Hornsbuck's lap and sighed deeply.

Tam crumpled like a body without bones, and his blood ran red over the hilt of the knife and puddled on the dusty floor.

Mika sank to his knees and lifted Tam in his arms, cradling the massive head and holding the wolf to him like a child. Tam's eyes were open, the magnificent gold now dark with pain. He looked at Mika and held him in his gaze as though imprinting his vision on his faltering heart and mind.

"Tam," whispered Mika, willing the wolf to live with all of his being. He started to rise, time still frozen, and saw the princess coming at him.

Without thinking, without premeditation, Mika held out his hand, the one that held the gem, and said the magic words, the wolf spell, at the very moment she sank her nails into his arm.

Time fragmented. Splintered apart. Then slowly reassembled. Everything was the same, but everything was different.

Hornsbuck sat on the floor still singing his song.

RedTail lifted his muzzle and howled.

The roan stamped his foot and snorted, tentatively nibbling a weed that had sprung up behind the broken altar. The warm sun filtered down on the strange tableau in the ruined temple. Shone down on Mika as he walked slowly out of the temple cradling Tam in his arms. Shone down on the small female wolf that followed closely at his heels, her thin pointed muzzle bumping into his legs at his every step. She whined uncertainly, as though afraid of being left behind. Her tail was held low, curled between her long delicate hind quarters.

She whimpered as the man walked away as though she did not exist. Then she sat down on her black furry haunches and lifted her dainty muzzle to the warm sun and howled. The sound echoed through the empty ruin, reverberating from one rounded wall to the next, a peculiar keening wail that held an oddly human quality of pain and grief.

As the last echo faded from the air, the wolf lowered her head. She turned her eyes, one green, one blue, and sought out the retreating figure of the man. Rising slowly, she stared after him for a long uncertain moment, then hesitantly, she crept forward, and followed in his footsteps.

FOR THE BEST IN PAPERBACKS, LOOK FOR THE 🐧

In every corner of the world, on every subject under the sun, Penguin represents quality and variety – the very best in publishing today.

For complete information about books available from Penguin – including Pelicans, Puffins, Peregrines and Penguin Classics – and how to order them, write to us at the appropriate address below. Please note that for copyright reasons the selection of books varies from country to country.

In the United Kingdom: For a complete list of books available from Penguin in the U.K., please write to *Dept E.P., Penguin Books Ltd, Harmondsworth, Middlesex, UB7 0DA*

In the United States: For a complete list of books available from Penguin in the U.S., please write to *Dept BA, Penguin, 299 Murray Hill Parkway, East Rutherford, New Jersey 07073*

In Canada: For a complete list of books available from Penguin in Canada, please write to *Penguin Books Canada Ltd, 2801 John Street, Markham, Ontario L3R 1B4*

In Australia: For a complete list of books available from Penguin in Australia, please write to the *Marketing Department, Penguin Books Australia Ltd, P.O. Box 257, Ringwood, Victoria 3134*

In New Zealand: For a complete list of books available from Penguin in New Zealand, please write to the *Marketing Department, Penguin Books (NZ) Ltd, Private Bag, Takapuna, Auckland 9*

In India: For a complete list of books available from Penguin, please write to *Penguin Overseas Ltd, 706 Eros Apartments, 56 Nehru Place, New Delhi, 110019*

In Holland: For a complete list of books available from Penguin in Holland, please write to *Penguin Books Nederland B.V., Postbus 195, NL–1380AD Weesp, Netherlands*

In Germany: For a complete list of books available from Penguin, please write to *Penguin Books Ltd, Friedrichstrasse 10 – 12, D–6000 Frankfurt Main 1, Federal Republic of Germany*

In Spain: For a complete list of books available from Penguin in Spain, please write to *Longman Penguin España, Calle San Nicolas 15, E–28013 Madrid, Spain*

The Penguin Science Fiction Omnibus

An exciting collection of stories from some of the best-known, best-loved science fiction writers: Harry Harrison, Isaac Asimov, Frederik Pohl, Arthur C. Clarke, C. M. Kornbluth, and dozens more . . .

Time Out of Joint   Philip K. Dick

Ragle Gumm is something of a local celebrity, something of a bum too. When he starts to think he is the centre of the universe, all the evidence seems to back him. The trouble is, which universe? Is it 1959 or 1999?

The Artificial Kid   Bruce Sterling

In the world of Reverie, the Artificial Kid is a notorious, affluent video star. His life takes an unexpected turn when mysterious forces come into play; the effects – both on him and on the lovely Saint Anne Twiceborn – are drastic.

Cat's Cradle   Kurt Vonnegut

Vonnegut's relentlessly deadpan humour makes this novel of global destruction chilling and extraordinarily compelling. 'A major novelist and a major novel' – *Sunday Telegraph*

The Day It Rained Forever   Ray Bradbury

Ray Bradbury is one of the few speculative writers to have created an identifiable and unified world of his own. This collection of lyrical short stories reveals that world in all its fanciful, gothic glory.

Bill, the Galactic Hero   Harry Harrison

When Bill enlists in the mighty forces of the Galactic Empire, he must travel to the steel labyrinth of Helior. On the way he discovers that 'war sure is hell' – and a man must lose his soul to serve the Empire.